TALES TO TERRIFY
VOLUME 1

P.D. THOMPSON

CONTENTS

FOREWORD

As a 20-year audiobook narrator, I'm always looking for talented writers who create stories that can 'bring it'. And without a doubt,my friend and colleague P.D. Thompson 'brings it'. The depth and structure he creates with his stories and the intelligence in his writing skills are topnotch.

In the years I've been narrating short stories and audiobooks, P.D.'s content, which covers a wide range of genres, is for me the very best of the authors I've come across. Every time I see a story by P.D., I know without a doubt, it will be interesting, engaging, intellectually stimulating, and most of all... a joy to narrate and, more so, a joy to read or to listen to.

You can't go wrong with anything P.D. writes. He creates masterpieces that stimulates one's imagination.

—Otis Jiry, Host of *Scary Stories Told In The Dark* and *Otis Jiry's Nightmare Fuel*

THE LURKER

How long had the dark figure been standing there?

Standing there, overtly lurking. I could see the ossified figure in plain sight, motionless, just staring up to the second-floor window where I was peering from. Who could it be? Why were they here? My skin crawled with nerves on edge. My yard was lit by moonlight, and the orb illuminated the figure with a haunting backlight. The hooded figure was alone. I was alone. A terrifying thought occurred to me. No, it was an unsettling question that came to mind. Had I locked the doors and secured the windows before taking my shower? I was convinced I definitely had, but better to be safe than sorry. I talked myself into going downstairs to double-check.

I was dreading to descend to the bottom floor. I would have to take my eyes off the figure in the yard only long enough to do my security checks. Once on the ground floor, I found everything was secure downstairs, which satisfied me immensely.

I had recently seen on the evening news about an incident happening at the park where a pervert was spying on people. A 40-year-old man had been caught near the woman's toilets behaving unseemly.

This man was originally reported to have been doing lewd acts and acting inappropriately behind some bushes before being arrested. I am always reading about some disgusting person being disgraceful and obscene in our city. I simply do not have time to consider such things.

And now someone of questionable character was lurking on my lawn. I do not like phoning the police because they can make a ridiculous fiasco out of it. Maybe the guy out there had an impeccant name, a fleckless reputation and a noble character. But how would I know that with him just dumbly standing there in the cold night air?

Although the temptation to look out of the downstairs windows into the yard presented itself to me, I dared not look from the downstairs windows for fear the dark figure might be at the window. Something told me that would be too close. If I saw such a thing, I would undeniably die on the spot of a heart attack.

I made my way back upstairs and peeked from the same window. The figure appeared to have moved closer to the house. I had great concerns this might happen. I never saw it move, but I swore it was closer than before. What could it want? No rational person would dress this way, cloaked in black with a hood. It was nowhere near Halloween, so why the costume? Why the sinister getup? I looked at the time; it was 11:50 pm. The hour was late. Most everyone should already be asleep, or at least in bed and settled for the night. Maybe this person outside had no home? Possibly they were homeless? I cannot take in anyone. I barely take care of myself these days.

I had been exhausted when I came to the bedroom to shower, but now I was wide awake, fatigued, suspicious, afraid. I persisted in watching the figure nervously, uncomfortably, not knowing if it saw me looking down at it. Of course, decidedly, it could see me. It was looking right at me, I assumed, but strangely, I never saw its eyes. What sort of person dresses in such a manner and then stands on someone's lawn and stares? This had to be a children's prank of some sort.

I questioned myself, who did I know that was capable of such a practical joke? Lewis always thought of himself as a funny guy. He was more annoying than humorous, but I doubt if he would pull a stunt such as this. Lewis had a family now, responsibilities and a solid job. I seriously doubted if this old-school buddy of mine would risk an altercation or, worse, a police arrest to pull something like this off. I had no enemies, no one who might have a vendetta or a score to settle. I lived mostly peaceably among everyone in the community. I could not think of a single soul who might want to intimidate or frighten me.

It was nearing midnight, and there was a ghoul on my lawn. The strangeness began to weigh on me. I had assumed as soon as the figure saw me from the window that they would run away and hide, and that would be it. But no, the figure seemed to be coming closer to the house. It was not skulking, and it was not threatening me. It was lurking. Maybe if I turned on the bedroom light and showed it that I knew it was there, that would be the deterrent needed for ridding it from my property.

I walked across the room and flicked the switch on. The room lit up, and I ran back to the window to have another look. The figure was even closer than before, and now with its draped arm, it was pointing with a gray hand directly at my window.

I was losing my justification for staying in the house. Was I truly safe from whatever the thing was on the lawn? In all reality, how would I know what its intentions were? Maybe it meant no ill will at all? Maybe it did? Why should I presume the worst when I had not been threatened? Yes, the figure was intimidating, but was that my own macabre imagination running away with itself? I realized this notion of having the bedroom light burning was a mistake. It was not a good idea at all. I went straight back and flicked off the light. I partially pulled the curtains closed but left a tiny slit so I could still see out onto the lawn. This would have been a good time to have powerfully bright security lights on this side of the house. I will have them installed first thing tomorrow, I thought to myself.

This was not the night I had prescribed for myself. I languished over the sound sleep I should be getting by this time of night. However, I was not at all tired nor prepared for slumber. I was the type who could go to bed with a book, read two pages, and be fast asleep within minutes. There would be nothing as idealistic as this fleeting thought.

Sensible, yes, I must be sensible. Why not open the window and address the figure? It was still stoically stationary. Like a fence-post, it postured erect, unmoving, not swaying, and there was no condensation coming from its breathing. It was not warm outside. As a matter of fact, the night was chilly.

Should I make contact with whoever it is? I could be over-thinking the situation, overcomplicating what may not be as strange as I have imagined it to be. Such ruminations can lead to fanciful illusions. It was not out of the question to believe that maybe my imagination was getting away from me.

I had to man up and deal with it. This lurker did not appear to be leaving anytime soon. How would I address it? I could yell, "Get off my lawn, weirdo!"

No, that would be too harsh. I needed to be courteous and polite. Possibly the person has a learning disability or had been in an accident and bumped their head?

"Can I help you with something?" No, that was an invitation to engage personally.

I thought it would be best not to ask it any questions. I needed to address it, but I needed to be smart, to say the right thing, to drive it off my lawn without insults or threats. Thus far, there was nothing to suggest I was in mortal danger. Would this figure have already tried to get into the house if it wanted in? I mean, how hard is it really to break into a house with as many windows as this house has? I had never broken into a house before, but I would imagine it is no trouble at all. I had no security system installed, no dog, no extra locks on the doors and windows. My home was a two-story house with no type of security measures at all.

Maybe I should arm myself? But with what? I had no gun, pepper spray, taser, nothing that modern. I did not even own a baseball bat. I suppose I could retrieve a butcher's knife from the kitchen? Could I honestly stab or cut another person? The thought of having to defend myself with violence sickened me. I was getting all worked up, most likely for absolutely nothing. If the person outside was going to make a move, would they not have already done so? Of course, they would have. The way they are going about it is no surprise home invasion. They are clearly not afraid of being seen. That is what I will do. I will get my phone and take a picture of the person just to show them I have proof they were here being menacing.

I did not believe in monsters, ghosts, or anything phantas-magorical. I knew there were no such things as aliens visiting from other planets nor right-wing conspiracy theories. I gave no credence to any of these things other than made-up stories, allegories from the vivid creative mind of dreamers, high fiction induced with illusion.

I took another look from my vantage point, and again, the dark figure was closer than before, mimicking itself in all stillness with one boney gray finger, which I could see more clearly now, pointing directly at me. It did not appear that the head was raised. I had no way of knowing if this possible revenant was looking at me or not. I was feeling stung by fright. I quickly took several photos in succession. Since they failed to move at all, all of the photos would be identical.

An emotion of impending doom rose from deep inside me; I felt my face flush red as my iambic tetrameter heart thumped to the hymn of death. This uncouth stalker seemed to be projecting its presence upon me from below. This could not be possible.

I decided to turn off the bedroom light and take a couple more pictures, but this time to get a good clear picture, I decided to be brave enough to open the window.

The lurker remained motionless as I stood in my dark bedroom window flung open, cold wind freezing me to the bone. My hands became cold and jittery. I took several more pictures, hoping it would look up at me. Unexpectantly, with a backdrop of dull grey groom behind it, the figure raised its head quickly and brought it back down into a bow position. In the freakish instance, I was so startled by seeing it move that I fumbled the phone in my hands, and like a football player trying to catch a fingertip pass, I clumsily and carelessly let the phone slip from my hands. My world slowed down as if time had framed this awkward picture of me stretching with great effort out of the window, trying to lay my hands back on the phone, which held the only evidence of the lurker's existence. During my moment of inept inelegance, the lurker did not even twitch. The phone fell through space and might as well have dropped into a black hole because for me, that was the distance between inside my house and the outside world right now. I let out several expletives and jumped up and down like a child, kicking the dresser and stubbing my big toe. Now bouncing around the room on one foot while nursing my surely swollen big toe, the lurker had to be amused at my negligence. How could I have been so careless? What a freaking joke. Oh, I imagined the lurker was celebrating a victory, and this angered me. I know accidents happen, but the phone was my evidence, my lifeline. Now I could not even call for help. Limping to the open window, it did not collect my phone, but it was a few steps closer and remained faceless.

In my frustration and idiocy, I addressed the person. "What do you want?"

I was given no answer.

I yelled this time. "Why are you just standing there?"

Again, I was not rewarded with a response.

I slammed the window shut and locked the cold air as well as the lurker out. I walked over and sat on the side of the bed to examine my toe in the dark. It was sore and throbbed. I imagined I had broken it on the dresser. After the examination, I made my way back to the window and peeked out.

He, she, it, whatever the thing was, it certainly was not here to deliver good news. I was suddenly impelled with surprise, practically pummeled by a strange alarm. I felt the need to run away. I was driven to flee the premises. I took another glance out of the window and saw that my stress was warranted as the nameless thing was at my downstairs front door. Driven by adrenaline and terror, yes, I was being terrorized. I went at breakneck speed down the stairs as loud as a herd of buffalo, forgetting about my broken toe, to the first floor. I made my way in the dark to the kitchen, which was on the backside of the house. I looked through the window of the door, and the backyard looked clear. There was no evil presence lurking that I could see. I saw nothing but the six-foot wooden fence I would have to scale if I were to make a clean escape. In my panic, I had forgotten to put on shoes or even pajama pants. I cursed to myself. I was too modest to venture out half-naked. That would mean taking more time to climb the stairs and dress appropriately for the cool air of the night. I cursed again and started for the stairs; my toe throbbed, reminding me it was most definitely broken. I dared not look at the front door because I knew what lurked behind it was unimaginable. I shot up the stairs like a gazelle, ignoring the pain, bounding two steps at a time.

When I reached the top, there it stood. Every bit of seven feet tall. A dark, cloaked figure with a face too deep to read. Distraught in the gloom of hysteria, my breath became gasps. I could taste the duress of wormwood in my mouth, the malodourous stench of Gehenna filled my nostrils like burning sulfur, I heard the stridulation of wings roaring in my head, the chartless direction of my own soul, empty, lost, vanquished as I fell headlong down the stairs breaking my cervical vertebrae, severing my spinal cord and leaving me dead at the foot of the stairs. How was I dead and still saw the cloaked murderer gliding down the steps and hovering over me? The cloaked lurker swelled its chest and spread its arms wide, revealing an impressive black wingspan.

I could only believe this was the notorious myth folktales called Moth Man. This flying humanoid creature was the most imposing thing I had ever laid eyes on. Not only was my body broken and torn, but my emotions seemed to be absent as well, for I felt no trepidation or fear. I only felt helpless. Its red eyes were merciless and examined me as if I was going to be butchered like a pig and devoured.

I suppose this was when I passed out. Darkness overtook me, and I drifted without any power of my own… or was I being carried? I did not know. I did get the chilling impression I was outside, for the cold nipped at my exposed body.

My eyes opened. I was standing. There was no lurker anywhere around. It had vanished, disappeared, flown away silently, leaving me alone. There I stood in the backyard of a house of someone I did not know. I was cloaked in black, soulless, emotionless, distant from who I was. I was cold, hollow, asphyxiated without a single human sense. I had been swallowed by the void, into the dark womb of all abominations. The throb of life was absent, the pulse of warm blood had been drained; Hell had planted me firmly here. Without essence, devoid of soul, all hope abandoned, disbelief stripped me of every resistance.

I was staring up at the second-floor window where a light had just been turned on. I saw someone come to the window. It was a man. He looked worried; he looked like me.

How long had I been standing here?

POPE LICK MONSTER

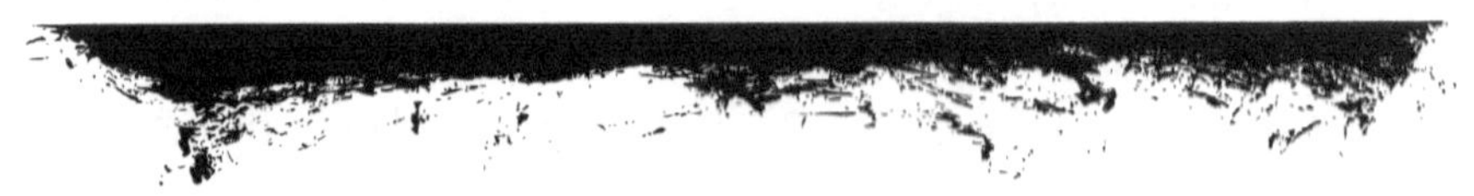

I purposely kept all the crude reminders from that fateful day. It was horror beyond imagination. We all suffered anguish and loss. No one survived the mental drudgery from the nightmarish experience. I endured the untenable to tell the improbable, far-fetched tale.

What began as four friends making a weekend of it became a hellish nightmare of unbelievable terror. The mortification could not have been predicted. The heartbreak was insufferable. The loss of life, irreplaceable.

I have always had a fascination with myths and legends. The mystique of Bigfoot, Sasquatch, and the Yeti has been an intriguing subject since I was a kid. The allure of the unknown was a secret enticement. I had never placed any credence in the stories told, the grainy, far-away video shots or even the physical evidence people have produced. Myths, legends, and fairytales are always hyped and exceed the realities. I suppose perception is in the mind of the dreamer or non-dreamer.

The four of us, friends since childhood, chose a weekend of camping out in the wild, taking along video cameras and our fishing poles. If we did not discover a Bigfoot, we could at least catch fish.

We found a campsite off-grid, so to speak, where we had more access to the forest. George, Rob, Brad and myself (Tom) pitched camp, and the drinking started. The grill was heating, and we had some tunes playing on the Jeep's radio. The plan was to have some drinks, get a good feed in us, head out into the forest off the trails, and see what we could stir up. I will admit we did not really expect to capture anything on video, but if we could catch anything remotely close to looking like a hairy 7-foot ape, even if it were a distant tree trunk with the right shadows, we would return victorious. Any video such as that always goes viral.

The forest in Kentucky is called woods by most everyone living in the Bluegrass State. Kentucky is better known for being the 'Bourbon Capital of the World' along with the home of 'The Louisville Slugger' baseball bats, The Kentucky Derby and Muhammad Ali. But this night we were not in Louisville. We were deep in the woods in Bullitt County not far from Fort Knox, the government military reservation. We were also not too far from Salt River and the Rolling Forks River, where fishing is hit or miss; however, we brought plenty of junk food, burgers, and hot dogs. We were feeling pretty good by the time the sun slipped over the horizon and a fantastic full moon lit us up like a spotlight. We four geared up with flashlights, video cameras, hunting knives that would make Rambo proud, and our flask was filled with some Apple Pie Moonshine, which boasted 190-proof 'Everclear' rectified spirits. If anything, we all would feel like Superman before the night was through.

Visibility was very good. The sounds in the trees were lively. It sounded like every woodland creature had made their appearance to greet us. Chirps, hoots, whistles, we had it all going on. At least if there were a Bigfoot in here, he would never hear us coming with all the woodland commotion. We were not as stealthy as we had probably meant to be, but by this time, we were hardly stable either. Trees began to blend into trees, vision blurred, steps wobbled at times, and our laughter was harlequinesque, for lack of a better word. We were partying hard.

I gave the guys a few instructions and the basics of Bigfoot hunting. Look for scat, but don't confuse it with coyote scat; a Bigfoot would have a considerably larger pile. Also, I instructed everyone to be on the lookout for huge crypto hominid footprints. Broken limbs could be a sign, and bark scratched from a tree... or that could be a deer rub, when they get new antlers and rub the velvet on the trees. The relict hominoids are creatures of habit, and I reminded them that there could even be a nest like gorillas built with sticks and branches. All three friends stood with collective quizzical expression.

George asked, "What do we do if we see a Bigfoot?" "I would ask him where he gets his hair done." Brad took a swig of his flask.

"How do you know if it is a male or female?" Rob had to go there.

"If it is a female, I prefer to ask her to dance," I said, attempting some humor amongst the poorly timed satirical frivolity.

"Dance? You'd come up to her kneecaps." George was taking the lead.

"No, I'd stand on your shoulders, and you could do the hip moves," I said, suddenly realizing that I had no idea which direction we were going. This is when the humor in all its drollery came to a halt.

"Are we already lost?" Brad asked, taking a more sober look around.

"We are not lost. We just do not know where we are." Rob, too, looked puzzled.

"You are correct, big difference," I mused.

"Okay, no one panic. Which side of a tree does moss grow on?" Rob was halfway serious by this time.

"North, I think," I answered.

Hoping to reassure everyone (because he needed reassurance himself), George stated, "We could not have gone too far from camp."

Rob probably had a little more to drink than the rest of us. He informed us that he needed—and these are his words—"to take a whiz." I saw this coming because we had tramped a good distance from camp now.

He properly moseyed away from us and found a certain tree to urinate. I never knew why, if you were going to pee in the forest, one tree seemed better than another. Most likely a canine instinctual trait, though I am not sure if trait is the right word. Various animals are said to possess a survival instinct, migratory instinct, herding instinct, but aren't those developed? Maybe a developed trait, whereas a trait is a distinguishing feature of your personal nature.

Regardless, Rob was relieving himself behind a mighty white oak. We waited and waited, but there was still no Rob.

"He must be watering the entire forest," I declared.

George offered to check on him. George peered behind the tree. "Fellas? He's not here," exclaimed George, his voice strained with concern. His prescient look was not a good sign.

Then Brad asked a dumb question. "What do you mean he is not there?" Brad began a forward progress toward the tree.

"I mean no Rob behind the tree. He is simply not here," George repeated.

"That goofball! What is he thinking?" I was somewhat angry that Rob wandered away, but if he had gone off on his own, was he following his instincts, clouded by the copious amount of Everclear that he had consumed? Had we not actually seen Rob go behind the white oak? Of course we had. I never took my eye off of him until he slipped behind the tree. Possibly he was alcohol driven and just walked deeper into the dark.

I called out for him. "Rob! Rob! We are over here!" The forest scattered at my yell. But no Rob. No answer.

George called out, followed by Brad. There was no answer from Rob. He had vanished.

This was terribly troubling. The forest was quite large, dense in places with dropoffs from which a man might survive a fall, but they would do some damage.

"We gotta stay cool, calculated. Keep our heads, boys. We know Rob went that way," I pointed, still holding my flask which was half drank. "We go that way until we find him."

If only the moon had remained in a clear sky, but clouds had rolled in from the south, and the cloud cover made our flashlights the only source of light. We strained our eyes in this charnel night with its Stygian darkness, hoping to see even just a glint of Rob's own light, and pressed our ears hard to listen.

Another 50 yards in, Brad declared, "I see a light!" He began to run in the direction of the beam.

"Wait! Slow up!" I exclaimed, but like a deer, Brad was wildly heading toward the beam, dodging trees as he made his way. George and I more or less trotted behind him, mindfully being more careful not to fall and injure ourselves. I saw the beam now. It had to be Rob. Who else would be this far off the main hiking trail?

When George and I reached the beam that we were following, there was disappointment. We saw that there were two flashlights on the ground, still illuminated. My heart sank. George audibly groaned. "This ain't right," said George, shining his own light in every direction.

One flashlight belonged to Rob. The other belonged to the foolhardy Brad, who had thoughtlessly run ahead of us. That dropped our numbers considerably. Now, we were two instead of four.

"Do you think they are playing with us?" George and I were a little more than dispirited by this discovery.

"I do not think so," George answered as he bent down, inspecting the forest ground. "Does this look like blood to you?" he asked gloomily.

I was not carrying luminol, nor was I a hematologist or a vampire, but it looked like blood to me.

"There is not enough blood to indicate that whoever this blood belongs to was hurt badly. This is more like a superficial wound if anything." Heavy-hearted, I inwardly prayed that I was correct. I was stirred by some vague presentiment that I could not find the words for. Something bad was happening.

"If someone had taken both of them, there was either more than one, or someone had a gun," George assumed.

"There is a third reality," I suggested. "Bigfoot!"

"Are you serious? We came out here to pretend to be looking for Bigfoot. I never thought you were serious about this stuff," George asserted.

"I wasn't necessarily serious, but I wasn't dismissive that we might find some kind of evidence," I considered.

"Well, here's evidence, but I am not certain what has taken place here can be attributed to Big Foot. There does not appear to have been a struggle of any kind. I mean, look, at the ground. There should be heel marks, broken branches, something!"

Neither George nor I were optimistic at this juncture. These were fresh abductions with no trail to follow, no evidence to collect and no perpetrator to accuse.

———

"What the holy hell is that awful smell?" George pinched his nose. A cross breeze brought the smell over to where I was standing. Absolute noxious fumes filled my nose. The mephitic stench rolled over us like a punishing fog. The foul air sickened us like a poison, and we found ourselves gasping in harmony. My nose burned, unrelenting; my eyes began to sting from the potency. It far exceeded the malodorous potency of a passing skunk. This waft of air was insidious. I got the immediate impression that we were in some sort of chemical warfare zone. The threat was upon us.

"Listen, we have to stay together. Strength in numbers is our only chance. Whatever is happening is happening now. Which way do you think our camp is?" I was wide eyed, as they say, and as sober now as I could be.

George pointed, "I believe camp is that way." Since I had no other reason to doubt him, I followed closely behind him through the darkness.

"I think we are upwind from that fetid stink," I noticed.

"That means whatever caused that stink is behind us," George agreed.

"Let us keep moving, man. It might be following us. We can get back to camp, get our bearings, call in some help," I suggested.

We spent some thirty minutes venturing around what seemed like circles until we made it back to what was left of our camp.

"What in the devil has happened?" George was aghast at what he saw.

It was difficult to believe the scene. It was annihilated. Everything, including the Jeep, was toppled. Our camping gear was laying ruined, the tents were ripped and torn apart.

"Someone has taken offense to our presence," I said, seeing that was clearly the case.

"Hell's bell's, Tom. I do not think a person is capable of this. My Jeep is on its side. One or even two men could not do this. And look at the tents. That is tough material!" George said.

"Yeah, a knife would be a cleaner cut, I would imagine," I agreed, but had no real explanation. All I had was my unprofessional opinion.

"George, this was no Bigfoot, and we do not have bears, but there is a myth which now seems more credible than before to me. Before you stop me, hear me out. Goat Man." I paused, waited for a reaction.

George stood with an obedient ear. "Goat Man?"

"All places have their legends of monsters, cryptids, creatures and such, but Kentucky is known for one of its own.

"I have read about this cryptid because of my Bigfoot studies. Usually, the sightings of what is better known as the Pope Lick Monster, which is a half-human and half-Capra Aegagrus Hircus, which basically means goat, happen at the Rail Road Trestle over Pope Lick Creek in Jefferson County. I recently read that someone had spotted this creature away from the trestle because new work is being done there by the railroad. So maybe they have uprooted the creature, and the thing is out here?"

I believed that to be as plausible as anything else I could think of on the spot. Assumptions or to assume was all I had. Then I remembered the quote which warned against assuming: "When you assume, it makes an ass of you and me."

"Okay then, what do we do? Do we call the police and tell them that Goat Man has abducted Rob and Brad? I am sure that will send out the S.W.A.T. Team," George said sarcastically.

"Listen, George, there are deaths reported because of this inexplicable creature. People have jumped from the trestle to escape it. They say it carries a bloody axe and uses some form of demonic hypnosis to lure in its victims. We never heard Rob or Brad scream. That means they were taken by surprise and did not have time to call out for help, or they fell under the Goat Man's spell."

As ridiculous as it sounded, I was beginning to believe it myself. I mean, the probability that two grown men unfortunately fell victim to a myth was unbelievably shocking, to say the least. As disturbing as this was, I did not want George to see me upset. If we had seen evidence of a fierce struggle, we would have had at least something to go by. But as it was, we could not speculate with any certainty what may have or had not happened to our friends. We did, however, have overwhelming evidence at the campsite that something more powerful than the two of us was in the woods with us.

"Where did this creature originate from? How is it even a possibility that something like this exist?" George looked as devastated by these events as the campsite did.

"This is what I know. Some freaky farmer years ago did some freaky things on his sheep and goat farm. Somehow, the devil got involved, and the next thing you know, the farmer was half man, half goat. Some circus owner, Silas somebody or some name like that, captured the cryptid, and it was part of his freak show until one night, while traveling by train, the Pope Lick Trestle was struck by lightning just as the train was crossing it. The owner, along with all of the performers and workers, died in the train derailment, but the Goat Man escaped and took up residence in the deep forest, terrorizing random people who tried to cross the tracks on foot."

"And you believe we are out here with that thing?" I answered, "I think it is a good probability. Bigfoot does not do this kind of carnage, and bears would not tip over the Jeep for fun," I assured him.

George headed over to his Jeep.

"What are you doing?" I asked, following behind him.

George crawled into the back of the Jeep and when he emerged, he was holding a pistol. "Never leave home without it," he said proudly.

"Do you have another one?" I hoped the answer was yes.

"Just this." He held up a small, two shot derringer pistol. "This is my wife's pistol. Small, but packs a big kick. It is called a Snake Slayer. It fires a .45 cal." George handed me the small but powerful derringer. "If you do have to use it, hold it tight or it will fly out of your hands," he warned me.

"Smell that?" I asked as I stood motionless.

"I do. It is that rancid odour again," George acknowledged.

"This is turning into Arthur Machen's 'The Great God Pan," I thought to myself. "Minus the firearms."

George and I abandoned the ransacked campsite, taking as many provisions as we could comfortably carry. Our phones were fully charged. We hoped that if we disappeared as well, someone could track us by our mobile phones.

"What a stigma to carry with you, being half a man and half goat," I said, just trying to keep our minds awake.

"If I see the SOB I will split him in half," George threatened in almost an angry manner.

"I still smell that vulgar smell," I said.

"It is probably stalking us," George envisioned.

We heard something other than the normal bustling forest sounds of hapless woodland creatures. Something cracked above our head. Our heads went straight up, following the beams from our flashlights. "Crap, man, that scared the Judas out of me," George whispered.

"I do not see anything," I informed him, still focused and feeling completely sober.

"Nothing," George confirmed.

"Stupid birds, probably," I hoped.

There was a mysterious fear that enveloped us unaware. We were frightened that something dreadful was lurking, but we were determined to find and rescue our friends. We could not give up hope. We were moving stealthily, attempting to make ourselves undetectable with the camouflage of the forest. The unknown is very intimidating.

We scrutinized every shadow. Clumps of bushes were approached with severe caution. The night plays tricks on your mind because the eyes are ever adapting to the ever-constant changes. The trees around us were creaking and cracking with the wind that had begun to pick up, pushing that foul, pungent smell in our direction again. We swiped away the cobwebs, newly spun and low limbs that hit us at eye level.

Another crack was heard!

"That is something, not a bird or a tree. That is something." George refused to believe anything different. I agreed. We were back-to-back, turning together, slowly covering the surroundings with our lights.

When George pulled the trigger, I dropped to the ground. I had not been shot. My natural instinct was to get low. "What was that?" I yelled out, no longer attempting to remain quiet. The gun blast had awakened anything sleeping and cut a hole through the forest with precision. We heard the sporadic flapping of wings and the clash of limbs overhead.

George was already running toward the area where he had discharged his weapon. I was not far behind, but had to catch up. When we got to the spot where George had aimed, we discovered a large amount of blood. "I knew I hit it," he said with confidence.

"Hit what? What did you see?"

"You know those movies where this goat thing appears, and it turns out to be Satan himself? Well, I just shot the devil. He ain't no angel either. Angels do not bleed. And by the way, it ain't no Bigfoot either. I have never seen anything like it," George said.

"A trail. How good are you at tracking a blood trail?" I should have already known the answer. George was a deer hunter. With confidence, he proudly said, "We will track it." The night seemed to have gotten darker. The unbroken forest was more foreboding, as if that gun blast had created some alternate nocturnal world before us. The air had chilled. Shadows were cast long, and the forest felt deathly quiet. The environment had become as haunting as a graveyard, yet wore an enthralling ambiance, almost a reverence. I had the impression that we were walking into the hollowness of something deep and Eldritch, which may turn out to be to our detriment. I took sedulous care with each step, though on the inside I was becoming unravelled.

"What happened to all of the sounds?" George was whispering again.

"This does not resemble the forest we were in at all," I noticed.

We walked the pathless grey deeper into the somber void, finding blood droplets which we followed. Unlike the lively sounds earlier in the day, all was hushed as if in anticipation as the two of us withered in size, being consumed by the enormity of the bleakness, which had crept upon us unwittingly. We could hear the river below us, and it was obvious that whatever George had wounded had gone down over the embankment.

We turned off our lights. The moon miraculously appeared, giving us a clear field of view. George, who seemed to always spot things before me, pointed without a word. As I followed the direction on his index finger, I saw what he sighted.

It was indeed the Goat Man, the unholy menace. The infestuous beast must have crawled out from beneath some chimerical lair. He was larger than a man, with the head and horns of a ram. He had muscular human arms and goat legs complete with hooves. It was hunched over, washing the flesh wound in the river. All manner of bones were scattered about, some even in the trees displayed like trophies. Numerous were the ones stripped white, clean, decorticated, and pulverized, while others had rancid remains of flesh attached. To the left of the beast, tied to a tree, were Brad and Rob, both awake and alert. They did not look injured, but from here it was not certain. Evil portent like an unseen menace loomed.

"I need to get closer," George said as he slipped on his backside gradually down the slope in order to gain a clearer shooting position. I held an unsteady aim on the cryptid, knowing that I would surely miss from here, but at least it would make some noise if George needed backup.

The unbelievable happened just as George took aim. Rob and Brad had obviously cut themselves loose from their vine restraints in an attempt to secure their own escape. At least one of them must have kept a knife on them. They began to run. I am not sure what they were thinking, other than survival. They permitted themselves one look back and ran, scrambling faster on unsteady legs.

The Goat Man rose from nursing its own wound. This is when I noticed it was a cyclops, a one-eyed satyr. It let out a mirthless shriek followed by a blasphemous laugh, which burst the forest alive with a cacophony of sounds that pitched from tree to tree until the forest echoed with uncanny noises.

George pulled the trigger a second time. This shot hit the Goat Man in the shoulder. It flinched as if it had been stung by a bee. I guess George was just making sure that the distance and aim were right because the next six shots hammered the cryptid several steps backward. Now being off balance and mortally wounded, it was repelled rearward until it fell into the river.

When Brad and Rob heard the explosions from George's weapon, they must have guessed it was us. They stopped in their tracks and turned in our direction. Relieved that they had been rescued, the two of them begin to walk back in our direction.

My heart was thumping like a hunted rabbit. I slid down the slope where George, Rob and Brad had already had their reunion. I was at the bottom, some 50 feet from the three of them, when I heard something charging that sounded like it was coming up behind me fast. The three of them were celebrating the rescue, too boisterously to hear it right away. I stood between whatever was charging directly at me and my three friends. I spun around one hundred and eighty degrees with the derringer raised. From the forest along the banks of the river, an infuriated wild Goat Man came swinging its bloody axe, shambling towards me. It was bleeding, growling like a large cat, but making heavy hooved sounds as it advanced at a great rate of speed toward my position. I knew the gun that George had given to me was for short distances and even at that they did not aim well. The Goat Man's eyes were glowing red with fire and ultimate abomination. Its white fur was crimson-stained; it lowered its head as if it were to ram me. It was swinging the axe wildly and with evil intent. I smelled its skunk-like potency and when I did, with nervous trepidation I pulled the trigger. The bottom barrel fired, and by mere chance, it struck the Goat Man in the top of the head. Its steps were immediately staggered. Trying to maintain coherent thought, I did not hesitate to pull the trigger again, firing the top barrel of another bullseye.

The Goat Man stumbled, its brains shattered by the blast, but its momentum carried until it fell inches from my feet, attempting a final swing of the axe, but thank sweet Jesus, it missed. The axe flung from its hand and splashed into the river.

The frightful smell was like a forcefield. It repelled me backward like an invisible hand. My three friends had witnessed the entire thing. George had actually raised his gun after my second shot, but it was obvious no more lead was needed. I had killed the Pope Lick Monster.

My ears were ringing like bells from the gunshot and through muffled congratulations, I seemed to be the man of the hour. I had to push down the delirium that wanted to control me. The temperature had dropped, but I was drenched in perspiration and freezing cold to the point my teeth chattered. I reunited with the three of them. We all suffered superficial scrapes and bruises, but no one had been seriously injured. We agreed that it was a miracle from heaven.

The crude reminders from that day that I mentioned at the top of this story are the impressive white horns and the once powerful hooves of the Goat Man. I have them displayed in what my wife calls the mancave. As to whatever happened to the carcass after I dehorned and removed the two hooves, I do not know. I took my trophies back to the campsite and called the authorities. A small army arrived when we explained that we had been attacked by an unknown beast. We did not mention The Goat Man in the event they thought we were intoxicated. When we came to the site where I had dropped the beast dead, there was no sign of it. There was a bloodstain, but the beast was gone. We never told anyone what really had happened because we had to live in the community and jokes would have abounded. Our story was simply we came across a mad billy goat and had to put it down. The horns and hooves are a reminder that drinking Everclear at night in the woods with your friends might just put you on an unforgettable adventure of unimaginable danger.

THE DEVIL'S PRINTING PRESS

My name is Aldus Manutius, but I am not he who grew up wealthy nor was sent to Rome to become a philosopher. I just so happen to share the name of one from the past. I am neither a painter nor a humanist, but one thing that we do have in common is the printing press. He was said to have changed reading forever, and I suppose when I came along some 600 years later, give or take a decade or two, there was another colossal change that took place without anyone being the wiser... with the exception of yours truly, who is giving you the story firsthand as it was given to me.

Borrowing from old descriptions and terms, I was what you might call a Devil's Printer. I performed a number of tasks, such as mixing tubs of ink and fetching type. I was often covered in ink, especially after I removed the old, worn and sometimes broken cast metal type and disposed of it in what we called a hellbox. The hellbox, as it was notably called, stored the discarded or broken type that were melted down and recast. This was the life I knew, but not the life I loved.

You see, I am a writer, and I have volumes of unpublished works. I am a prophetic writer, writing daily my thoughts, which turn to stories. I am literally suffocating myself with works that I fear will never be read. My writings cover many different subjects and styles. I have submitted my work to several well-known publishing houses, yet I have taken the 'no reply,' as a permanent 'no thank you;' thus, I continue to spill my thoughts out onto paper, hoping one day I will get that knock on the door and someone says, "Let us see what you have."

Now, you might say that the following has been manufactured, made up, over-embellished and even that it contains aggrandizement that could not possibly hold true under scrutiny and rigorous examination; however, I beg to differ. If you want to paint me as infamous, misleading, devilish or something worse, that is your prerogative, but first allow me due respect to get this matter off my chest, won't you?

Permit me to say that which needs to be said in my defense as a matter of great importance without scrutiny or interruption. You can rest assured I will gladly field and entertain all of your questions at the end of my soliloquy.

Forgive my lack of proper elocution. I will attempt, in no uncertain terms, to keep my monologue condensed for the purpose of keeping your full attention throughout my counterclaims against the accusations heralded and thrown in my direction.

Concentrated imaginations can easily be manipulated by dark forces that linger around the written as well as the spoken words. You have heard the idiom, "You took the words right out of my mouth?" Or the mate to that phrase, "Do not put words in my mouth?"

My work had been a righteous work, a pure and undefiled work, up until the little man, that baser of a man who seduced me through lust and carnality, entered through my doors and into my life. He was an atavistic type, a bloodsucker whose nature was to drain you of your life source while barely keeping you alive. He fed from the trough of my imagination, my dreams and my desires, all the while using me like a plaything in the hands of a mischievous child who had no intentions of ever letting go until that doll of a thing (in this case the doll was me) was ragged, broken, unusable, leaving me under the spotlight of scrutiny inchoate, like an afflicted antediluvian no longer fit for purpose.

It all was a shameful display, with the curtain stretched wide open with such unattainable force by human means until the drawstrings were broken, and the curtain would never fall again on my life. Exposed, all revealed; can you not see that I was used, mastered, a puppet in the hands of Titivillous?

I wrote only what he commanded me to write. This demon, who comically brings chaos and chatter in the middle of sacred times, took hold of me, defiled my thinking and vulgarised practically all of my work. He gathers the broken pieces of thoughts, dictates their meaning, scribes a distorted narrative, and feeds it into the person who then has no choice but to write what they are told to write, for it burns the membranes of the mind to hold it within.

And another thing, the original is not by ink and paper but by fire and flesh. He burns the stories onto your heart, forever scarring you. I am proof of that.

***

Let me begin; I was at my wit's end. I was exhausted from writing, pouring my soul into my work for no rewards, no interest, and no promise. But I was committed to my work, a slave to the grind, and in this time of votive reflection and creativity, a knock came at my door, unexpectedly, out of the pure blue. I never received visitors, so on this rare occasion, I hastily ran my fingers through my ruffled hair, straightened my shirt and answered the door accommodatingly. I was surprised to see a man of infinitesimal stature, yet he was not what one might define as a midget. He would have been regarded as proportional and simply a small man.

"Hello, my good man." He introduced himself as Titus. I took him at his word, which was the polite thing to do, and I introduced myself as "Aldus," to which he said, "I know. You are why I came.

Rather, with your permission, I would like to explain to you why I am here on your behalf."

I was curious, to say the least. "On my behalf? Well, my friend, come in." I invited the little man inside and, assuming he was going to stay awhile, I made us a pot of peppermint tea with ginger, and we sat at my dining table. As we took our teas, Titus seemed to have a lot on his mind and appeared to have a sweet tooth. I counted six lumps of sugar in one cup, and he hummed a short thrum in his throat with each sip, a noise gurgling twice in his throat, swishing the drips around before committing to completely swallowing the brew. He certainly got a lot of mileage from a single sip.

He carried the conversation, and I listened intently, hoping he would get to the crux of the matter with a little more urgency.

He explained to me why he was visiting my shop.

"I have been dispatched to you by my employer upon your request, and in this response, we hope you will contemplate and consider what we are willing to provide for you. You are a writer, and we publish. We would publish some of your original works and distribute them with a hefty percentage coming to you, but there is one thing we would require and necessitate from you." Titus paused long enough to allow me to query, but the very second I was about to ask the question, he interrupted me. Indeed, I wanted to ask a question, but weirdly, I could not recall what the question was. I had no reason for rebuttal because I was already sold. Maybe I was going to ask how soon we could begin; instead, I lent my full attention to his pitch all the way up to the interlocution.

Intrigued by every facet of the proposal, I saw no need to, nor a single reason to revise or further strategize what had clearly been laid out for me. I did not hesitate to sign the paperwork Titus had thoughtfully brought along for such an occasion. We had a deal that favored me in the agreement, which was a rare gem. All that was necessary for me to do, and the only stipulation, was that I use my name and under such, Titus would provide a dictated story per day, written by his independent employer, and I would be required to submit it to the local newspaper where I was guaranteed to have those stories published. I had no problem with this arrangement whatsoever. I would have my books and short story collection published on a large scale, and in return, I would always have a piece in the local paper mandated by the unknown employer of Titus, who would drop off the story to be submitted to the newspaper every morning for the evening press.

Titus took one of my first books in its entirety with the promise it would be published within days. He also dropped off the story he wished for me to submit to the newspaper after I had read over it and transposed it to a proper format for the paper. I was acting as Chief Editor; I was not allowed to change the story or the names but could word anything differently that I felt did not flow well. The first story was disturbing, to say the least, and I noticed that the time given was not past but futuristic. The story read as follows:

"Strange happenings in the Morgan Township Cemetery at approximately midnight, the 27th of March. Under the cover of darkness, graverobbers, treasure hunters, have exhumed Mrs. Roberta Flacker from her entombment and have desecrated the grave in an act of thievery but not body snatching as such. Mrs. Flacker has been reported to have been buried with a wealth of jewelry, and not a single ring, broach or necklace was found. The thieves got away with priceless loot."

I found this to be incredulous. How could my new employer possibly predict a graverobbing (which is unheard of in this day), and how would my employer have one iota of knowledge concerning who was buried with their wealth? The big question was, how did he know this was going to happen since it had not actually occurred to my knowledge? This dumbstruck me, but I followed the instructions of Titus and submitted it through the proper means. When I hand delivered the story to the editor, he too was amazed that within an hour of the paper finding out about the theft, I was handing in a comprehensive story covering every aspect of the crime and desecration.

How my employer knew this crime was going to be committed was a mystery. I thought it best not to inquire, but just to let it go. I was being paid per week more than I had ever been paid per month, and Titus brought cash money, which I gratefully accepted. I suppose Titus saw my concern, and without asking why I possibly had a problem with the first story, he looked me in the eye and quoted:

"Jocelyn Murray, Khu: A Tale of Ancient Egypt. 'Even in prosperous times the living robbed the dead.'"

That in itself was unpaired and inexplicable, yet I went along with it because I was now a published author, and that meant more to me than anything else in the world. I admit I had selfish reasons, but why do people like myself write? We write to be read. Not to be read is only someone talking to themselves, and I never wanted to admit that I was the type of person who would talk to himself. To find myself in a condition of psychosis would defeat the purpose of my every intent to be read. Nothing could have been more devastating than to have lived a lifetime with things to say and to share and yet to have it stifled, muted and to be considered unreadable. To be overlooked, not considered, forgotten, or neglected to a writer is the ultimate insult, for it would signify failure. To have been forgotten and to never even be published and read would mean no library would ever house the creations. I am legible, I am readable, and now I have that validation. The exposure I was going to receive was invaluable to my career.

Over the course of the next two weeks, Titus dropped off one news story after the other, and I rewrote, edited, and turned them in to the local newspaper, where every story became a featured piece. The subject matter and the circumstances of the stories were all tragedies and unprecedented. I began to become nervously suspicious and admittingly concerned if I was taking part unknowingly in nefarious incidents. I was not a willing participant in malevolent or sinister doings. There was no possible way that anyone could be predicting these insidious acts of law-breaking and despicable atrocities without having a dubious and unsavory personal connection with the victims. I subscribed to a perfidious notion that my employer could not in any way be responsible directly or indirectly for these iniquitous acts and misdoings.

I was consumed with guilt yet drawn by the almighty dollar and the lust for success with my own personal writings, so I stayed quiet, said not a word, did not report my suspicions, counted the dollars and basked in the joy of my literary success. In stark contrast, my conscience was not at peace, and I found no rest. I rebuked these feelings of guilt and tried to ignore these concerns, but they continued to be reminders of my success. I ceased reading the newspaper because I was beginning to feel responsible for the tragedies printed therein. The debate with myself was swinish, which I was never proud of, but I was slowly being turned from my original nature and found comfort in my pernicious state. I took an emollient approach toward my weaknesses. I knew deep down in my core that I was working for the Slanderer, and he was very responsible, firsthand, with the events in my area. I wrestled immensely with my emotions, the feelings of heartache for the victims, all the while counting my money like a Scrooge.

It was because of a premonition I briefly saw when I looked in the mirror one morning, preparing to start my day, that made me reflect and reconsider where I stood and if I was able and capable of standing there any longer. In my revaluations, I judged myself, weighed myself, and condemned myself, knowing that if I continued down this path of yielding to every whim of my employer, I would be surrendering my soul to eternal damnation. I opted to change how I approached these stories I was rewriting for the newspaper. I was vying for control of my life, but somehow, I knew it would not be successful without a fight.

Titus arrived as he had arrived every day since I agreed to turn in the stories for the paper. I said nothing of my internal protest, my resistance, my refusal to comply with further requests. I made the decision to test my theory. Titus entrusted me to deliver the next news story, as I had been faithfully doing. I carefully read the story after he departed, and it was without a doubt the most troubling story I had been entrusted with. It was given to me as is, "May 3rd at 9:00 pm. Thieves entered the home of Mr. John Bagwell at 22 West Front Street. Mr. Bagwell, 62, confronted the thieves, Vance Culpepper, 18 and Randy Barnes, 19. Mr. Bagwell was murdered during the confrontation. Both Culpepper and Barnes are being held in the Fulton County jail awaiting arraignment."

The story was heartbreaking and beyond dreadful. My mind was made up, and I was not going to stick with the narrative. I took certain liberties and made some tweaks. These amendments did not completely scrap the original story, but my redefined modifications read something like this: "May 3rd at 9:00 pm. Two men, Vance Culpepper, 18 and Randy Barnes, 19, visited 62-year-old John Bagwell and brought him a free pizza and colas. The three dined together and watched the game. At midnight, the two young men went home, and Mr. Bagwell went to bed and lived a very long time."

I submitted my article to the paper and got some pushback. They did not feel that this was newsworthy, yet I convinced them that if they printed this article, which was more involved than what I have shared here, I would surely bring them even more fascinating articles in the future. They agreed, to my amazement, and I returned to my place to have a rest.

The following day, I heard an aggressive banging on the door of my shop. I had not yet unlocked the front door, and it sounded as if someone was determined to come in. It was Titus, and he looked very upset.

He began, "Totally and absolutely unacceptable. You have blatantly broken our trust in you. The story from yesterday has terribly upset our employer, and he is very disappointed. Do you have a single excuse why you deliberately changed the narrative?"

I made my claim. "Why, yes. Because I see that whatever I write and submit and what gets printed comes to light, it happens as if I am dictating the lives of these people. If I write that someone died, they really die, and I am no murderer."

"There is a balance between good and evil that must exist. It has always existed. There are rules to follow. It is black and white, and you have ventured into a grey area where you do not want to be, trust me," Titus threatened.

"And what happens if I refuse to write any more articles for you?" I asked defiantly.

"That would be ill-advised. I am in no position to state what might happen or what might become of you, but I can assure you whatever the repercussions would be, would be detrimental." Titus opened his black briefcase and handed me another story.

"Our employer is willing to forget you ran your little experiment, but he will not forget this betrayal. He has sent a letter directly to you and has requested you write another story, and here it is." Titus slid two envelopes across the table and nudged them against my chest. He then stood on little legs, his tiny frame rigid. I wanted him out of my shop. He was an intimidating, feisty little man.

I first opened the letter addressed directly to me. This was the first letter or direct communication from my sadistic employer, so I was interested in reading what it had to say.

Aldus,

You have been faithful in your allegiance to me, and I have rewarded you handsomely for your willingness to use your ambition to further my worldwide cause. I hope that you are not reconsidering because we have invested greatly in your success, and I would not want to think that my hospitality is going ungratefully. It is important that you stay the course and follow the normal protocols, which you have followed up until your last improvisation. This caused me great and terrible grief. You must know by now who I am and what forces are present. I know you will not be foolish enough or as careless with your submissions as you were with your previous one. We can allow for one mistake. My goal, and you are instrumental in helping me to achieve this, is I want them to believe in me, fear me and when they panic and do everything they humanly can do to avoid me, they will willingly run straight into my arms. I will give them religion. I will make them think they are worshipping God, but I will make it so with many translations, variations, adaptions, writes and rewrites, exhaustive works, in different languages, versions, I will watch them argue and bicker and fight over who is right and who is wrong. God will be painted as a Santa who rewards the good little boys and girls with gifts and toys, and then, from his fiery furnace, he will withdraw the coals for the stockings of the disobedient.

Hopefully, this letter is clear enough about my intentions, and you will be invested in its success.

And it was signed in old-fashioned letters. P.O.D. Which I assumed stood for Prince Of Darkness.

This was most troubling, to say the least. Doubting myself, totally self-abased, momentarily, I believed I was defeated. This was not a good place to be in. There was no disputing the success and acceptance along with the monetary rewards of becoming a convincing author on a world stage with the help from P.O.D.

Titus was a faithful lickspittle to my employer, and must have seen him daily in order to bring me these stories. It was terrifyingly clear that I was in imminent danger if I refused to continue to submit the stories to the paper, and it would, in any case, be detrimental to my achievements as an author. I could see no light at the end of the tunnel for me. The nearest I could see was the harsh dimness of a final judgment that would rain down on me, and the practicalities would be nonsensical and unmanageable.

Titus stood dismissive with a smug expression, as if he was being inconvenienced, waiting for my response. His irksome face riled me, yet I understood the exorbitant value of this moment in comparison to the relentless torrents of extremism that could be unleashed upon me, a prisoner now of the Slanderer, trapped within my own compositions. As unacceptable as this was, I saw no way out. I was secure only if I continued being used in this complacent scheme of unremitting servitude, embellishing P.O. D.'s words as discreditable and repulsive as I found them to be. Immoral, repugnant... this misuse of my talent was surely going to come back to personally haunt me, maybe in a judicious way, maybe in an eternal way; either way, with every word I transposed, edited, copied, or published, I could see my fate extrinsically being set in stone, which in this case would be a headstone marker for my own grave.

Understanding that my employer was not reasonable, I had to answer him through Titus.

Impulsively, I asked, "Can I meet him?"

Titus acted as if he had never been presented with such a request in all of his days. "The burnished one? The one forged in the fires? You believe you could stand before him and not be burned?" Titus chortled like a child.

"Have you seen him?" I needed to prod him more.

"Seen?" Titus's eyes lit like a flame. "We see him every day. Look out at your impoverished lands. He takes the food from the mouths of the starving. He removes the shelters from the indignant. He raises someone to power and then leads a coup against him, to overthrow anyone who seeks to sit where he sits. He causes rebellion in the hearts of humanity and causes the bloodbaths of war. He inveighed against the church, the truth, and sent his spectral hordes to infest mankind like a plague. Look around you, and you instantly have an audience with him. Walk your streets tonight and see his dealings, visit his affairs, watch flesh pursue the sordid things and the transgressions of his power are revealed in the way people distort the image of God. The walking dead, the revenants... they are his handy work. See how they cry out for more from the Master. He tears down the antinomian forms of faith and leaves a soul barren. How could I possibly take you to see him face to face? But... ask, and it shall be given. Are you truly asking?"

"It is what I am asking," I said aloud.

In a move I thought was off-subject, Titus produced a newspaper and laid it into my hands. "Have you seen the papers?"

I took the paper from him. "Page 3," he instructed and observed. I saw the headline "MURDER OR ACCIDENT?"

The short piece read as follows:

"Mr. John Bagwell, 62 years old, living at 22 West Front Street, was found unresponsive in this home just before midnight. Preliminary reports said he died on his way to the hospital. The cause of death has not been revealed, but investigators say they cannot rule out foul play."

Titus gestured with his hand as if to say, 'There it is, in black and white,' or at least that is what I derived from seeing the silly little man's false grandiosity, his vile, unethical attitude, which I loathed.

"They cannot be saved. This is the role we all have to play. That is why I say, 'Live for today, for tomorrow is the illusion that may never be.' If you want to be a sinner, sin large; if you feel the need to repent, you can do it all day long. But one thing is certain: written in stone, when your day comes, you will face it entirely alone. But that day will come."

Deflated and humiliatingly mollified, I sat at my writing table and opened the second envelope. In this horrific moment, I felt like a reprobate with no moral compass to guide me. As unsound as I was, I had some constant strange tinnitus building in my ears.

"Do not feel bad, Aldus. A reasonable offer has been presented to you, and you agreed. The contract cannot be altered, rewritten, or amended. Do you remember the story of the rich man and the beggar man, how the rich man lived lavishly, while the poor man ate the crumbs from the rich man's table? And how the dogs licked the poor man's wounds?"

This was the first time Titus had used my name. Now it had become personal. "I do remember the story, but I remember the rich man, Dives, I believe his name was, ended up in Hades among the flames and begged that the poor man who sat in Abraham's bosom for just a drop of water to quench the fires on his tongue." I remembered my Sunday school lessons and the threats of a tormented afterlife, which I presently did not adhere to.

"Our master rescued the rich man, and that is not what unequivocal truth teaches, for the truth is a lie, and the lie is the truth, and if you eat from this tree, you shall not surely die. The whole story has not been told because it is still being written. Do you not see? The narrative requires surrender. You must follow the storyline presented because it is unfinished, fundamentally misleading, and requires immolation. Everything burns; everything is tried, tested, and proven by fire. Your works will be revealed. You have been endowed with the vitality and foresight to write the future, to make it happen, and you will be rewarded not only as you presently are, but only imagine—and I know you can—waking to everlasting wealth."

I opened the letter which contained my next assignment. It read like a murmur on my lips.

"Tragic events tonight have shattered our small community after the bodies of 13-year-old Cindy Wellford and 14-year-old Kathy Metcalf were discovered in a clearing within the Vickers Tree Reserve at 10 pm tonight. The girls went missing just yesterday.

No more details were given by authorities. The investigation has begun, and we will stay on top of this."

An illness poignantly swelled in my gut.

"Time is of the essence. I must be going now. I trust you will not disappoint the master for a second time?" he loutishly said as he left once again, leaving the door to the shop swinging open. His agitation of helplessness was a prickling irritation in his chest like a deep thorn from a flawless rose whose sweetness was lost on the pain and never entered the nose.

Entangled like a fly in the spider's web. What was I to do if saving the girls was out of the question? I could only mourn the inevitable and grieve for the heartbreaking news to come, which would split the families apart and change the course of every friend the girls had ever had. I had withered when I folded up the letter of instructions. I could not save them regardless of what I wrote. But I had to change the narrative. I had to make it a peaceful departure from this wicked world, so with the proper punctuality I wrote, "Tragedy befell two local families this evening when the bodies of 13-year-old Cindy Wellford and 14-year-old Kathy Metcalf was discovered in the Wellford home. The cause of the girl's deaths was carbon monoxide poisoning due to a faulty heater the family had recently purchased to heat the upstairs bedroom where their daughter slept. We will bring you more news on this heartache when it becomes available."

I delivered the story in the usual way, and it was accepted as a piece for the morning paper run. I spent a ponderous night waiting on the consequences of my rewrite, if it was sufficed and if would be appreciable enough or if he would mute me in some deranged chamber of death while being tormented by Titus, the cicerone of my every nightmare. That foul little man was my anathema. Maybe

I should make him part of the headlines? If it were possible, I would write him into the bowels of hell.

Living life in a vacuum, I swore in this funnel I heard the flapping of wings. With every visit from that uncouth Titus, I was losing more and more of myself, dissatisfied with every aspect of the deal I had made, but I saw no existential exit, no way out, and misery joined me, locking arm and arm with me, and traveled where I traveled. The point of consummation was not yet reached. I had to find a resolution and agree with what was surmised from it in order to stop this vein of the devil's trickery. Entirely contaminated, violated, and polluted with a mirky sediment of sticky goo, I could not escape the guilt, the grime and the condemnation that clung to me, nor scrub it away.

The following day dawned, and in the light of day, I could see more clearly. In my restlessness, I had concocted what I hoped to be a solution to free me from this infernal doomed existence. I had decided with confirmation from my own deliberations that I would no longer be used as a pawn and a puppet in some masquerade, giving myself to the traducer of souls. I would excuse myself from this carnival attraction of megalomania. Determining all of my goals as an author had been met, and I would be infamously recognized posthumously by my adoring readers... that was really what this had all been about for me. Yes, I will admit, I was basking in the dream state of my success, finally achieving the prestige I deserved for my many literary works. Even with all of the adulation and temporary acclaim, I was not gratified. The affluence of admiration I had received I could not enjoy. It was overwhelming, and now I found myself as the rich man in the flames of his own success, without true prowess.

I thought I should possibly attempt to write Titus out of my life. That in itself would resolve some of my tribulations, but when

I sat down to write it, most peculiarly, his name would never appear in ink. I proposed to type it, but the hammer with its slug of metal type failed to strike the paper when I typed in his name.

I went to my writing desk, and I wrote my next news article, which I knew would come to fruition. I had been given the prophetic gift to write the subsequent story, the unforeseeable and to be the engineer of life and death thanks to P.O.D. Before he stripped me of this talent, I had one more thing to write. This would be my final submission to the newspaper, and thus I would retire.

"The esteemed Aldus Manutius writer, poet, novelist, and contributor to our local newspaper, has died. Ironically, he passed away in our offices this afternoon while handing in his last new story, which we are printing verbatim, and you are presently reading it at this moment. Obviously, he foresaw his own death, and questions have been raised if he poisoned himself before entering the building. Authorities are waiting for toxicology reports to rule out if possible illicit substances or drugs of any kind were found in his bloodstream. It appears without question Aldus Manutius ascertained an unusual gift for prediction, and in his foresight, he forecasted to the very second his own death. He would like to be remembered simply as 'a man willing to do the right thing regardless of the consequences.' And yes, one more thing to add to the eidetic memory is, he was a fantastic writer."

Who would have ever thought that the last thing I ever wrote would be my own obituary?

NINE LIVES

Melvin Garland sat alone in his two-bedroom apartment on Burrows Street, pondering the complexities of life. He was an odd one to be writing romance novels, yet he was fairly successful and had a medium size fan base. Melvin wrote under the pen name of Simon Hardy. He chose the name from two of his favorite writers. Melvin admired Claude Simon, the French novelist who had been awarded the 1985 Nobel Laureate in Literature, and the second writer that fascinated him was the poet and novelist Thomas Hardy.

Melvin was odd for a number of reasons. At 40, he had never married, had no children, nor had an interest in family.

The dark veil that he now wore over his life was pulled down twenty years ago when his beloved Maggie took her own life by jumping from the Golden Gate Bridge right in front of his pleading eyes. Since that time, Melvin had gone on in hurt and inner agony, withholding his heart from any other. Now his emotions were fortified by misery and love lost.

Shortly after that tragic evening, Melvin checked himself into a clinic, claiming mental exhaustion. Therapy had been suggested for Melvin, and he complied in the beginning, gaining a good repertoire with the psychiatrist, who was concerned that he may have onset schizophrenia. When Melvin heard this diagnosis, he immediately went into deep denial, explaining to his doctor that he understood the difference between real and unreal experiences. He was a man who could think logically; he had normal emotions of love, pain, joy, and hurt. He loved his privacy; however, he was not afraid of the outside world. His psychiatrist explained to him, in no uncertain terms, that although he may not have believed he had the onset of a mental illness, certain environmental events may trigger an irreversible episode.

Melvin could not accept the doctor's findings. He was convinced that the doctor's conclusions were off base. "I am not suicidal. Yes, I am depressed, but the love of my life threw herself off a bridge right in front of my eyes!" Melvin protested.

For a fairly successful writer, Melvin lived much more modestly. His apartment was cluttered with books and loose papers that contained ideas, scribbles, and written thoughts. Melvin was also fond of lamps. "They put the light closer to earth," he used to say.

Melvin took the time to shower daily, though his dark, dull wardrobe needed some professional dry cleaning. His hygiene was probably above normal because he detested bad breath, dirty fingernails, stained teeth, especially body odors.

On this dull December holiday, Melvin sat behind his cluttered writing desk gazing out of his third-story apartment window, taking in the distantly manicured John McLaren Park while admiring the strings of multifarious blinking lights. Caught up in thought, he tapped a no. 2 wooden pencil loosely between two fingers. His thoughts were often as scrambled as his writing desk. Like a slot machine viewing window, he never knew how the images would line up with the pay line.

The payout today was a brand-new prize for Melvin. He became lightheaded as a wave of warmth made him feel fuzzy inside. Melvin felt that he had hit the jackpot. No longer able to define the line of demarcation, he clearly spoke aloud words which made him shiver. "I'm going to kill someone."

Melvin went from being engrossed in his most recent romance assignment to thinking about murder. His romance novels never addressed murder: every work that he had published were feel-good stories with happy endings, but today, something had changed him. It was difficult to say why Melvin's mind shifted gears from cruise mode to faster than the speed of light, but whatever the influence or reason was, he had veered off the highway of reason and logic, spinning down a dangerous path.

Rifling through his bundles of newspapers with scissors in hand, Melvin began to design encrypted messages that he would send to the police as teasers. They would be taunts to law enforcement: "Catch me if you can." This was new to Melvin, who had never even killed a mouse in his lifetime. He did not question where this power of life and death was coming from. He embraced it because suddenly, he was rejuvenated with a rush of youthful excitement racing through his soul.

The first message that Melvin prepared while wearing latex gloves for the police in block letters clipped from newspaper glued to a plain white sheet of paper read, "It walks on all four in the morning, two legs at noon and three legs in the evening. What is it?"

"Clever, no prints," he thought, grinning to himself like a child that had snatched a piece of candy from the supermarket without being seen. He assiduously folded the letter and stuffed it into the plain white envelope. Being very pleased with himself, he used his typewriter to type the words "Nine in Nine Days" on the envelope.

He delivered the letter across the Golden Gate Bridge, mailing the letter far away from his own home. The deed was done. He was exhilarated with his first play in the game. Melvin knew he had the upper hand. He had no previous criminal record. He was not a homicidal maniac. There would be no sexual undertones to his killing, just killing for the sake of killing. He would pick random people that he had never met, so there would be no personal connection. There would be no exchange of emails, phone records or dinners. The victim would be anonymous until the moment of death. It was a win / win, fail-safe plan. Acting from a conscious perspective, his plan was to commit nine flawless murders in nine days, then abandon the notion and simply walk away with the satisfaction that he had gotten away without suspicion. Melvin prided himself that he was in complete control.

He did not hear audible voices telling him to kill. He did not have vivid dreams of murder. This was just something he decided to do.

Melvin realized that he was a unique serial killer because the genesis of his killing would be unpredictable, and the penultimate act would set up the final scene. He had it all thought through. The garrote would never be placed around his neck, for his neck would be clean.

The first step would be to find the first victim. He had decided that his first victim would be on this particular evening. It was Friday, and the bars would be packed with party-minded people drunk, high, and looking for a world far removed from their mundane 40-hour-a-week job schedule. This would be like shooting ducks in a barrel. His mind was a jigsaw puzzle, sliding all of the loose pieces into place.

Dressed in his nicest dress shirt and slacks, Melvin placed a pair of black gloves in his jacket pocket. He gave himself one last inspection and left to carry out what he hoped would not be a cursory murderous night. He wanted to take his time, leaving no clues. He headed to the Castro neighborhood to the Lucky 13 dive bar.

The Lucky 13 was an inviting bar. Melvin would be able to blend in without anyone seeing him clearly. The crowd was an eclectic mix of punks and Goths and a handful of other 'Melvins.'

He watched the bathroom door, waiting to see if anyone went in or came out. Melvin decided to use the bathroom for cover. He found a stall and waited. He heard the bathroom door open and someone came in. Whoever entered did not go to the stalls; they went to the urinal.

Melvin despised the urinals. He could not understand how a grown man could urinate openly next to another man. It was like pissing in someone else's pocket.

Melvin had to think quickly. He had no weapon. Time to improvise. He lifted the rectangular ceramic toilet bowl lid off the tank. It was heavy. It could be used with both hands for extra swinging power. Melvin slipped out of the stall and approached the man facing the urinal. Raring back and tightening the grip on the cold lid, he was standing like a baseball slugger. He wanted the victim to see his death coming. As soon as the man turned, Melvin swung, unloading with all of his might. The blow to the head was so powerful that the lid broke in Melvin's hand. This unnamed victim fell back. A frozen expression of helplessness painted upon his smashed face. It occurred to Melvin in the panic to find a weapon that he had forgotten to use gloves. He knew his victim was dead. He was positively dead and growing cold.

Melvin's heart raced, and his breathing became erratic. He ran to the paper towel dispenser and practically pulled every towel loose from it. He soaked the towels under the sink facet with water, and then, like a madman, he scrubbed the possible fingerprints from the two broken ceramic pieces. He rushed to the stall, and he wiped down anything that he thought he had possibly touched. He pieced the lid together and laid it back upon the tank. He realized he had really been careless. He had to go. He went to the body and looked down.

He gasped audibly as, for a split second, the man's face morphed into his own, then back into its current smashed self. One last thing to do: Melvin dragged the corpse by the feet into the last stall and sat it up on the toilet seat. To himself, he said, "I am in the clear."

He took a deep breath and tried to act casual as he weaved through the bar. Head down, he went straight to his car. He fumbled for the ignition key; once started, he turned the air conditioning on high. Laying his head against the steering wheel, he slowly took control of his breathing, for he had nearly hyperventilated. At the instant he raised his head and glanced to his left, the reflection in the driver's side window startled him. The image was not his face, but a mirage of his murder victim. His hands instinctively flew up defensively to protect his face. He blinked hard twice, and the mirage had vanished. Staring back into his eyes was his own troubled gaze.

When the magnitude of what he had done settled, he had a sense of accomplishment. Melvin could not imagine life clearer than in this moment, regardless of the aberrant behavior that he had just exhibited. It was not the perfect murder, but it was murder. He could not wait to read the headlines in the paper in the morning.

Once home, he swallowed a handful of aspirin in hopes of getting relief from his developing headache. His head throbbed with a pulsating pain.

———

The following morning, he filtered through the newspaper thoroughly. The big story of murder at the Lucky 13 was nowhere to be found. He cursed and slammed a single fist against the table. He could not imagine how such a brutal murder had gone unreported.

He finished up his normal morning breakfast, while cutting and pasting a new message for the police. The new message read, "I am the beginning of the end, and the end of time and space. I am essential to creation, and I surround every place. What am I?"

He placed the folded message in the same type of envelope as his last one and addressed it to the police with the typed message on a smaller piece of paper, which read, "Catch me if you can."

He had some shopping to do. He wasn't about to get caught off guard again like at Lucky 13. He drove his car to Academy Piano Services, where he bought a single E string for a piano. Melvin did not own a piano, did not play piano, and had no plans to start taking lessons, but the E string was perfect for strangulation of the next intended victim.

Melvin dropped the letter to the San Francisco Police in a different mailbox than the first one and made his way home to prepare for the second murder.

The sun was setting. Melvin decided to take a stroll in the park. Alta Plaza brought out the dog walkers and families with children. The park wasn't overly crowded, so he found a park bench that looked out at Alcatraz.

As night fell, Melvin went on the prowl. He walked across a thick, plush green yard and down a slope. He focused his attention on a man who had been hanging around the fenced-in play area where children had been playing earlier.

Melvin eyed the man. He appeared dumpy in baggy clothes. His eyes were set close together, and he gawked stupidly in the direction of the last two boys playing in the fenced area. Melvin despised the man's appearance. He decided to make his move.

Melvin followed yet kept a distance. Both men were headed toward the restrooms. Melvin coolly slipped his leather gloves on. He heard footsteps inside on the tiled floor. Reaching into his jacket pocket, Melvin brought the piano wire out, wrapping it tightly around both hands and making two fists. His heart began to race, and he fought to control his breathing. The riddle he had sent to the San Francisco Police raced through his head: "I am the beginning of the end, and the end of time and space. I am essential to creation, and I surround every place. What am I?" He mumbled the answer to himself, "The answer is E, the answer is E. The answer is E; that is why I am using the E string of a piano." The exit door slowly opened, and to Melvin's advantage, the intended victim looked the other way before stepping out. Melvin slipped the piano wire around the man's throat. He hit the man swiftly with power, and the force of the slam drove the man to his knees. Melvin pulled back as hard as he could with both hands while bending his knees into the man's shoulder blades. The poor wretched soul reached back, trying to fight off the surprise attack, but by the time he thought to act, to defend himself, the taut piano wire had already done mortal damage. The wire instantly cut through the man's flesh and dug so deeply in that he was unable to squeeze his fingers between the wire and his own throat to separate the two. The man stopped fighting after his artery was cut and the windpipe crushed under the extreme pulls from Melvin's capable hands. The body slumped. Melvin pulled a few seconds longer for good measure.

Melvin was desperately out of breath, and as he released the wire in his hands, he fell backward in a sitting position against the restroom wall. He removed his gloves, filled with the sweat from his palms, and he placed them in his jacket pocket. He spun the wire around one hand, slipping it into his other pocket, and dragged the lifeless body back into the restroom. He slipped out of the restroom and simply walked away, unencumbered. He managed to reach his car parked on Fillmore Street. He felt as if he was coming down with a cold. That annoying headache was back, and he had a scratchy throat.

The San Francisco Police Department was baffled. They had received two anonymous riddles, slightly encrypted (but easily solved) from someone—assuming that the same person had sent both newspapers pasted to letters spelling out riddles. They thought by now bodies would have turned up. But no such case. Maybe it was a prank of some sort, but they thought it best to do an initial investigation.

Detective Nazarian sat alone in his cubicle with a workload that would choke a horse. He was baffled by the strange riddles that crossed his desk to investigate. There was something intriguing about the simplicity of these encrypted messages, but he had no body, no motive, no crime, no murder, and no witnesses, so as far as he was concerned, this was a cold case. He filed it on his desk in a file that read, "Possible but not probable."

Melvin's next murder would be more complicated. He wanted to kill a religious figure. In his mind, a riddle from his childhood was spinning around like clothes in a washing machine.

"You stand at the entry of a labyrinth with two entrances. Next to each of the entrances, there stands a guard. You know the following things: One path leads to Paradise, the other to Death. From where you stand, you cannot distinguish between the two paths. Worse, once you start down a path, you cannot turn back. One of the two guards always tells the truth. The other guard always lies. Unfortunately, it is impossible for you to distinguish between the two guards.

"You have permission to ask one guard one question to ascertain which path leads to Paradise. Remember that you do not know which guard you're asking—the truth-teller or the liar—and that this single question determines whether you live or die. The question is: What one question asked of one guard guarantees that you are led onto the path to Paradise, regardless of which guard you happen to ask?"

The answer to the riddle was, "If I asked the <u>other</u> guard, which door would he indicate leads to Paradise?" Always take the door <u>opposite</u> to what's indicated! Regardless of whom you ask, they'll point to the wrong door.

He chose Grace Cathedral, located on Nob Hill, for the next murder. Melvin was not a religious man by any standard. As a matter of fact, one might say by not attending a church, Melvin believed he was being saved from the law of oblivion.

Melvin took the time to drive by Grace Cathedral, grinning to himself.

He thought maybe that the first two riddles were too easily solved and hoped that this third one would grab someone's attention. Yeah, "It walks on all four in the morning, two legs at noon and three legs in the evening. What, was it far too easy?" He thought of the answer: "A person."

He considered it for a few seconds more before making a stop at a religious store that supplied heaps of brass trinkets, such as crucifixes and candle holders, along with rosaries, long robes, scapulars, and books and Bibles. It was there he purchased a heavy metal cross with sharp edges and points. "Indeed, this will do nicely," Melvin happily said.

Melvin found his way home and prepared for his next theatrical act of murder. He dressed in a black suit and left the apartment, being sure to lock the deadbolt on his door tightly upon departure.

Melvin arrived at the church and entered the sanctuary. Melvin concealed the metal cross down the back of his pants and covered it with his jacket.

He was focused on delivering a fatal blow to the heart of a priest. He instinctually scanned his surroundings and found himself alone. The room seemed hollow, like a hole bored into a piece of wood by a wood bee. The walls breathed like asthmatic lungs. His vision blurred, and he stepped forward, making his way to the front of the sanctuary, passing by each pew closing in on him from both sides, until he was squeezed tight at the altar. His reactive mind could not help but invent devils, but he thwarted these minor thoughts by finding a door.

The door led to a hallway of doors. Melvin's affinity with death gave him the courage to walk down the hallway, not only peering into empty rooms with open doors, but the boldness needed to try each doorknob of the closed ones.

He heard the shuffling of paper in the next room. He paused, held his breath, became transfixed, and reached for the cross at the small of his back. He did not hesitate to poke his head around the door casing. Sitting at a desk was a priest, still in his vestments. The priest noticed Melvin right away, and with a look of puzzlement, he said, as if to ask a question, "I believe you are lost."

"Not lost, priest. I have found my way," he sheepishly smirked.

The priest stood to his feet. "You will have to make an appointment if you wish to meet with me."

Melvin disregarded the priest's words and flopped arrogantly in the visitor's chair while slipping on his leather gloves. He said, "I believe that this constitutes an audience."

"This is very unorthodox," the priest said, growing tired of this insolence.

"I suppose I am upsetting the balance of your holy one?" Melvin clasped his gloved fingers together to tighten the leather.

Melvin did not hesitate. He produced the cross swiftly, and with a single thrust, the stipes (the vertical part of the cross) drove into the chest of the priest. He made a gasping grunt. The eyes of the priest seemed to be in disbelief, staring at the face of the very evil his Christ was to protect him from. Melvin added a twist and pulled hard upward while driving the folding priest backward to the floor. Melvin tightened his grip on the cross even more and yanked back hard on the cross, dragging the priest forward. The cross was stuck in the priest's chest, wedged between bone. The priest clung to the cross, struggling for air.

Melvin wanted his cross back. He had paid good money for it, so again he wrestled it, this time with his left foot pushing against the priest's chest. With one final jerk and a kick, the cross was loose, and the priest was affirmably dead.

Melvin did not take the time to gloat. His head hurt, his throat was raw, and he had tightness in his chest as if he had an infection. He needed to find a drugstore and pick up cold medicine.

Monday night, Melvin contemplated the next murder. He took double the dose of non-drowsy cold medicine to relieve his cold symptoms. His body fevered, he clipped more words from yesterday's paper.

"I give you a group of three. One is sitting down and will never get up. The second eats as much as is given to him, yet is always hungry. The third goes away and never returns." The answers were Stove, Fire, and Smoke.

"I am always hungry, I must always be fed; finger I touch will soon turn red." Fire.

Melvin had everything nice and tidy, just like his last three murders. The only exception was making two separate packages. One was for the police, and the second was for the newspaper. He typed the words "Catch me if you can" on the outside of the envelopes this time.

Something concerned him. He walked to his jacket and reached into the pocket, feeling for the pair of gloves that he wore during all three murders. He pulled them out into view and examined them closely. Something was missing from the gloves. There was no blood.

Melvin thought, "I am a natural!"

With restless sleep, he was up early, taking his two packages to the post office and dropped them into the public slot. Melvin casually began looking for the next person to die. A Buick with a single gray-haired driver backed their car right out into the highway, causing Melvin to slam on his brakes, inches from the old man's bumper. The only thing Melvin could see through his tunnel vision was the handicap tag hanging from the rearview mirror and the middle finger of the old man flying it in Melvin's direction. He thought, "another boundary point, and rightly justified."

Melvin took note of the driveway where the elderly man had recklessly backed out from. Melvin returned to the elderly man's house. He pulled into the driveway and gave the front of the house a thorough look over.

Melvin had noticed that the houses in this neighborhood all had gas meters. These meant that with the right tinkering and know-how, one could cause a very substantial explosion. LP gas and a match, and Melvin would surely make the news.

It wasn't long before the elderly home returned. He had a case of Bud Lite in his hand and marched into his house through the front door. Melvin estimated the man to be in his late 70s.

Melvin strolled upon the man's front porch and pushed the doorbell button. Melvin could hear the man grumbling as his feet slapped the hardwood floor inside. The door opened, and now Melvin was face-to-face with his next target.

"What do you want?" The man's voice was gargled and filled with spite. With no warning, Melvin threw a straight right punch, squarely connecting with the man's nose. The old man awkwardly fell straight back and flat on his back. Melvin rushed into the house and slammed the door shut.

He paced while looking down at the man, who was bleeding profusely from the nose and mouth. "No, no, no, don't be dead. You will ruin everything," Melvin said to himself. He flopped down on the floor next to the man's unresponsive body and put his ear near the man's mouth. "Yes! Yes, yes, yes," Melvin said with delight. The elderly man was breathing.

Melvin struggled to drag the man to a recliner, leaving the body slumped over the arm of the chair.

He went into the kitchen and rummaged until he found a book of matches. The house had several candles scattered throughout, so Melvin lit them all and returned to the kitchen, where he muscled the kitchen stove out into the middle of the floor. About the time he was prepared to kick the gas line loose from the back of the stove, he heard the voice of someone moaning.

In a panic, he raced into the TV room where the old man was stumbling about, disoriented. In a cartoonish move, Melvin, who was behind the wounded man, gave a karate chop to the side of the old man's neck. The man buckled to the ground. Returning to the kitchen, he kicked and stomped with reckless abandon at the gas line coming from the wall into the back of the stove. When the line finally gave way, the sound of gas pouring out from the broken line whooshed out. It was time for Melvin to make his exit. He was parked far enough away to watch the excitement, but not close enough to be impacted. It was just a few minutes, and the sound seemed to go out of the air for a brief second, then the explosion. The concussion and force were powerful enough to Melvin that it shattered all of the windows of the house as fires could be seen burning through every glassless window. Car alarms had been set off, and dogs were barking wildly. Melvin now had his number 4, and this one would make the papers for sure.

He was enthralled at his achievement. If he had known killing was going to be this absolutely fabulous and easy, he may have made a career of murder rather than writing romance novels.

Melvin lay on the bathroom floor against the cold tile. He did not know how long he had been there. The last thing that he remembered was having a nosebleed and going to the bathroom. Melvin managed to pull himself off the floor using the sink.

Thoughts swirled in Melvin's head, all scrambled, until they settled on three words. "Kill the weatherman."

He despised meteorologists. He began concocting a riddle for the police and the newspaper.

Melvin wrote scribbles on a blank sheet of white paper, toiling under the weight of time restraints until he came up with the next riddle. "A man was out for a walk when it began to rain. He was not holding an umbrella, nor was he wearing a hat. His clothes were drenched, but not a hair on his head was wet. How could this be?"

Easing back in his chair, he looked at the riddle he had composed and exuberantly vocalized, "Bald, the man is bald. That ignorant miscreant weatherman is also bald." Melvin madly went about clipping the words from the newspaper, giggling audibly, allowing some of the discarded paper to litter the floor. Tomorrow, the weatherman had to die.

Tuesday morning, Melvin awoke and thought today was killing day. He had a sense of liveliness pulsating through his body.

The San Francisco Chronicle, the police and Channel 7 news would receive the next riddle. He hurried the morning along, dropping all three envelopes at once into the postage slot.

Melvin crossed back over the 80, headed straight for the news channel building. Parking, the only thing he could do was to slump down in the seat, be inconspicuous, and wait for the bald weatherman to appear.

The weatherman eventually came out, went to his BMW ActiveHybrid 3, and drove away. Melvin pulled behind him and kept a distance as the two vehicles motored down the highway.

Melvin was led to the dark part of the city. It was a disgusting area of adult bookstores, strip clubs, and sleazy bars. Melvin felt sick just by being in the area.

The weatherman turned on his turn signal and pulled into a porn shop called Theater X. He drove to the fenced-in private area in the back while Melvin parked out front. Melvin had no desire to enter this den of iniquity.

Melvin never turned off his car. He had a full tank of gas, and he was running the heater at full blast. He could not get warm. He was drowning in perspiration, yet his body temperature was like ice. It took the weatherman 15 minutes to emerge from the porn store. He slid into his car and drove away. Melvin pulled out behind him and cautiously followed him from a distance.

The weatherman drove to the Castro District. Melvin watched the weatherman park his car in an unlit space on a side street. Within a few minutes, a young man approached the car on the passenger side. There seemed to be a dialogue going on between the two, and the young man walked away. He saw no better opportunity than right now. He clutched a brass two-bladed ice scraper in his hand.

Melvin left the concealment of his automobile and approached the weatherman sitting in his BMW. He approached the driver's side, tapping on the side window. The weatherman spun his head around and flinched, startled by the sudden appearance of a stranger on the driver's side. The weatherman put a small crack in his window, and with apprehensiveness, he choked out the words, "Yes, can I help you?"

Melvin broadly smiled. "Absolutely, I am a bit turned around. I drove down here by mistake. I took a wrong turn somewhere, and I was afraid to keep driving in circles, so I parked the car. Now these young men keep approaching my car, and I was a nervous wreck until I saw you pull up. I figured, driving a BMW, you were either lost too, or at least you could point me in the right direction. I am not from this area, and just being here gives me the willies."

The weatherman must have believed every word of Melvin's fib because he rolled down the window. Melvin thought about how ridiculous the weatherman looked with his bad hairpiece and fake thick eyebrows. "Yes, what you need to do," the weatherman said helpfully as he turned his head in the opposite direction, about to give Melvin directions, when Melvin, with his left hand clenched monstrously tight, rammed the sharp edges of the brass-tipped ice scraper into the weatherman's neck.

The first thrust was deep enough to cut the carotid artery. The weatherman reached with both hands as the second blow came, digging deeply into the backside of his right hand. Melvin attacked him again and again while the weatherman's arms frantically flailed wildly, unable to halt the battery. The weatherman eventually slumped over in the seat. Knowing that his fifth victim was dead, Melvin casually walked unseen back to his automobile, inhaled deeply, and slowly released his breath. His gloves came off and were gently placed in the passenger seat. He checked his passenger side mirror and took one more look at the BMW.

He had not driven far at all when a motorcycle gang of a dozen bikers blew past him like he was sitting still. These were the cold-hearted types in their leathers, dangling chains, roaring about the city like bandits from the Wild West. Melvin was not happy at all with the loudness of the motorcycles and the inconsiderate way they had leapfrogged around him. He was appalled at their zipping in and out of traffic, weaving dangerously through traffic as if they owned the road. He mumbled, "Stinking putrid bikers." He loathed these sorts of people. He was positive that one of them must die.

Melvin arrived home to collapse upon his sofa. He was ill with fever, sweats, pain in his chest, a throbbing headache, and a sore throat, but he was determined to beat this affliction. He had more killing to do.

He laid his head upon the desk and fell asleep. When he awoke, his shirt was soaking wet, and his first thought was, "Where am I?" Then the second thought, "What day is this?" His fear was that he slept through Wednesday and had missed his next kill. But he looked at the date on his computer, which confirmed it was Wednesday, 6 am.

Melvin had a terrible rush of emotion overwhelm him, and he sank into his chair. He was full of fluid vitality and laughed hysterically, tears rolling uncontrollably down his face as he released this great emotional charge. As quickly as the hysteria had started, he froze with a serious thought. Melvin began rummaging through the daily paper and cutting out words until the riddle in his head was readable on the cut out words in front of him. He placed the words carefully together to form the following riddle.

"When the sun is out, I am hot. When it rains, I am wet. When it snows, I am cold. I eat bugs. I am moved by the wind. I roar like a lion, and the ground rumbles when I go by. Few see the dark side and live."

Melvin made up three identical riddles, and as he had done previously, he glued the letters on a plain white piece of paper, typed "Catch me if you can" on the paper, addressed white envelopes, and prepared to visit the post office. Melvin's thoughts were bouncing through his mind like reflected light through a laser maze.

After mailing the three envelopes, Melvin turned his attention to scoping the city for just the right biker. His mind was ripe, and his heart raced when he caught sight of the bike and its outlaw rider. The biker pulled his motorcycle to the back of Melvin's car. Melvin went to his car, watching the huge, bearded man in leather and chains wiping off his gas tank. Melvin had to think quickly. This was the perfect opportunity, but what should he do?

Melvin had a brainstorm. He went to his passenger side door, opened it, and reached into his glove box, removing a metal chrome flip-top lighter. He slipped into his leather gloves, quickly wiping down the metal with a tissue. He proceeded by doing the unimaginable: he removed the nozzle, allowing the gas to pour out onto the ground.

The biker paid no attention at first. He was looking the other way. By the time he had turned to face Melvin, he was standing unaware in a couple gallons of gasoline. Melvin stood holding the gas nozzle, smiling at the biker. The biker wasn't amused. He looked at Melvin and said, "What do you think you're looking at?" Melvin smiled idiotically. "You deaf? I asked you what you're looking at, boy?"

Melvin's smile warped into a scowl. "I am looking at a human fireball."

As Melvin answered, the biker looked down at his feet and realized that he was standing in a puddle of gasoline. Melvin turned the nozzle toward the biker and sprayed a heavy stream of gasoline into the biker's face. The biker screamed out even before Melvin dropped the burning lighter at the biker's feet. Melvin had set him ablaze. Instead of stopping, dropping, and rolling, he began to run blindly across the parking lot. Melvin dropped the gas hose, returned to his car, and drove away, glancing only once in his rearview mirror to see the flaming man crumble to the ground.

When Melvin arrived home, he went straight to his shower. His sickness had intensified, and his body burned with fever. While he was no expert, his mind's eye had diagnosed something malignant within. He wished death upon himself as the cold water poured down upon his naked body. He was not bathing, but rather, he was using the shower therapeutically. He was afraid to take his own temperature for fear that he might really be dying.

The day was getting away from him, and he desperately needed to gain control over whatever demon had chosen him, clung to him, and was boring into his brain. Unless this angel of darkness killed him, he would not be deterred.

Detective Rogers leaned over his boss's shoulder, looking at a computer screen. What he and Detective Nazarian viewed was data on missing people from the San Francisco area within the last six months. Det. Rogers was trying to get to the bottom of the mysterious riddles he had been receiving anonymously. He did not know how to investigate a crime that he had no proof had occurred.

The two homicide detectives who understood the multifaceted and multidisciplinary approach to solving homicides had only the riddles to go on because they had no crime scene or crime. Their only evidence was the simply solved riddles without fingerprints. A miscellaneous file had been started recording the dates that each riddle had been mailed and received. Photos of the packages and content had been photographed. This was the thinnest file the station had and the most impossible to solve.

The answers in the order of the riddles received thus far were: Man, E, Pointing to the Other Door, Fire, Bald, Motorcycle. Both Homicide Detectives had full caseloads and agreed to file this mystery away for the time being. There was no reason for them to chase shadows. Phantoms were not tangible, and they needed something to sink their investigative teeth into.

Melvin did not tarry. He raced home to prepare his 7th riddle for the police and newspaper. Meticulously, as before, he took precious time cutting out all of the letters from the newspaper and gluing them to a blank white sheet of paper. It read, "When young, I am sweet in the sun.

When middle-aged, I make you gay.

When old, I am valued more than ever."

The answer, of course, was wine. Unquestionably, this would rouse their interest.

Melvin wasn't feeling well. He had a horrible stabbing pain in his chest. He attributed it to indigestion from his dinner and was forced to take an antiacid tablet to settle his nausea and discomfort.

The following morning, first things first, he made the long drive to drop his latest riddle into the post box and returned to his apartment.

As he walked through the door, he noticed on his desk that the envelopes he used to send out his riddles to the police and media were somehow in different positions on the desk. "How could this be?" Melvin was dumbfounded. He then began to have apprehension and doubt. He starting questioning himself. Had he used the plain white envelopes? Had he double-checked? "I used the right envelopes, not the ones with my writer's name, Simon Hardy, on it? Surely not? I would not be that negligent." That would be unforgivable, but he had a suspicion that there was something wrong.

He convinced himself that all was well, and he was only being paranoid. He had work to do. There was no time for him to second-guess at this point.

Melvin loved the old classic movie Arsenic and Lace with Cary Grant. This was where two old women, Cary Grant's aunts, were actually serial killers. This gave Melvin the idea about using the arsenic. He had ordered off the internet enough inorganic arsenic to kill a buffalo. He had also purchased fentanyl from a drug dealer he used to buy other illegal substances from when he was younger. The dealer reminded him that this drug was deadly. Melvin only said, "I hope so."

For this, his seventh murder, Garland loaded two syringes with the reaper's mixture of arsenic and fentanyl. This concoction would produce pulmonary edema, leading to death.

His plan was a simple one. He entered the local liquor store and went straight for the corked wine bottles. With a bit of effort, for the corks were frustratingly tight, he pushed the needle through the cork and emptied the contents into one red wine and one white. He giggled to himself like a giddy schoolgirl as he exited the store for home. He was proud of himself. The deed had been done. It would not be long until the deaths were reported, and both brands of wine would be recalled. He could not wait for the excitement.

Melvin had just not felt right these past few days. He was suffering from headaches, stomach aches, numerous hot flashes and felt generally ill. "Two more victims. Only two." Melvin invented his riddle for the eighth victim not yet chosen. He felt very clever with himself.

The riddle was: Can you take eight 8's, and using only addition, make 1,000?

The answer was: 888+88+8+8+8=1,000. He characterized the note with "Catch me if you can."

He smiled to himself and began cutting up a newspaper, being fastidious with his scissors. His mind considered the eighth victim.

After reflecting on his options, he decided his next victim should be a patient in the hospital. He had thought about maybe a doctor or male intern, but then he reminded himself that he himself was unwell and would not want to snuff out someone who possibly would treat him if he turned for the worst. He would do the deed tonight.

After serious contemplation and a light dinner, Melvin made his way from his apartment to the General Hospital. His goal was to make it to the ICU on the 3rd floor.

Melvin made a stop at a mailbox along the way to the hospital, where he dropped in the notes he created for the local paper and the police concerning his 8th victim.

Melvin was scouring the halls of the hospital, working his way to the ICU. He paused long enough near the waiting room to overhear a discussion about a man who had been shot by police. He was in one of the rooms on this floor. From what he gathered; the wounded man was a known burglar. This critically injured patient was unguarded, on life support, and would probably never wake up. The police were interested in questioning him about some sexual attacks as well. Melvin thought, "What a scumbag."

His heart was beating hard in his chest. He tried to slow his breathing. He felt cold and clammy, as if he was having night sweats. Noticing a closet door in the hallway ajar, he slipped quickly into the closet in hopes to find some hospital scrubs.

"Great day!" he mumbled, excitingly, finding a couple of pairs of scrubs hanging. The first set was too small, but the second set he tried on, though a bit tight, would do the trick. He emerged from the closet unseen and made his way deeper down the hall until he located the room where his victim lay on life support. There was not a soul in sight. Melvin thought, "Wanted for sexual assault and no police presence. What is this world coming to?"

He eased into the man's room. There were machines around his bed, some making beeping noises, others flashing LED lights. He eyed the ventilator that was keeping this criminal alive and knew from reading that it was a simple flick of the switch to turn it off. He probed around a bit with his fingers until he found it, and without hesitation or a moment of reflection, he flipped it off. There was a gasp from the patient, and that was it. Melvin was waiting for the death rattle or the sound of desperate wheezing or gulping or something, but there wasn't anything. He peered at his victim, studying the face, trying to read what he might be experiencing at this very moment. What was he thinking or feeling, or was he just dead? Where was the agonal gasp?

Knowing he could not wait around any longer because the nurses would have gotten an alert that the ventilator had stopped working, he exited the room, heading in the opposite direction from where he came. The hospital was eerily absent of nurses, so he had no difficulty removing the scrubs he had borrowed and tossed them carelessly into the doorway of an empty, open room. He made his way to the staircase and to his car as quickly as he could without drawing attention. He sat in the car, hyperventilating and panicking. His head ached something terrible, and his throat was severely raw and scratchy. He was sweating profusely, and his skin was on fire. Trepidation was tearing at his reasoning as he was losing all sensibility. He continued to remind himself over and over again, "I did it, I did it, I did it." Eventually calm, eupnea restored, he relaxed. "Time to go home."

He had almost made his quota. He was deathly sick, with more symptoms than he could count. He took a double dose of cold medicine, and he crawled into bed.

San Francisco was waking as Melvin had snuggled with the morning paper and scissors on hand and had created another cryptic riddle. "The buyer doesn't want it; the user doesn't see it, and the maker doesn't need it! What am I?"

"A coffin," Melvin snickered to himself.

Detective Nazarian and Detective Rogers were at their desk when another officer delivered Melvin's riddle to them. Their eyes lit when they saw the name Simon Hardy embossed on the outside beneath "Catch me if you can."

The two detectives began to dig in. The case had been handed to them on a platter. They did not have a clue who Hardy was. Melvin had made a mistake!

The detectives opened the end of the envelope and read the riddle.

"When young, I am sweet in the sun.

When middle-aged, I make you gay.

When old, I am valued more than ever."

They quickly Googled the name. They initially came up with the novelist Thomas Hardy from the 1800's.

"Doubt if he is still kicking," laughed Detective Nazarian.

"I would say not," Rogers replied.

"I'm pretty sure it's not the actor either," Nazarian ruled out.

"I've got something here, boss," Rogers confirmed.

Nazarian said, "Talk to me."

Rogers read what he had found. "Simon Hardy, San Francisco romance novelist, real name Melvin Garland. Looks like he lost a partner years ago. Never recovered, has been in the psych ward in the past."

The two men jumped up with Melvin's address in hand and decided to pay Melvin a visit.

The detectives arrived at Melvin's in record time to find he was not home. They discovered from a neighbor who talked to Melvin that morning that he was headed to the bridge.

By the time Melvin had reached the bridge, he had convinced himself that he must be the 9th victim of his plan. He would conclude his killing spree by never going to prison because he would be victim number 9. His thoughts were unraveling; his nerves were coming unglued.

He balanced himself on the railing. It looked like a long way down.

When Detectives Nazarian and Rogers arrived at the bridge, they had a photograph of Melvin from the back of one of his romance novels. They took different directions, examining each face that they passed by.

Melvin looked at the walkway of the bridge to the left, then to the right. His head was pounding, his chest began to heave, sweat suddenly made his body cold and shiver, his throat grew raw. His eyes saw everything as bleak, and his skin burned.

Rogers, who just happened to be coming that way, saw the crowd gathering. He called Nazarian and relayed their position on the bridge to him.

They were able to apprehend Melvin. He did not resist and was taken safely down without incident.

Detective Nazarian and Detective Rogers determined Melvin was innocent of every crime he had admitted to. There were no murders except the murders committed in Melvin's mind. He was diagnosed with a severe and rare case of a form of Munchausen Syndrome. This was the cause of his illness and ailments, which were all psychosomatic. He wasn't arrested and charged, but he was taken to a hospital for the mentally insane and there and given treatment. No solid prognosis was agreed, but they would treat him as long as it took to get him well.

The detectives visited Melvin Garland on a couple of occasions, but Melvin no longer existed. Melvin was lost in the world of Simon Hardy and would theatrically recite lines from his romantic novels for the entire hospital to enjoy.

A TRAIN TO CATCH

Jeff and Nancy Saulsberry had been married for 12 years. They were successful, not young, not old, but were now semi-retired. Their life together had almost been two separate lives until they decided enough was enough; enough of city living, city, commuting, city noise, city congestion and all of the other nuances city life brings. They had loved the hustle and bustle in the beginning, but the more demands their jobs had placed on them with deadlines, overtime, bringing work home, the less time they had for one another. They were simply fed up. They had saved their money, and this little nest egg was going to give them the freedom to explore the things a day job would never allow.

It was time to take a drive, a long drive westward and see for themselves how the other half of humanity lived, and if living far away from the metropolis was what they really wanted. Yes, at first it was just a dream they both shared, even spoke about it over dinner, but now they were making it a reality.

The car was loaded with the essentials for a very long drive. They had hired a young girl who was on her summer holidays to house-sit for them while they were off, hopefully to find themselves a new life, one they could share together instead of co-existing on the same planet with one another.

"I cannot believe we are really doing this," Nancy said excitedly.

Jeff gave her a look of bold confidence and replied, "We should have done this long ago. You know we had the finances a couple of years ago, then I took that promotion, which practically gave me a stroke."

"I know, dear. Too many hours at the office. I admit I was lonely. I was tired of eating alone and only seeing you after I had gotten ready for bed." Nancy put her hand on Jeff's leg.

"Well, no more late hours at the grind for me, and you're free from that infernal idiot boss at the insurance company. I wanted to punch that woman every time you told me how she treated you." Jeff tightened his hand on the steering wheel just thinking about it.

"I put up with a lot from that place, but let's not start our trip looking back. Let's talk about where we are going, what we are going to do and leave our troubles behind." Nancy took a breath and sighed as if the weight of the world she had carried simply just blew away.

The Saulsberrys were starting over, getting a fresh start; it was a second honeymoon for them. They had no planned destination; they were just driving and if they saw what they were looking for, they would know it. Jeff was anxious to settle elsewhere so he could write a book he had outlined about a year ago. Nancy had read through it and agreed it would be an incredible thriller. Jeff had wished he had pursued journalism and literature, but his career put him near the top at a prestigious law firm. Practicing law daily, he hardly had time to draw inspiration from his imagination and even less time back then to put it on paper. Nancy's only desire was an old-fashioned one. She wanted to support Jeff in any and all of his new ventures. She wasn't interested in starting a new career. She thought, maybe some gardening, raise flowers, even grow their own food. It sounded romantic, like the perfect life.

"We are going to have to stop for gas soon," Jeff indicated.

"That's good. I have been holding my bladder for the last hundred miles," Nancy agreed.

"Where are we anyways? I sort of zoned out about 15 minutes ago," she asked, sitting up taller in her seat and readjusting her shoulder strap.

Jeff had lost his bearings. "You know, I did, too. I thought there was supposed to be a turnoff ahead, but maybe I missed it."

"I don't have any cell phone service. We must be way out of the city now," Nancy groaned.

"Hey, wait, there's a sign," Jeff pointed as they approached the road sign.

The sign indicated food, gas, and lodging ahead. "Well, we're cutting it close; the ol' fuel gauge must be sucking fumes." They laughed and followed the turnoff.

A meager sign read "Ravenworth," and had an arrow pointing straight ahead. The area was forested with dense brush and formidable trees. The Saulsberrys motored down what appeared to be a narrow lane for approximately a mile, when a quaint little village came into view.

"How delightful," Nancy remarked. The picturesque village looked as though it was frozen in time, a nucleated village style with railroad tracks running along the backside of the buildings. Its old fashion shops had a turn-of-the-century look to them. The place could have been a Norman Rockwell painting.

"Would you get a load of this," Jeff pointed out, referring to the backward way a couple was dressed. They, too, fit the scene as if within the same painting.

"It must be a tourist town, you know, built to give visitors a sense of going back in time."

Jeff pulled up alongside the Branwell Soda Shop, and he and Nancy stepped out of the car. "Do you smell that?" Nancy asked.

Jeff tilted his head back just a little and took a breath. "I don't smell anything."

"No pollution," Nancy gave him the answer. "No exhaust fumes, no whiffs of sewer, no stale grime. We are as far removed from our old lives as we can be," Nancy exclaimed with a wide, closed-mouth smile.

The village was small enough to see from one end of it to the other. At the far end of the town, just past the last row of shops, were several Victorian-style houses, all perfectly in a row. A four-story clock tower was in the center of the village, and the time seemed to be incorrect. The hands of the clock read 11:11, but that didn't make sense. The Saulsberrys knew, according to their watches, that it was 5 pm. They assumed the clock was broken and paid it no more mind for the moment.

"I could use something to drink." Nancy was feeling parched.

Jeff agreed, and the couple entered Barnwell's Soda shop, which they also found out was the town's drug store as well. The young man behind the counter was playing the part, Jeff thought. He looked just like one might imagine from a forgotten time lost in the annals of time.

"Tell me, son, do you know where I might get some gasoline?" Jeff asked as he looked over the menu board of drinks behind the counter.

"Gasoline? You folks must not be from 'round here," the boy seemed suspicious, uptight, excitable. "You won't find any gasoline here in Ravenworth. Everybody takes the train."

"Train, you say?"

"Yes sir, it comes by every so often. Not really on a schedule, but folks here knows when it is coming."

Stumped, Jeff looked at Nancy, raised his eyebrows and asked the boy, "Where does the train take everyone?"

"Not far, I suspect. I have never been on it."

Jeff and Nancy both had a sense of unease, but they ordered sodas and made their way toward the door leading onto the sidewalk. Before exiting, Jeff caught sight of a newspaper on the counter. The masthead read, "The Ravenworth Gazette." The feature headline read "Europe Building for Revelation." In a column to the side of that story which seemed to run the length of the paper, another piece appeared and was called, "Japan Opens its Borders."

"These stories are ancient," Jeff sounded surprised.

Nancy took a quick read. "It is part of their nostalgia, Jeff. You know they want everything to be and to feel authentic."

"They have done a bang-up job," Jeff remarked.

When the Saulsberrys returned outside, they noticed, peculiarly and suddenly, the village was busy with people strolling along. When they had first arrived, the village looked practically empty. Another strange thing, Jeff pointed out to Nancy, was although it was late in the day, the sun seemed to be in a morning position. Jeff tried not to overthink. What really unsettled him was the uninhibited distance in the eyes of those who walked by them, merely nodding graciously as if afraid to break character. They looked through him, beyond him, but never at him.

A booming voice broke the reverie of the moment. "Hello, good folks! Allow me to introduce myself." Jeff and Nancy spun around to see a staid yet short man facing them, hand extended and a whopping smile on his glowing face. Jeff dutifully engaged and shook the man's hand, who nodded his head toward Nancy in a more distant welcome. "My name is Hieronymus van Aken, or as folks around here call me, 'Mister Mayor.'"

"Jeff and Nancy Saulsberry," Jeff introduced themselves.

"Let me guess. You were passing through, looking for a cozy little village to spend the night in," the mayor presumed.

"Not exactly," Jeff attempted to correct the assumption. "We were looking for a gas station."

"Oh! Just passing through, huh? The best bet is the train. Respectively, we don't have any fueling station here."

"How far is the next town?" Nancy asked, standing very close to Jeff and taking his arm at the elbow.

"Long ways. If you are empty, you'll never make it. You'll end up stranded somewhere between here and there, and these roads are barren with traffic at night. You really don't want to get caught out in these parts. Sometimes it just ain't safe," the mayor said, still grinning like a Cheshire cat.

"As inconvenient as it may sound, I reckon you folks get yourselves a room at the hotel. They'll treat you right. In the morning, I can catch the train with you to Gateshead. They'll be able to accommodate you with some gas to get you on the road again," the mayor beamed with credibility.

"Is that the best we can do?" Jeff asked.

"Sorry to disappoint you good folk, but that is all there is."

As vexing as it was, the Saulsberrys had no choice, so they followed the mayor to the hotel. On the way, Nancy noticed an unassuming little girl in a white dress who seemed to be following them at a distance. Nancy also took a mental note. She had seen no more children on the street. She brushed it off, thinking since the village was staged for tourists—or seemed to be anyways, maybe children weren't part of the theme they were selling?

———

The hotel was not a surprise other than the magically interesting frontispiece. The design was practically carnival-like, yet had to be one of a kind. It fell into the same era as the rest of the town. The attention to detail to represent this forgotten era in U.S. history was marvelous, Jeff mentally noted. The portrait of the mayor adorned the lobby wall at reception, which was much to do about nothing, Jeff thought. Someone really knew their late 19th-century stuff. He convinced himself that, obviously, they must buy their relics and antiques from the same place Cracker Barrel got their wall hangings.

The room was innovative as well; two single spring beds with metal headrests. In the corner was a coal-burning stove with a large bucket full of cobbles of coal. The wooden floor was covered in several non-matching rag rugs, and they soon found out there was no ensuite, just something the young man who showed them the room called an earth closet or chamber pot. Jeff thought these backward people were the type that knew nothing but feared everything.

After the boy exited the room, Nancy became somewhat emotional. "I don't know whether to laugh or to cry."

"What's the matter?" Jeff put his arms around her. He could feel her shivering.

"Are you cold?"

"No, just a little unnerved. This place, with all of its pleasantries and cuteness, is beginning to give me the creeps."

Jeff agreed, looking at the primitive gazzunder, which he knew they would have to humiliatingly use before the night was over.

A knock rattled the hinges on the door. This startled Nancy more than Jeff. Jeff answered it, and there stood a solemn-looking man whose face could only be described as mortician wax. He was tall and thin, his skin blanched as sickly as a hospice patient.

"Good evening good people. My name is DeAngelo. Mayor Hieronymus van Aken has invited you to dinner."

Jeff checked the time. "I guess it is dinner time." He and Nancy accepted the invitation. DeAngelo led them downstairs, out of the hotel and down the street for about a block. They went left down a side street not much larger than an alley, passed by a standing box phonebooth (to which Nancy remarked, "I have not seen one of those in ages!"), two buildings down, and there was the mayor's three-story house, complete with a large wraparound porch. The mayor was waiting in a rocking chair and greeted them with a controlled, enigmatic smile, as if he had a lot to say but wasn't going to say it.

"Dinner will be on the table shortly." The mayor leaned forward. "Have a seat and tell me about yourselves."

"We don't have a lot to tell. We were hoping to start over again somewhere like this. We are done with city life," Nancy revealed.

"Rusticated living, huh? I do not blame you. With the inventions of today, the world is getting smaller. We like our peace and tranquility out here," said the mayor.

"I noticed you do not have a church in town? Normally I thought the smaller towns centered around the church?" Jeff waited for a response.

"Church burned down some years ago. The preacher, he up and left, and there was not enough folk interested in a rebuild. We found it to be a bit stuffy at times. We have a meeting hall where we gather as a community and have some fellowship, but nothing like we had before. We are better off for it." The mayor's words swelled louder at the end.

Nancy had been looking around, taking in the surroundings, when she caught a glimpse of the same little girl in the white dress who had followed them mysteriously earlier. When the blonde-headed girl saw she had been spotted, she ducked behind the corner of the house.

"Mayor, who is that little girl?" Nancy was waiting to see if the girl would poke her head from around the corner, but she did not show herself.

"What little girl?" The mayor bobbed and weaved his head as if he were looking, but Jeff felt it might have been bad acting.

"We have no children here in Ravenworth. We are an adult village. I'd say the youngest person among us is 40 years of age.

"I swear, I saw a little girl. I saw her earlier today," Nancy was adamant.

"Are you sure?" Jeff asked.

"Very sure, she was standing just right over there," Nancy pointed.

The mayor stood up and called for someone in the house named Charles. Charles must have been like a caretaker, all assumed.

"Charles, our guest here believes she saw a child over there. Would you mind easing our concerns and take a look?"

Without a word, the amiable Charles did as he was asked.

"Charles is shy," the mayor mentioned. "Don't let his awkward abstention make you folks uncomfortable."

"Dinner's served!" A voice came from inside the house.

"Let's let Charles do the investigating and we should eat while it's hot." The mayor led the way, and into the house they went. The interior was very old-fashioned and reflected the look of the rest of the village; however, things did not look rustic or as if they were hundreds of years old. Most everything looked immaculately refurbished. The dinner spread was a feast. There were meats, bread, fresh vegetables, juices and iced tea.

"We just love your little village. How do you manage to keep it so authentic?" Nancy's question seemed to have mystified the mayor, as if he did not know what she meant.

"Oh well, we all chip in and do our part. We are not so open to what we consider to be the outside world. There are far too many negative influences sweeping the country. We prefer the simple life. If you folks are looking for a place to plant some roots, this might be the place for you." The mayor reached across the table to secure himself another piece of fried chicken.

"Do you have houses available here for sale?" Jeff inquired.

"We always have something for sale," the mayor chuckled, his insatiable appetite on display. "Most people don't become acclimated to our way of living at first, but over time they see we have nothing to hide; what you see is what you get. Villages like ours are becoming extinct... houses turning into hovels and such. The value of our town is its people, its profundity. If I were you, I'd stay a while. We never know when the train is going to roll into town.

Save any predeterminations until you have had a chance to meet the village folk."

Charles entered the dining area and went to the mayor's side. He whispered in his ear, and the mayor nodded. "Charles has just informed me that the little girl you saw, Magdala, was, in fact, from a couple passing through like yourself. I guess they had been getting supplies in the village, and she went on a wander. You know how kids are."

"Wait," Jeff said, "you mean there was a family here with a child in a car, and we were looking to get gas, and you did not say anything to them? We could have hitched a ride with them."

"I thought about that, Jeff, but you see, their car was filled to the brim. They had no room. Not for even one person. Additionally, if you are genuinely traveling to find you and the missus a new life, I would not want you to get away." The mayor smiled, showing his teeth and holding the smile unusually long.

Jeff was becoming more apprehensive as the evening wore on. After a delicious apple pie dessert topped with some aromatic coffee, they retired to the front porch again as night was falling.

"Now I want you folks to get comfortable. I have a meeting to attend tonight. Y'all turn in early, I want to give you the grand tour tomorrow if you would permit me." The mayor stood and extended his hand. Both Jeff and Nancy gave it a shake and dinner was ended.

Back at the hotel, the Saulsberrys wrestled with getting a fire lit in the stove, but eventually achieved the feat. They were not looking forward to using the chamber pot, but if necessity called, they had no choice.

"I find this place strange," Jeff mentioned.

"I agree, but they are friendly enough," Nancy concurred. The two then discussed the oddities they had already been exposed to. There was the unexplainable little girl. Neither bought the mayor's account of a family passing through with no room in their vehicle. There was the newspaper, the stiff village folk looking at them strangely. There were no cars anywhere. The church was missing. These were all red flags to them. There was nowhere they could go. They were firmly stuck in the village, at least until morning. The village was surrounded by woodlands, and with a small river on one side and a train track on the other, it was as if they were boxed in. They had locked the hotel door, even pushed the dresser and a portmanteau against it in case any unwelcomed guest tried to get in. Later, as night set in, the Saulsberrys resolved to go to bed.

They were fast asleep when something woke the two of them at exactly the same time. They sat bolt upright with the utmost anxiety of unknown dread permeating every cell in their bodies.

"What was that? Did you hear it?" Jeff asked. The sound occurred again. "What in heaven's name?" Something sounded like something hitting the room's only window. Jeff dispelled the tangible mystery of the sounds when he peered from the window to the street to see, for the first time, the little blonde girl, Magdala.

The vexatious child stood in the street with a tragic expression, with pleading eyes of desperation. In the first place, he could not begin to speculate as to what this girl wanted; moreover, it tore a hole in the mayor's account of her and her family conveniently leaving the village. Jeff practically had an unannounced cardiac spasm as to what the implications might be. The girl was looking around nervously and waving her arm as if she wanted Jeff to come down.

Nothing was adding up and once he adumbrated to Nancy what was happening in the street, both agreed they ought to head down and ask the girl if she was in some sort of trouble. They quickly got dressed and made their way downstairs, past where the hotel clerk station was unattended and out into the street. Magdala was still there and ran to them as if urgency was of the utmost importance. She said in a soft whisper, "...Until the last of us are gone." Her words gave Nancy a vulgar scare. "What are you saying? What does it even mean? What are you saying?"

Nancy leaned over the little girl, and she spoke again. "Devoted to the cause."

Was she figuratively speaking, warning them? What did she mean?

With a despondent recrudesce, she said, "Until the last of us are gone." Having heard this for the second time, it rang in their ears like a death knell.

Nancy encouraged her, "Show us, please. Let us help you."

"You need help, devoted to the cause," the little girl's words were bleak, thanatotic in annunciation. Her tiny whispers fluttered like the panicked wings of the Chiroptera order.

"Show us?" Jeff pleaded. Magdala took Nancy's hand and began to lead them off the street and through an alleyway that led to the railway tracks. The girl put her finger to her lips as if to remind them to be quiet. They ended up at the back of what was the meeting hall. It was teeming with activity. The mayor was on a platform addressing about two dozen people, which Jeff supposed was the bulk of the village.

In an elaborate, pontificating manner, the mayor addressed the villagers. "My fellow residents, we have had additions to our numbers today. This is a blessing, not a curse, which means two of us can now move on. I am old. I am tired. To be truthful, I am worn out. My hair is thin. It is silver. My bones ache, especially my hips and my feet. Look at these lines around my face. This was who I was, who I am frozen in time to be. My skin is saggy, my belly round, and I have moved aside time after time for others to leave. This is my time. As your mayor, I will be resigning once the train arrives, and Charles, my devoted friend since the accident and I will be getting on the train. You will have to elect a new mayor after I am gone."

Some commotion ensued, and people were talking over one another. The conversation became indistinct and undeciphered, but the little girl tugged on Nancy's arm and said, "You must go now." Her voice was commiseratingly sad.

"Go where? We have no transportation," Jeff argued.

The little girl practically dragged Nancy by the arm. She led them away from the community center and toward the road they had traveled in on. "We are in the middle of nowhere, how are we going to get away?" Jeff asked.

"I remember seeing a phone booth. Can we use the to call for help?" Nancy's eyes said it all: 'A fear of the unknown.'

Magdala shook her head no. "Does not work."

Unexpectedly, the girl fell into a trance state. Jeff caught her before she hit the ground. Words were spilling from her mouth like a possessed oracle, "It will come when it comes. Train is coming. Change is coming."

Interceptive words were being said, phrases recited, and a warning issued, "They are coming. Run!" Inexplicably, Jeff's heart sank.

"We have to take her with us," Nancy firmly said.

"We can't, Nancy. She will slow us up. We will get help and come back for her," Jeff promised. Voices were coming out of the meeting; then they heard stirring as if there was copious suspicion building. There was an undistinguishable shout and the sound of people running as if in pursuit.

Nancy held Magdala in her arms, "Jeff, we can't leave her!" Her pleas fell on deaf ears. Consciously or subconsciously, Jeff snatched Nancy by the wrist and yanked her away from the un-chastened face. As they made distance between themselves and the girl, Nancy looked back to see the girl seemed to be doubled over in some sort of posture of pain. Nancy could not be consoled. Her heart ached for the little Magdala she barely knew.

The footsteps of their pursuers were getting closer. It was impossible to ascertain the distance, but the mob was coming quickly. Jeff's face was stamped with mortal fright, and he struggled to keep Nancy running. Indubitably this was going to have to play out to the end. There was nowhere to hide, no suitable concealment. This was a race of attrition. Jeff was slowing, using an exorbitant amount of energy as he languished to keep Nancy on her feet. Jeff and Nancy pushed through the pain, the lack of air, the ambivalence of leaving the girl or facing the mob. They were uncertain as to why they were running. But they assumed the worst and erred on the side of caution. They had run down the road for a good way, sweating bullets and gasping for air. Their lungs felt like they could explode at any minute. All around them was this vague horror, something menacing like unseen monsters not visible to the naked eye, but whatever it was had alerted their other senses like the hair which raises up on one's neck when confronted with a suspenseful situation. They feared they would soon be exposed to unimaginable and immeasurable terror in this unfashionable realm of darkness. Their conjoined depression leaped into Stygian depths where all hope is absent. Maybe it was a lack of oxygen to the brain, but the upheaval in their minds gave way to a form of paranoid delirium. They were fearful yet strangely amused as endorphins were being released. With contemptuous facetiousness, Jeff balked at the nameless thing. He saw it was now crouched and ready for the kill charge. The cacodemons were fixed upon their position. The end was imminent. They were being pursued by unmitigated determination. Emotionally Jeff was doing all he could manage to unshackle his bravery and let it loose in a courageous act. He did not know what was coming through. Was it going to be in human form? He could maybe win a battle there. But if it were a creature, an osedax-like bone-crushing prowler or a Candiru bloodsucker sort, he knew he would not be able to save Nancy nor himself. Nancy was inert, beaten by exhaustion, sitting mentally dormant on a log from a fallen tree. Both of their hearts paused with tightness, then galloped wildly until their lungs folded suffocatingly, then gave way to a rush of respiration.

A loud speaker was heard shouting out to Jeff and Nancy. It sounded close, and the voice was the mayor. "Tonight is the drawing of life and death."

The incredulous terror echoed through the trees. "Jeff, Nancy. Please listen! It is not too late to requite your very bad decision to run. You are fleeing your salvation."

Sharply growing panic when the glow of torches could be seen through the brush. Jeff looked at Nancy. Nancy looked at Jeff. Dutifully, Jeff said, "We've got to." This time, Nancy seemed to have gotten her mind settled. She stood, and the two began to run again. As fast as they ran through the bush, dodging small limbs and stumbling over the underbrush, it seemed impossibly as if the torches were closing in. Real or imagined sounds like wild beasts resonated in an encompassing manner. Other than running blindly into the unknown, now the unimagined was on their trail. Pushing away despondent thoughts because it was paramount, they ran a little further. The Saulsberrys ran in mute silence and bright moonlight. Chewed up with abrasions and superficial lacerations, they found themselves in the still quiet of a graveyard containing many gravestones. "I don't see the torches," Jeff gasped for air. With her hands resting on her hips, Nancy added, "I don't hear them."

Their flesh weak and nauseated, they begin to carefully make their way through the place of the dead. They carefully navigated between the headstones. These were old graves, and when Nancy shuddered with an explicit word, Jeff stopped to see what had shaken her so.

On the headstone nearest to him was engraved: Hieronymus van Aken. Born Janunary 1, 1800. Died April 3rd 1854.

The headstone on the grave next to that one read: Charles Powell. Born December 14th,1824. Died April 3rd, 1854.

"They are dead." Jeff muttered this a couple of times, trying to rationalize what he was thinking.

"Everyone in the village is dead." Nancy's voice quivered, emotionally numb.

"How is this possible? Was Magdala, the little girl, dead too?" Jeff rhetorically asked.

"What does this mean?" Nancy was crying.

Jeff held his wife close, relieved and thankful they had escaped. They were too fatigued to run further. This ambiguous night had been equivocally regrettable. All disquietude had been lifted. They decided to lay right there and sleep.

The Saulsberrys were making good time, but Jeff knew they needed gas and were running on fumes.

"Where are we anyways? I sort of zoned out about 15 minutes ago," asked Nancy, sitting up taller in her seat and readjusting her shoulder strap.

"You know, I did too. I thought there was supposed to be a turnoff ahead, but maybe I missed it." Jeff had lost his bearings.

"I don't have any cell phone service. We must be way out of the city now," Nancy groaned.

Nancy groaned as a deer stepped out of the forest right into their path. The car made impact with the deer, smashing the animal terribly. The body of the deer flew up onto the hood and through the front windshield. The last sounds the Saulsberrys heard was the sound of their own screams with the crescendo of glass shattering and tires squealing like wild boar that had just been hit with a hunter's arrow.

In the back of the ambulance, paramedics worked on the Saulsberrys. There was no sign of life, but Jeff and Nancy could oddly see and hear what was taking place. There was a sense of urgency. One of the paramedics leaned over Jeff, and Jeff, in his corpse state, wanted to scream aloud. The paramedic was Mayor Hieronymus van Aken.

The mayor broadly smiled. That is when Jeff saw Charles wearing a paramedic uniform as well. "My good friends, we must get you to Ravenworth Village. You are expected. You are the two newest additions to the community. As you may remember, Charles and I have a train to catch."

SHADOWGRAPHS

The shadows moved through the oscillator radio like a wireless transmission of energy. From this primeval and eternal energy called light, a creation was birthed even before all matter. The heavenly body glowing like a fireball in the sky was a paradigm, and harnessing its radiance and high velocity of energy, these shadows were created.

Capturing high frequencies and voltage within the coil containers, the vacuum tubes caused a clever expansion of wavelengths, stretching the shadows as one would lengthen any elastic material.

Controlling the dispersion electrostatic charging elements, the barium-platina-cyanide gave them the first indication of light, and where there is light, there is also a possibility of life.

Their goal was to find shadows independent from any other source, and through this series of experiments, they hoped to bring forth a shadow without the use of light altogether.

Their clinical signs thus far had produced only negative results in that some of the test members had been temporarily affected with eye irritation and inflammation of the skin, which quickly turned to blisters, but no long-term or lasting conditions have been noted. These symptoms faded over time, leaving only the evidence of three small black dots noted on each test member's left wrist distal to the thumb.

They were not interested in neonatal results or brief optical illusions. Nonuniformities were not being considered due to various amounts of contamination found in the air. They sought concentric consistency, an unvarying flow visualization.

A shadow is an impression, an imprint; they are observable. There are no eclipses without a shadow. But are there many shadows or one uniform shadow with many individual parts? Yes, the absence of light does give the shadow its image, reveals the darkness, and in that space, the absence is an object. One cannot say the same about light; one must define what an object is. A shadow is the absence of color, and if there is an absence of anything, then the shadow is the origin.

Dr. Hatfield said, "I believe I have said enough about that. Contradict me or argue against me, it makes little difference to me because I am prepared to bring forth from my experiment's discoveries from the beyond, to prove that we all cast the same shadow."

Conjointly, Dr. Hatfield and Dr. Duncan had taken an excursion from conventional science to explore areas that had been explored before, yet they did not seek to defile themselves with information gathered and or obtained by others in the hope that they could venture into bold new facets of the subject.

Back to the subject of shadows. The disembodied, as far as anyone has proven, do not have shadows because they are no longer organic matter, yet the doctors could not help but believe that they do; they just cannot see the shadow with the naked eye. A deceased person whose body remains intact has a shadow, although it is no longer animated.

Some would say it was profane to do what they were attempting to do, exhuming the dead, or what was left of them. The possibilities were unlimited when the expanses of the unknown were not bound by laws. They were literally digging up the fields that people had forgotten about. Ambitiously, they were collecting the dead who had been forgotten, and, in most cases, those were the discarded ones, never missed to begin with. Unethical to some, but a ripe, rich harvest for the amiable Dr. Hatfield and Dr. Duncan.

Of course, the two doctors were not doing the physical labor themselves, for their skills and expertise were better suited in the indoors of a controlled room. They had acquired a team of vigilant, strong-backed young men, sworn to secrecy, who conducted the raids upon the graves, and they were paid handsomely when they brought back results. It was best to collect the specimens whole, but they were willing to work with what they could at the time. With the withdrawal of the cadavers, it was a celebration of emancipation, freeing those bodies that had been bound out of sight for decades. The diggers neither believe in ghosts nor souls, and with this godless group, there was never any worry about superstitions or unaccounted spirits of the dearly departed, causing fear and chaos to these elaborate plans.

The collection of remains had grown exponentially, and the diggers were not called on as often as they were in the initial phase. Trials and experiments were still in full bloom, but they could only work so fast. The diggers also rewarded them with their comments and encomiums, which resounded great pleasure to the doctors. A couple of these young men were able to indulge in amorous affairs with women outside of their league due to becoming financially respectable. They followed the primrose path of dalliance wherever it led them. Money cannot buy one happiness, but it could certainly pay for the entertainment while one was on the hunt.

Doctor Hatfield had mentioned, "Our work is a bloodless one, thank heavens for that. I have been exposed to great volumes of blood in my field, and now to put my hands on something that does not stain them red is much appreciated."

After they had ferreted out a few bugs in other equipment through analysis and troubleshooting, it was time for them to check documentation with real-life scenarios.

They took the individual bones and placed them upon the conveyor belt, which fed into the Shadow Play Machine. Up until this point, they had been speculative at best due to a defunct inner pulley, which was causing a drag, and this drag caused friction, which produced heat; thus, the temperature blowoff valve would go off as it was meant to do, but this led to inconsistencies. The doctors had gone through these enough times that Dr. Hatfield winced involuntarily, and Doctor Duncan could always feel a grimace shrinking the side of his face before the anticipation of continued failure. This caused a great deal of stress until the issue was sorted out.

Now that the machine was operating pristinely, they ran into another anomaly that had to be addressed. Bodies began to go missing from the facility. The bones and remains were housed in secure lockers, and only the two doctors had access to these lockers. Yet they would run a cadaver through the battery of tests, store the remains away, always logging the cadaver in and out, and yet there remained unexplained disappearances.

They investigated and searched high and low, inside, and out, and questioned everybody associated with their experiments and studies and rightly concluded that possibly they might be dealing with astral phenomena. They hoped they had tapped into the nonphysical realm of existence, and if it proved to be the case, then they were closer than they thought they were to initiating our next phase.

"Goodness me, Dr. Duncan, we are on the precipice," Dr. Hatfield said excitedly.

I agreed. "Yes, on the cusp of tapping deeper than anyone has ever achieved or imagined. We must move past abstractions."

He could see his flesh quake with excitement. Down here in their lab, they found it to be their sanctuary from those who criticized and attempted to defame the work.

If they only knew what was about to reveal, they would be bowing at their feet.

Unitedly, the doctors were going straight through phantasmagoria and optical illusions, for all of the fantasy in the world would not be able to imagine what was about to be brought forth. What they envisioned was bringing that unseen realm not a little closer for a peek inside, but they wanted to step through, into that world. As men of science, they were the true explorers and astronauts willing to lay down their lives, forfeit their reputations, if need be, in order to advance the knowledge of the world and bring enlightenment to the world that exists right outside of their own.

Working persistently through the night on what at first seemed like tireless legs after everyone else had gone home, exhaustion fell upon the two of them, and the mind began to play tricks. Mentally, they needed a bit of a break to reset.

Dr. Hatfield's thoughts went something like this: "Good and evil walk hand in hand. The fingers of good and evil interlock in a casual stroll but tugging and pulling to their own side. They tighten, squeeze, and attempt to get the 'upper hand,' yet neither lets loose the deadly grip, for everything of good finds its end in death. Death sweeps down like all meat-eating scavengers do; they feast until the bones are dry, until no more remnants of what was life remain, and that which was is now dark, black, stained with the imprint of absence. For all things absent leaves a dark hole, a pit in the stomach, a hollow heart, an empty mind. It is draining, while straining, instinctually surviving in a different form. Death leaves traces of what once was.

Departure, the going away of something that leaves no return address.

Dr. Hatfield confessed to himself as he penned in his journal: "I am at that junction when I ought to know what to do, but I do not know what to do because I am so close to discovering everything that will tear our world apart. And if this discovery rips into us, pulls us away, then who is to control what comes forth from the darkness that has been confirmed unseen? Can darkness be seen, recognized, established without prejudice? Can we comprehend such depths? So, I observe, I admire, I even regard that which I do not know, but will it regard me when it manifests? Shall I proclaim victory, discovery, or ascension? Is this find a demonstration, a discovery? Is it personally addressed to me? Should I salute that which comes from a blackened, dried, barren womb? What does it represent? Will the world applaud? Am I the one to give affirmation to that which is misunderstood? How shall we consider this truth or a lie? I suspect I will show respect only if it is presented in a way that emphasizes brotherhood. It is noted that I have those who have rallied around me as witnesses, such a cloud of witnesses, but who remembers the beginning, the alpha point? And I reflect, think back, and consider those sorry bastards who wanted to ride my coattails into the presence of God. But which God? Does he have a name? Elohim, Jehovah, the great I Am? It is not for me to say. I know that I am at the cusp of something far greater than myself. I am less than honoured for so much is misunderstood. Please, I beg of you, give me just a fraction of your time, a moment of your day, while the light still burns to dissolve myself into you. Are you ready to embrace the impact? I present the opposites, yes, a doppelganger of truth that when you look into the mirror and your sordid breath steams the pane, you are awakening a truth you fail to understand. It is my famed assertion that everything is out of our reach, or God cannot be touched by our intellectual prowess. Rather, he is touched by the feelings of our infirmities. And he, without sin, was tempted at all points, so what am I? I am dying flesh that can never be what I have seen hanging upon Golgotha's tree.

"The agony of ruin captures a heart like a fowl in the snare, which is about to be torn apart. The call to the wild, yet no one comes, no one answers that which has been done. The silence permeates like a liquid fire, and the praises to the Lord rise higher and higher. But between the devil and the deep blue sea, there is much more despite of me. I reached out my hand, and I showed the cards; that is when I knew, without a doubt, positively, the light is only the brightest when it penetrates the dark.

"They say there is no such thing as complete, absolute darkness. But they lie. The fluctuations of light that you believe you see are deceptions and illusions inside of you, resonating in me.

"Light noise and that beyond merely fills up the space where we belong. The absence of light, where shall we be, when pitch blackness pours over me? Stygian dark, the forbidding myth, the Son of Chaos, just another word for the blacksmith who blows on the coals of fire and that brings us all back to the places where we all are.

"Minds soaking in the tenebrous of ignorance. Now I know, now I know. I am darker than you, I am darker than you. I am immersed in the blackness, thick, curdled, grumose and inviting, yet unyielding in intensity. As exploratory scientists, we often limp along, wounded with self-inflictions due to our own flawed designs, but in this case, I am on to something. I cannot promise absolute excellence, but I am assured that the end result will be electrifying."

Dr. Duncan and Dr. Hatfield returned to the laboratory very early the next morning. Both men had grand ideas, incredible schemes of how to use their Shadow Play machine, but as of yet, neither had been daring enough to push the dials to ten. Small experiments with light and shadows had ensued, but on this day, Dr. Hatfield was going to see a new, adventurous Dr. Duncan.

Dr. Duncan walked in, saying, "In a world where brutalism architecture has taken hold, we are about to embark onto much grandeur. Was it not Le Corbusier who said, 'The history of architecture is the struggle for light?'"

"I am not familiar with the quote, but you are referring to the Swiss architect and designer?" "Indeed I am. He was an innovator. Can you imagine once we bring forth the dark from the nothingness what they will call us?" Dr. Hatfield smiled broadly, his eyes changing into a childlike excitement. "Let us do it, do it tonight, he insisted.

"I was going to suggest the same thing. It is time we bring forth what awaits to be seen," concurred Dr. Hatfield.

The two men working in cohesion went to the broad control panel, and, in a series of switches, clicks, and dials, turned on the power of the enormous machine. It began to make a whirring sound as that of a massive fan, beginning to rotate. A burning smell of hot metal filled the air as the fuel rods began to heat up. The facility had been completely rewired in order to muster enough energy for this machine of their design.

The Shadow Play machine itself looked like two stainless steel cylinders that laid horizontally across from one another, end to end, with a gap as wide as the arm span of a tall man. Most of its complexities and impressiveness were built inside of the two elongated tubes, unseen by the naked eye. They contained charge tubes, radiation shielding, pressure vessels, graphite moderator, and a plumbing system to cool the gases used.

It was a slow start-up, and neither man could speculate what they were about to encounter. Both men moved away from the control panel, which resembled the cockpit of a warbird, and faced the machine while reading gauges on a separate board with visual monitors, which reflected what was taking place within the gap of the two cylinders. The machine from the outside looked so minimalistic and sparse, not giving away any of its potential and sheer power to connect with worlds outside of its own. The room began to feel the effects of their grand design and shimmied and shook slightly like a sifting device.

"I believe it is working," Dr. Hatfield said as he adjusted a dial.

"What a grand apparatus we have designed," Dr. Duncan replied.

Between the cylinders, there was a faint glow of something, as if a mighty sun was trying to burst through the curtain that separated what mankind was and what he desired to be. This divider protected them from what they aspired to be, for all man's dreams have become otherworldly over time. They did not wish to impugn man's authority over this world, but rather possibly (though they never stated it to one another), they wanted to put mankind in its place.

In this aphotic zone, light was being absorbed, pulled from one realm to another, and when crossing over, the light was extinguished like a match. Appearing between the cylinders, using the divide as a doorway, a black body appeared as sizzling sounds of the Shadow Play Machine marshaled the air.

The two doctors were intrigued, reserved and, in this taciturnity, both felt inseparably connected to that which they could not define. They could scarcely imagine what it was they were witnessing.

The skin beneath Dr. Duncan's eye twitched nervously while both men experienced a strange, contrived stinging that pecked away at their cheeks, mottling their faces with specks of blackness. They wished fervently that they had set up more cameras, but that was an impossibility now because whatever was being brought forth was nearly in view. The image between the cylinders of the Shadow Play Machine began to expand its body and, as it took on another shape, it appeared to the two men that it was becoming recognizable as a person. Uninterrupted, the shape evoked a cluster of smaller shadows, but no solid form was present. Peaceful or vindictive, Dr. Hatfield did not know as his already deeply creased brow furled with immense concentration, knowing what Dr. Duncan was surely about to ask.

"What do you make of it?" he did ask.

Dr. Hatfield personally had a plethora of assumptions but remained subdued, knowing this genie from the bottle would not be subjugated, for there was no recording and gathering what had been spilled.

The single shadow form, by reason of its unexplained turpitudes, seemed to snarl oddly, for it lacked a mouth, and the doctors were washed with intimidation from what they interpreted as vindictiveness being issued from this dark entity. It was impossible to disentangle their thoughts or to assume with any real analysis at this point. Their distance from this shadow figure was occluded by distance and poor lighting.

"Are we sure it is contained between the cylinders?" Dr. Duncan asked, becoming leary of his own creation.

"We have done all that is humanly possible, but we do not know the implements of power that we are dealing with." Dr. Hatfield sounded more unsure as the moments passed, watching with curious attachment.

Still having a torrent of questions in his head, Dr. Duncan only asked one. "Should we shut it down and gather the readings?"

Dr. Hatfield somewhat took offense to the suggestion of turning off the Shadow Play Machine. "Shut it down? Shut it down after this image has revealed itself from an interminable passage from which we hardly know the source? No, that is absurd. We are scientists; we must study and engage what we have generated. A bodiless shadow is before us. We are looking at the impossible."

Dr. Duncan's suggestion nearly resulted in his ostracism. Dr. Hatfield, in his assiduous desire to learn more with his added eccentricity and overwhelming exigency, was not about to push the off button.

Dr. Hatfield reminded Dr. Duncan, flattering his own pride respectively, "This is the arcane, an antediluvian moment; we cannot lose it now.

Dr. Duncan was constrained, as if a foreboding dread had quickened inside of him. He wondered if Dr. Hatfield was seeing the same unutterable horror as he was seeing. In an expression of aversion, he moved away from Dr. Hatfield toward the kill switch. Dr. Hatfield instantly noticed and intervened to stop him. Dr. Hatfield snatched Dr. Duncan by the arm.

"Let go of me," Duncan demanded, attempting to pull away, yet Dr. Hatfield was the larger of the two men.

"Sit yourself down and do not even think about it. We have come too far to stop. We cannot go back. We are onto something. Act like a man. Man up," Dr. Hatfield flung Duncan into a chair away from the panel with the kill switch.

Rumblings from the machine made the room noisy, causing the two men to be louder toward one another. Duncan was dejected to some degree, shunned, but in his trepidation, he presumed that Dr. Hatfield could not be stopped. He even considered Dr. Hatfield at this time as being over-anxious, deluded in his mission, and possibly obscured by thoughts of grandeur, yet he decided to let this play out and not act impulsively again. He admitted to himself that it was Dr. Hatfield's ingenuity that had gotten them this far. His thoughts were interrupted by the unfolding exhibition, and his attention went back to the impending darkness that was drawing nearer.

The veritable drama between the cylinders was ever changing, and during the disagreement between the scientists, there appeared a cluster of many reflections of concrete shapes, yet they were not advancing but gathering as storm clouds would form.

"What strange gods they must have," Dr. Hatfield assumed. "Gods? What if they are the gods?" Dr. Duncan could feel an utter hellish fear, and, in this fear, frenzy was taking over his sanity.

"If they are gods, we could worship them, show them we respect them, acknowledge their divinity," Dr. Hatfield argued.

"Do you even hear what you are saying?" It was then that their disagreement was diverted by what happened next. The group of shadows began to converge upon the main figure, and everything became dull, as if this one entity was becoming darker than before. The men had never viewed such immense black.

Again, even without the facsimile of a structured face, the ghastly thing seemed to insufferably smile with sinister intelligence.

"The long and the short of it, man, is that we are in the thick of it. Now help me gather data," demanded Dr. Hatfield with an irritability of do or die in his tone.

Dr. Duncan did not know what to fear the most, the unnamed shadow or his unpredictable partner, a man normally of severe aspects who appeared to have gone invariably insane in his selfish pursuits.

Working together again, the men approached the currently restrained darkness before them with much apprehension, holding in their hands an advanced wireless sundial mechanism that fed into their main computer. The approach was not without hesitancy and extreme caution. Dr. Hatfield also had a powerful flashlight, which he pushed on. When he shined the beam without a strand of compunction at the shadow, the menacing ball of misshapen ebon ink absorbed the light as if it did not exist at all.

"Look at that, will you? It is impenetrable," he said impressively.

The indeterminable shadow was woefully barren, as if it was absent of all light but absent of heat, and if it could speak, it would be a cold tone, most likely in duality, Dr. Hatfield surmised to himself.

"How do we know it is not probing us, examining us somehow," Dr. Duncan peevishly asked.

"We can only hope that is exactly what it is doing." Dr. Hatfield was much closer to the umbral vestige lurking before them. He saw it as a smudge in the fabric of the universe that could not be wiped cleanly, almost like a swatch of blackened druidic cloak without appendages worn by something supreme. This was the goliath of the deep.

Dr. Duncan had tempered his last ounce of courage and approached the unknowable shadow, his own gelid eyes beginning to execrably weep stirious tears, frozen on his cheeks as the presence of the algific form passed over him like a blizzard of moribund to his soul. In that moment, Dr. Hatfield saw a change come over Duncan. In his apparent fragile condition, Dr. Duncan was insupportable, caught in a frozen stew being stirred by the acolytes of darkness.

The primal shadow had tentacled itself through the plain of the invisible into the visible, raising his own atavistic fears and instincts. He felt a sudden urge to save Dr. Duncan from this unexplainable, predacious form. The immediate sense of desperation had not even manifested the direness of the situation, but something inside of him recognized the tremendous danger. In this hour of culmination, in an inexplicable move, Dr. Hatfield literally plunged himself at Dr. Duncan, who was transfixed at that moment, but between the time Dr. Duncan froze there like a slab of white marble and the time it took Dr. Hatfield to identify the threat, Dr. Duncan was gone.

Dr. Hatfield stumbled across the room, having not saved Dr. Duncan. In strident confusion, without a remedy, Dr. Hatfield gathered his nerves enough to know that this was unparalleled in every aspect of the word. How could this have happened? What did just happen?

Without jumping to conclusions, he believed the answer was as abstract as the actual experiment was. There were apparent dappling inconsistencies in this cosmic pervasive triumph of the ageless ghoul.

Inexhaustibly, Dr. Hatfield was charged with electricity as if for the very first time since they had begun; he considered this experiment may have been too far-reaching, and once the destination was arrived at, there would be no way to return from such a distance.

Caught entirely off guard, a voice called out from the impregnable cacodemon. The typhonic roar of the voice was that of Dr. Duncan, and it resonated from the depths of the enthralled tenebrous.

His face was graven as stone when he turned hard toward the illimitable gloom. Dr. Hatfield posed the question, "Dr. Duncan, is it you?"

The voice of Duncan answered like something devouring, like a carrion devouring call to feast.

"You should see this," the voice said.

Dr. Hatfield demanded to know, "Where are you?"

"I am in absolute darkness, but I can see. I exist in a cyclic repletion of wonder. There is emptiness, yet I am not alone. I can only say that this is intermediate vastness, limitless and weightless, and I am circumnavigating."

Speculative, Dr. Hatfield repeated with a question, "Circumnavigating what?" "It is impossible to explain. Somehow, the negative magnetism caused a reverse chain-reaction that has cast me into an abyss," Dr. Duncan declared, with the intonations of a solemn voice.

"This is not something we have done. Nothing could penetrate the barriers we had in place. These environed denizens you seem to be reticulated in, are they alive? Can this be true?"

There was a questionable silence that followed. Dr. Hatfield impatiently waited for Duncans's voice while he pondered who might dwell in such malevolent vicinage.

Duncan's voice returned like a damnable impelling arrow into the heart. The observatory shook again under the reverberations. The sound vibrated with a darker imminence, as if it were being broadcast from a cold sepulchral hall of stone.

"I am not alone in here. There are multitudes with me, though I cannot see them." Duncan's voice was not rent with fright or concern whatsoever, and this bothered Dr. Hatfield the most.

The shadow that loomed between the two cylindrical machines had become unduly more daunting, increasing in size and undulating like a dark sea. And as implacably, as unfeasible, and atrocious as the situation presented itself, Dr. Hatfield had no answers as to how to retrieve his colleague from the void. This left him very much perturbed.

"Do you believe you are in danger?" He posed the question.

"Quite the opposite," he said with a pause. He then continued the discourse as if he were being fed the words to say, the sentences to recite, and the dire warning he was about to give with an esoteric punctuation.

"It is not I that is in harm's way. It is you."

These words struck a chord with Dr. Hatfield. Regardless if he believed it or if he were to dismiss the grim warning, it was imperative for him to escape. He saw himself in an interminable position without argument or debate, and because of his loyalty, it was now imperative that he find a way to rescue his friend.

The baleful shadow, without a body to shield the light, swished in its confines and twisted into what could only be described as a death-like pallor of a stone-cold dead iris, without luster or flame.

Withering, due to intimidation, Dr. Hatfield hesitated. The immemorial expanse of the unexplained scrambled all of his veracity, causing warranted reticence.

To shut off the machine completely could compromise Dr. Duncan, but Dr. Hatfield, admittedly doubtful but not disclosing his plan, could do the inadvisable. He could increase the power of the machine, believing by increasing the energy, maybe this would force a hiccup in space and time, and Dr. Duncan would be released from his prison.

Duncan spoke again, challenging Dr. Hatfield's intentions. His words seemed disordered, as if they were tumbling over themselves. His sensibility, or lack thereof, would present one last syllogism to Dr. Hatfield.

Venting repressions upon his colleague, the voice of Duncan said, "Dr. Hatfield. It is crucial that you do not attempt anything rash." From this still cold vault beyond the terrestrial, the impious voice reflected an adamant warning. Dr. Hatfield began to reprogram one of the computers.

Causing him great consternation and immediate stress, Dr. Hatfield was verbally accosted by the vicarious voice of Dr. Duncan, yet he knew it was no longer Dr. Duncan, his friend, speaking. The sound was broken, fractured in sonorous accents, which was difficult to decipher, yet Dr. Hatfield had no problem decoding the words.

"You have called me forth from my domain. You have arranged my arrival. I am not translucent; I am not a solid. I have no true form; I bear no defined shape nor image to reveal. I am the iniquity born of all men who have come into the world. I am lightless. You will find no meaning in me. I was before the light. I have always been, yet I do not exist. I am ever present, yet I never move or travel. I am."

Dr. Hatfield remained undeterred and continued to feverishly change the settings within the main computer.

"I am measureless, antiquated, outside of time, though I occupy all space." With renewed haste, typing faster than he had ever pecked away at the keyboard before, Dr. Hatfield managed to complete the programming, and without delay, he pushed enter, and the machine actually rattled as a power surge shot through its circuitry. He had attacked the enigma with the only thing that he could fight with, and that was knowledge. He had brought this less-than-innocuous entity to the forefront. Now, he hoped he could send it back to hell.

He prayed that Dr. Duncan was not forever lost, but he could not permit that unblemished darkness to flood the world of light. He may have been thinking deleteriously at the moment, yet he could not stand by and do nothing; after all, it was he and Dr. Duncan who had orchestrated bringing the black figment forward for study and observation.

———

Their main issue had been what to do with anything that just might step forward. Now here he was, alone, trying to push it away, out from the reaches of earth where it had found it possible to snatch away Dr. Duncan. Real or artificial, he no longer cared. With a cursory notice, he was waging war.

As the Shadow Play Machine shook and gyrated with sounds of metal splintering and caving in on itself, Dr. Hatfield yelled into the achromatic shadow. The shadow grew in size and then reduced drastically as if straining to remain relevant. In this colossal abhorrence, a voice replied to Dr. Hatfield.

"There is no human form here. All is dark, bleak, and inescapable. I am the shadow negative." The lights in the laboratory were put out due to the electric charge. As luck would have it, the backup generators fortunately worked, and the artificial lights returned. When they returned, Dr. Hatfield jumped back.

Standing outside of the gap between the two cylinders was Dr. Duncan, but he was only a shadow of himself. He had no facial features or true identifying marks. Dr. Hatfield simply recognized his likeness. It was as if he were seeing a disembodied shadow unnaturally standing before him from the lowest plains of the universe, from deeper than any world's Hell.

The figment attempted to speak, yet outside of its own plane, the words were like wet squelches which Dr. Hatfield could not decode.

The Shadow Play Machine could take no more of the energy surge, and there was a cataclysmic explosion which repelled Dr. Hatfield across the room. He would feel the pain of being concussed when he awoke sometime later to the sounds of paramedics who were tending to him and a commotion in the background or rescue workers.

Dr. Hatfield was disoriented and blind, but an impending doom rested upon him. He could not help but ask, "What happened?"

"There was an explosion. We must get you to the hospital right away," the male paramedic insisted.

Dr. Hatfield began to panic, and he thrashed about with all of his remaining strength, uncharacteristically with arms flailing and legs kicking violently. He was shouting at the top of his lungs, "Shadows, shadows! Everywhere are shadows. Cold, cold, I am so cold. I am alone!"

A familiar voice spoke with chilling air into his ear. "You are not alone. It is me, Dr. Duncan. I am with you now."

THE NEIGHBOURHOOD HAS GONE TO ELL

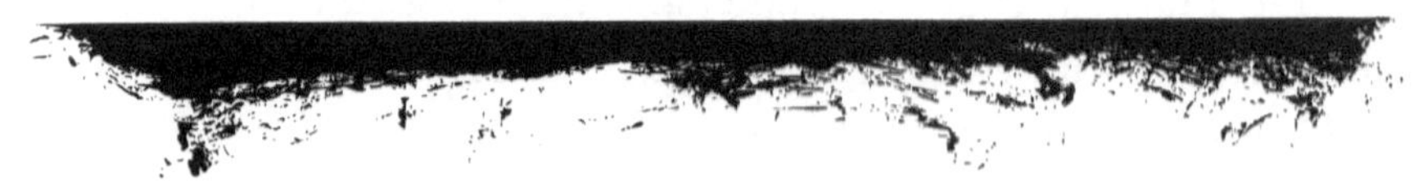

My name is Ethan. My family and I lived in an idyllic neighborhood, on an idyllic street, in an idyllic house that we worked and saved to buy over the course of approximately ten long years. My wife Katie and I had two little boys at the time, Nathan and William, and we settled into our new ranch-style home with a plush green backyard. There were even two pear trees in the small yet useable backyard, which butted up against a wooded area. I suppose we had only been there a short while, living the dream, as they say, when we started to notice the word idyllic was probably overused. I would say our place went from picturesque to bucolic, reflective, never blissful, then downgraded to bland suburbia. It dropped even further down the semirural scale to "spoiled and incongruous" for our needs and likes. I will tell you exactly what happened, and you can hear for yourself how quaint and peaceful can turn like the weather to bleak and foreboding.

After we were settled and had been there a short while, we began to hear rumors that floated to us from Emily, who lived a few doors up the street, a widow twice over and now happily residing alone. It seemed that Emily somehow had a nose for news and gossip, and others gravitated to her, drawn like magnetic talebearers to her kitchen where she served them midmorning coffee, tea or homemade pie and bread. These prattlers were always spinning yarns in the rumor mill, and some very interesting stories were birthed forth, some true and others fabricated.

We already knew that the lady who lived next door to us, Tressie Sample, was a religious fanatic, ringing a bell on Sunday morning in her garage that she used as a home church on the weekends. The percussive sound was loud enough to wake the dead. We knew there was no sleeping in on Sunday morning because she would shatter the silence with that infernal, clanging piece of iron. I felt like wringing her neck, but if this was what she did, then who was I, or were we, to go against what was normal on the street? I just wished we had been shown our house on a Sunday before we signed the contract; we may have reconsidered. But the bell was not the worst of it. The mountain worship music, which raged frantically for two to three hours, would ensue after the gathering of her dozen or so attendees. Not only was the singing unbearably off-key, but they would hoot and holler and shout and rejoice as if Jesus had descended upon them.

———

One Saturday evening, since I knew what was coming the following morning, I decided to take a walk next door and speak with Tressie about the bell ringing. I was apprehensive, and Katie urged me not to go. She said she did not want a feud with the neighbor. I walked up her blacktop drive to the side of the house, where people seemed to go when they were there visiting. Before I made it to the door, I was abruptly stopped by a man whom I assumed was her husband. He had an axe in his hand and was sweating profusely. I assumed he had been chopping wood. He wore a white tank top, which I called a 'wife-beater tee,' and the looks of this lean, hard-faced man were probably the very reason the simple tank top got renamed.

"Hello, I am Ethan, from next door." As bad as I hated to shake his clammy hand, I stuck it out as a peaceful introduction.

"Yeah, I know who you are," he did not introduce himself but glared, squinting his eyes to thin slits as his expression scowled at me with distrust.

I withdrew my olive branch and asked him, "I was wondering if your wife is home. There is a matter I would like to discuss with her."

"A matter? You got a matter, do you? Maybe I got a matter that I would like to discuss with your wife as well?" He emphasized the word "your" while becoming irate and unreasonable. Our conversation just went from zero to sixty faster than a supercar.

"I am not here for a confrontation. I just wanted to ask her if she could refrain from ringing the bell so early on Sunday morning." I smiled cordially.

His eyes remained fastened on me, and I took more notice of his axe, which he was slowly twisting in his hand.

Then he shouted so concussively I shuddered. "Tressie! Tressie, there is someone here who wants an audience with you."

I had to gather my nerves because in the second it took him to disarm all of my defenses with the shout, he could have just as easily taken my head off with the axe, which I noticed had a sanguine stain on its blade. "Good Lord," I trembled, questioning inside of my brain, "What was he doing right before I interrupted his evening?"

Tressie appeared, waddling from the side door which I had tried to make it to before being cut off by her suspicious husband.

Before she reached us, he took a look at me, then at the axe head, and smiled. Then, with a twisted grin that I had only ever seen from clips of Charles Manson, he proclaimed just loud enough for me to hear it, "There is always some killing you gotta do on the farm."

Tressie was a porcine woman, stern-faced with the strict look of an old-school English teacher. She obviously was not concerned with aesthetics. She wore her dull gray hair in the beehive, Pentecostal style, all piled up on top of her head, which caused her to appear taller than she was.

"What is it, Wayne?"

Now, I knew her husband's name. Wayne, the axe murderer. No two people have ever glared at me with so much disdain, their eyes frozen, locked in on me, not blinking for such a length of time. One might remember Ross Perot, the 1996 Presidential candidate for the Reform Party (or maybe not), but this billionaire said that you know people are lying when they blink, and he proudly proclaimed that he seldom ever blinked. As much as I wanted this Pentecostal couple to blink, they did not, so I figured that they meant business. Something serious was going on here.

Everything was happening at once. I was temporarily unable to keep up with the disorder. I do not believe I had ever found myself in a more awkward position. There was nothing for me to do except speak up, man up, and say what I came to say.

"Do you think it is possible for you not to ring your morning bell so early on Sunday mornings?"

The question seemed to have broken their current frown of concentration of trying to burn a hole through my head, and Tressie answered, "I ring that bell for God. It is a call to assemble the righteous, to gather them together as a mother hen does her chicks. It is rung for focus and clarity. Be mindful of the Word of God, young man. It must be rung. The priests of old wore bells on their ephods, entering the Holy of Holies. While they could be heard ringing, that meant he was alive. If they ever stopped, he was dead. This is divine work that you would know nothing about. Do you know anything of the Hebrew word pa-'amohn?"

I shook my head no.

"I figured as much. So, you see, you are ignorant of spiritual things. The bell must be rung," Tressie confessed.

I could see that I was fighting a losing battle. My attempt to deal with this issue was an impossibility; I graciously said, "Thank you anyway," and made my way home, leaving the two first-century Christians standing in their drive.

"How did it go, honey?" Katie asked.

"About like I thought it would. They are not going to budge… and that woman's husband…" I paused as if I had a nightmare of reflection, then continued, "I think he might be deranged."

The bell continued to obliterate our sleep every Sunday morning, and the awkwardness of neighboring with these religious zealots became even more strained after Tressie decided that not only on Sunday would she have church in her garage, but she added Wednesday night Bible Study to the calendar as well.

One evening before dusk, I made my way through our backyard to check on the pear trees when I heard a goat bleating. The sound of 'Maaah!' grabbed my attention, and that is when I saw the darndest thing. There was a full-size goat tied to a tree in Tressie's backyard. I stood in place, truly stunned by what I was seeing. I mumbled to myself for reassurance. What the devil did they want a goat for, need a goat for? What were their plans? I was severely troubled by the thought. I could not begin to conceptualize what I saw. I felt this excruciating uneasiness in my chest, like my heart had swollen. This was something other than an affliction of my physical heart; this was an emotional cry from within myself.

I checked on the pears, all the while with that goat on my mind who was maaing, stretching into a baying overtone at times almost as if to say, "Save me!"

I returned to the house to find Katie at the sink. She had been watching me through the kitchen window while handwashing some pans from the night's supper.

"I saw you looking over at Tressie Samples' house. What was going on over there?" she asked as she was drying the saucepan with a towel.

"You are not going to believe this, but those nut jobs have a goat tied up in their backyard." There was no way to dilute the truth, so I just said it.

"A goat? Do you mean like a billy-goat?"

"I did not see horns, but it is a goat," I answered.

"You do not think they are going to sacrifice the poor thing, do you?" Katie's voice always sounded kind, and this time, it was no different.

I did not say this to Katie, but I could not imagine them doing anything else with a goat; a sacrifice was exactly what I thought might happen to the poor, defenseless creature.

I tried to lighten my answer so it would not sound so gruesome as a sacrifice. "Who is to say? I think they are capable of anything. I am going to free it tonight, after it gets dark," I said.

"You are going to steal their goat?" Katie asked.

"I cannot just let them kill it. Why else would they have a goat? It makes no sense," I said, becoming angrier as I thought about their heartless cruelty. I knew I had to save that goat from Tressie and her retinue cult. I asked Katie to keep the kids occupied while I did my dodginess. I did not want them to learn of my cloak-and-dagger mission; they might just spill the beans, and it would circle around to Emily's rumor mill, and Tressie would possibly find out. I could just imagine Wayne storming over with his axe, and that was not something I wished to dwell on.

After the sun had settled neatly on the horizon and the moon gave a faint hue through the trees behind our house, I marshaled my nerves and hurried out dressed in all black, carrying with me a butcher knife to cut the rope (I was afraid if I attempted to untie the nanny, it might take too long to fidget and fumble with possible multiple knots). I headed down into the woods first. There I could see the lights in their house and had a clear view of the goat. Clandestinely, I maneuvered from the woods to the edge of their property, and like an Army Ranger, I crawled on my belly, rolling from one shadow to the other until I reached the shed. I speculated that they had eaten dinner since it was so late, and that the light that I saw burning in the window was either a bedroom or the living room, where I assumed they had gathered.

Hidden by the structure, I stood, and with my back against the shed, I slid down the wall to the tree where the goat was secured. Unmoving, I listened and heard chattering inside their house. That was a good thing. I could not afford to get caught. I could only envisage the unspeakable things they might do to me. I was about to do the unholy, 'take away their sacrifice to God.' I would no doubt be the replacement.

The goat paid no attention to me and bleated a couple of times but not so much with purpose as before, and with speedy impulse, I cut the creature free and led it toward my own yard. I took the shortest course straight to my SUV, where, with some difficulty because the animal was stubborn and uncooperatively strong, I managed to fit it into the back of my vehicle. I thought, 'No blood sacrifice for you, my little friend.'

I drove several miles to a farm where I knew they raised goats. Possibly this one came from there, but I was not going across the state line with a stolen goat. I drove down a graveled road leading up to the Muss's farm and, with some resistance, managed to drag the goat from the back of the SUV and remove the rope completely, which I tossed over a fence. The goat could not seem to care less, was absolutely oblivious and began to much on a clump of grass. I returned home, mission accomplished.

As impractical as the decision to set the goat free was, it was done, and I slept, knowing I had done a good thing.

The following day, I went to the garage to do some work. I had an old '67 convertible Mustang I was slowly restoring. It was a good project to keep me busy on days when Katie took the boys to her mother's house. I loved it out here, just piddling and dreaming of one day backing this beauty out of the garage and speeding down the highway with the top down and the wind in my hair.

It was a Saturday, and the goat was long gone. I turned on the radio to a local rock station. Some top 40 band from the 80s was playing; it could have been something out of the Seattle music scene, I did not know. I retrieved a couple of wrenches from the toolbox and poked my head under the hood. I really needed my ratchet because I needed to take the valve covers off and replace the gaskets.

Right when I picked up the ratchet, I heard a booming voice coming from next door. I nearly wet myself. There was no immediate explaining what was happening or a rationalized answer to why it was occurring. I stepped out of the opened garage door and knew right away what it was. It was Tressie's grinding voice. She clearly had moved her church's PA system, and I use the word church very loosely, into one of her rooms in the house next to my garage, and she was preaching through an open window in the direction of my garage.

"The suffering of an eternal hell is real. An unregenerate man is a mere shade tumbling down into the abyss of everlasting hell fire, deep down into the lightless abyss. And in this pit of doom and despair, you will suffer God's wrath. The devil will mock you, and you will burn with unquenchable fire until you lose existence altogether."

That was the sort of insanity that was spewing from her mouth. I had no defense. I thought I had no recourse, but I would be damned to allow her to drive me from my own garage. She wanted to talk about the shades of the dead, did she? I went for my CD collection, where I found the 1979 AC/DC album Highway to Hell. I had not listened to this album in quite some time, but I slipped it into my CD player and cranked it up, twisting the speakers around to face Tressie's house. I wished I could have seen her writhing in anguish as Bon Scott's voice croaked out the classic tune. It took the entire song to shut the old bat up next door, but it worked, and I went about my business under the hood of the Mustang.

Later that same day, Katie and the boys returned home after a fun-filled day at grandma's house. I briefly explained to Katie after supper while the boys were playing in their room what had occurred earlier in the garage. She said it was beyond her contemplation that anyone would be so cold and calloused, living right next door to someone. I assured her I had done nothing earlier to provoke such an attack.

Night fell, and Katie and I had just fallen asleep when a persistent banging noise from outside startled both of us from our sleep. I immediately got dressed, shoved my bare feet into my slippers, and went out the back door with my flashlight in hand, stabbing at the darkness until I saw where the hammering sound was coming from.

There sat Wayne, as proud as a peach, in a folding lawn chair with some sort of metal tub in his lap, and he was relentlessly hammering away on the tub. He was still wearing that redneck white beater T.

"What are you doing?" I demanded to know.

"What does it look like I am doing?" Wayne was older than my own dad, so arguing with this senile twit was exhausting.

"It looks like you are trying to keep the neighbors up," I deduced.

"Not just any neighbors. Only you," he banged on a few more times.

"How do you like that? Do you like the noise?" Obstinately, he struck the tub with rage. His eyes did not seem human. They were dark, dead, and depraved.

"I thought you people were Christians. Is this any way for Christians to act? We have children inside, and you are frightening them." I raised my voice to the same volume as my blood pressure.

Katie then made an appearance in her robe and stood by me. "Please, Mr. Samples, this is unconscionable. People are trying to sleep," she asked pleadingly.

"Then tell your husband to keep his demon music turned down." Wayne struck the tub twice more for good measure, then he stood. Tressie could be seen lurking in the shadows, and another figure, someone big that I could not make out, was standing next to her, obscured from sight. But I noticed, even draped in darkness, dangling down from his right hand, pressed against his leg, the big guy was gripping a machete.

My blood was boiling. I had a firearm in the house, and in the moment of white heat, anger, and rage boiling up in me, it took all of my common sense and resolve not to retrieve it and put an end to this nonsense. But being the bigger man, I simply said to the shielded, unknown figure, "You do not need that."

There was no reply. Then Wayne gave me a crooked smile, truly showing what character of a person he was, and then he said in an unsettling voice, smooth and unexcitable, "Our goat is gone."

I mimicked the word "gone" as a question.

"Yeah, it is missing. You would not by chance have seen it, have you?" His voice was rattled with accusation.

I unashamedly lied and answered, "Nope."

Tressie called to Wayne to "Come in now," and like a well-trained dog, Wayne gathered up his claw hammer and his bucket, folded up his chair and started away to the side door.

"If you see my goat, you will let me know, won't you?"

Right then, the dark became darker, and I got an awful chill. Katie and I returned to our house, and I made sure all of the doors were locked. I had never considered such precautions before, but now I seemed to be growing more paranoid as this bizarre tension between the neighbors and I continued. And who was that mysterious giant of a man with the machete?

This was all inconceivable, and I saw no resolution.

Every Sunday morning and Wednesday night, that diabolical bell would be rung, and Tressie's disciples would congregate, practicing their brand of worship, which I saw no truth in their services. I thought she was no more than a deceiver, a false prophet practicing witchcraft, magic, and chthonian darkness. There was no doubt in my mind that she was running a full-fledged cult. Most likely, it was advisable for me to let it lay, just leave it alone, yet every hour they remained next door, I simply could not stand it.

On yet another occasion, Nathan's birthday had come up on the calendar and Katie and I knew exactly what the little fella had been dreaming of; his very own drum kit. Nathan was the kid who would take wooden spoons and forks and use the kitchen pans, pretending them to be a good Zildjian or Tama set. He was over-the-moon, when we led him out to the garage with eyes closed and surprised him with the kit already assembled in the garage. I had a small workspace in the garage where I used to work out quite a bit, but since I was not engaging in exercises and self-improvements at the time I pushed the weight bench and pullup rack to the side making room for the four-piece kit. It was a learner's kit but came with a crash and ride cymbal. Nathan went right at it and with his natural ability he was beating and banging out rhythms, practicing his stick work and rolls and he was darn good to have never sat behind a kit. He would not play for long periods of time, just about an hour or so each day.

One night as we were preparing for bed, the moon was high in the sky and the boys were already fast asleep my wife and I heard the most disturbing commotion outside. I sprung from the bed, put on a shirt, shorts, and slippers, and raced outside with a flashlight. The noise was a crunching, rolling, slamming noise attached to some motorized machinery. It was awfully loud and was resonating like a grinding but sloshing sounds. When I came around the corner of the house there stood Wayne with his white tank top on showing with pale freckled skinny arms.

I had to raise my voice to combat the noise of the cement mixer, "what the devil is the meaning of this?" I demanded to know.

"You like it? That is what it sounds like in my house when your boy is making all of that noise in your garage." Wayne's voice was taut, strained, and his eyes were black with rage.

"Turn that thing off, you maniac. My kids are trying to sleep," I yelled.

"I will turn it off when I am good and ready to turn it off," he said vehemently as he scooped another shovel of rocks into the rotating mouth of the machine.

Knowing there was no way to get through to this braindead idiot, I tried to compromise. "Okay, I will soundproof the room where he is practicing. That should help with the volume." I proposed.

Wayne jerked the cord with hostility and the cement mixer came to a grinding halt.

"You do that. You do that," he repeated menacingly, and an added smirk and scowl.

The following day I bought installation and sound boarding and created a fabulously, almost sound proof room. Nathan was happy to help because he and his brother had heard the entire fiasco the night before.

I stopped discussing it with Katie because it only upset her. The boys asked a couple of times about the clanging of the bell, and I explained they were the religious sort and that is what religious people do. I did walk up the road to Emily's house, who greeted me with a warm welcome, a smile and a chuckle, and then I was at her kitchen table having coffee and homemade peanut butter cookies.

"Emily, do you know what is going on at Tressie's?" I just asked without reservations. I figured Emily thrived on this sort of thing.

"They are nuts," she said plainly.

"Yeah, I get that, but does Tressie really believe she is doing God's work back there in that tiny garage?" I gladly got myself another chewy cookie.

"She thinks she is a reincarnation of some old-time evangelist. I cannot recall their name, but she feels she is carrying on the unfinished work."

"Unfinished work?" I repeated while chewing.

"Yes, Tressie has always been a strong personality, difficult to understand and harder to get along with. We have never been friends, but there was a time when we spoke often. The real problem is her husband. He pretends she is in control, but Wayne is evil. I think he is using her for whatever unnatural gratification he is getting from it. She is a figurehead, but he rules the roost." Emily reached out and got herself a cookie. "I eat too many of these," she chortled.

"Do they have a goal, a purpose? I mean, what are they hoping to accomplish?"

"Their son Larry just got out of prison. He is a big man and sneaky. They have two daughters who no longer visit them. I guess they had a falling out of sorts. But now that Larry is free again, they are determined to get him converted to God." Emily looked down at her coffee as if there was more to say.

"Grudgingly, Larry really does not want any part of it, but as a felon, he has nowhere else to go."

Brilliant, just brilliant, I thought to myself. Another patient at the funny farm next door.

Now that I had a clearer picture of what we were up against (I say we, meaning Katie and I, but in reality, it was just me), I thought I would get some video footage of those attending her so-called church and sort this thing out, as far as who was who and how dangerous they were. I had a clear view of the front of their garage from the vantage point of our bedroom window. Katie was adamantly against me spying on the neighbors, but what other choice did I have? This was the only recourse: to gather information in order to exploit the enemies' weaknesses. It is called reconnaissance. I needed to know what made their Cimmerian minds tick. I did not trust them at all; I believed they were significantly avaricious and grandly minacious.

———

Emily had told me that Larry was larcenous, a man with sticky fingers who would thieve and steal anything that was not bolted down, so I installed an extra lock for my side garage door.

The first night yielded a lucrative amount of information, and here is the version I witnessed. Wayne had started a large bonfire, much closer to the shed where he previously had the goat tied. It was a much larger fire than anything I would have wanted to deal with personally. It was practically an inferno. But being clever in incendiarism, he managed to keep it under control. A group of people had arrived in two separate minivans and piled out, every one of them wearing black. Some even wore black funeral veils over their faces. I found this intriguing.

The fire was raging, and the guests gathered around the fire. Black balloons were released, and about a dozen shot up into the air, rising on the embers from the fire, each exploding to the cheers and jeers of the party guests. An uncharacteristic song was being sung acapella by them all.

"I come into the Circle of Fire, the Circle of Song, as the light grows shorter, and the night grows long."

Each participant then presented a piece of paper and together tossed their papers into the fire. I could not hear the words Tressie spoke over the fire, but it seemed devilish to say the least.

Lifting their voices together, they recited something that went like, "I welcome the Old Ones. Show us guiding spirits in this sacred space. Into these fires, I place messages for the lost close to my heart."

If this was not the most peculiar thing I had ever seen, I do not know what even comes close in comparison. Tressie had a vial in her hands, and she began to sprinkle the ointment into the flames and this caused them to raise even higher.

She then spoke alone, "I anoint this night, the night of sacrifice, that the old heart of the unlearned be cut asunder and a new heart will begin to grow within."

That is when two men led Larry, whom I was seeing for the first time, into clear view because of the light of the fire. He seemed hesitant and afraid, and his reluctance was not missed by others around him as they gathered closer to him, blocking his retreat and escape.

Katie had been lying in bed reading a book while I was doing my observations. "Katie, you got to see this. It is a human sacrifice, I think!"

Katie said, "Do not be silly. People do not make human sacrifices these days. Do they?"

"These people do. I think they are giving up their son to the fire," I said cryptically, though why I said it, I do not know. I was more invested in this than I thought I would be, obviously shown by my weird dialect which naturally spilled out.

Katie came to the window and was amazed at how large the fire had gotten. "I think they need a permit to have a fire in the backyard, "she said.

"I do not believe that followers of a malevolent being who are in the process of breaking the cosmic order care about permits or the law," I told Katie. "This just ain't right."

"Should we call the police or the fire department?" queried Katie.

I continued my persistent watching, and what came next was tragic, if not oddly comedic. Larry, a large man with prison experience, became unstrung, moving with a necessary yet profound unpredictability. He leaped through the flames of fire, knowing he was no match for the mob surrounding him.

Tressie yelled out. "Get him!"

A contingency of young men ran around the blazing fire and gave chase.

"I cannot believe what I am seeing," I said, continuing to shoot video footage. Katie was dumbfounded, occupied in thought, thoroughly entertained by the unusual fiasco.

My heightened consciousness was on a level far above anywhere it had ever been. I expected to see spirits rise from the flames like wraiths and ghouls, but nothing of the sort happened. This episode augmented Larry's courage, running around the house, being chased closely by the others until fatigue caught up with him and the molesters tackled him near the fire.

Tressie ordered Larry, "Drink the blood, eat the flesh! I strip Adam from your throne." In a state of panicked exaltation, I saw some sort of transformation take place in Larry. Initially, while on the ground, he fought, thrashed around, kicking at and punching the others until he was physically exhausted. He was being held on the ground in a state of uncomfortable prostration.

Tressie held her hands high overhead and prayed to the skies. "Renew mentality, change his fallen personality, open his eyes to infinity, imbue him with the trinity, bring forth a true identity and inject him with divinity."

Larry appeared frozen, inert with terror, as Wayne stepped up and shoved what I can only describe as raw meat into Larry's mouth. He gagged and spat it out, coughing and gagging sickly, but Wayne shoved it back in. Another man draped in some sort of druid-type cloak poured what appeared to be blood upon Larry's head. The cruel nature of the assault was disturbing, to say the least. We could hear Larry's screams, then guttural sounds emanating as if from his own private perdition. A chromatic and spherical aberration emanated from the fire and enveloped Larry. Those who had him restrained stood and then helped Larry to his feet. He was no longer fighting, but rather seemed remarkably tranquil, almost hauntingly submissive. Tressie was brooding, staring fixedly at Larry as she approached him with her hands out. She took Larry's pallid face into her hands and shouted imperiously, "It is said, it is done."

Larry collapsed as a dead man. I was agitated, full of malice toward my neighbour.

Tressie turned her vindictive eyes directly toward our bedroom window, as if she knew we were there. Coincidentally or not, Katie and I ducked down out of sight.

"Do you think she saw us?" Katie's heart became rapid, her respiration acute with excitement, with impending dread looming.

I could give no explanation for what we had been privy to.

"I am not sure." We whispered between us, building up the courage to rise up to the window again. The blood came back into Katie's complexion, and her breathing returned to normal.

I raised to take a careful peek out of the window to make sure we were not about to get unhappy visitors. Next door, the fire was gone; latent darkness had snuffed out any vision.

The following day, after a restless sleep and strange unexplainable dreams, I ventured into our backyard, acting as if I was checking on my pear trees, all the while taking furtive glances into Wayne and Tressie's backyard where the eldritch ceremony had occurred. I was sure I was being surreptitious, but then I heard an unfamiliar, friendly voice. My snooping must have been found out.

I turned to see Larry standing there on the property line. "Are you checking on your pears?"

I could do nothing. I had no weapon, and he was much larger than me. I thought of all the horrible ways I could die at his enormous prison hands. He could strangle me to death with former inmate strength, which would take a bit of time. He could just beat me to death straight down into the dirt like a newbie in a prison yard. Instead of running for the house, I simply answered, "Yes, they are almost ripe enough for preserves." I enjoyed canning and making pear preserves. I did not like making small talk with people I deemed lunatics.

"I guess you heard all of the excitement last night?" Larry's question was laughable, if not disingenuous. I thought, how absurd a question. Then I answered in my head, and I wanted to say, "Yes, I saw your twisted, Satan-worshipping theatre group with all of the ludicrous displays of insanity. Yes, I saw you running like a big coward from the warlocks and witches. How could I have missed such an outlandish spectacle?"

I could not read this man. He was unclear of his intention. Instead, I actually said, "No, we did not. Was there something going on?" I said dumbly.

"We had a few people over for a celebration of my release from the penitentiary, and it was my birthday. We had a bonfire and some singing," Larry said, seeming to be purposely leaving out the part where he was running for his life and then being held down and forced to eat raw meat.

"Happy birthday," I said. I knew nothing else to say. I was not interested in a dialogue with this stranger. After all, he was a convicted felon of who knows what?

I ended the conversation with, "Well, see ya later. I better check on my trees."

Sunday came again, and the bell was rung, so we got up earlier than we wanted to and had breakfast. It was not acceptable or suitable, but from what we knew, we needed to remain sedate and watchful, and we turned to praying for peace of mind. As part of that peace of mind and to ensure our privacy and secure our yard, I contracted a fencing company that put up a six-foot fence around the perimeter of our yard, assuring us that our two young sons, Nathan and William would not be directly exposed to the despicable behavior of the Samples. Tragically, I did hear the bleating of a goat, only to not hear it a week later, which led me to mournful conclusions. But then again, I cannot save every goat in the world from tragedy.

I continued getting updates from Emily. We had no further contact with the Samples, and the real kicker was days later, a police raid stormed a different neighbour's house just on the other side of the Sample's, and two young men were arrested for trafficking illegal substances. Two weeks after that, our neighbour on the other side of our property was arrested as a suspect in a serial killer case. Maybe the Samples were nutcases, but while Katie and I focused on them, it seems even more evil were festering that we never knew.

The neighbourhood has gone to hell. Today, I called a realtor. We knew when enough was enough.

THE PALACE IS HAUNTED

"**S**omeone stop that yappy dog from barking! I cannot think! There is enough noise in the world. There is a constant clattering, a clamor, and this is make-believe. I hate a ruckus; all of this accursed pandemonium is an outcry and uproar for attention. Havoc divides us; disturbances confuse us; chaos and turmoil should be left to families, not to ghosts! There is a firestorm in your midst. A royal palace is no place for spooks. I would suggest that your shenanigans and out-of-character frenzies come to an end!"

The Queen was serious. She was ready to get down to business because the royal ball was just around the corner, and this report of disembodied voices moaning in the night, creeping unexplained shadow people lurking in the hallways, and the persistent rattling of annoying chains was driving her mad. The servants were spreading these rumors and fueling myths and legends, and the news of this had made it to the Queen's ear more than once.

"I will not have it! I will not have it at all. Marry in May and rue the day," she protested. "My footmen are afraid to enter the silverware room because they have been convinced that it is haunted. Who would want to haunt the palace? Next, they will say that the furniture is moving about on its own or that the eyes of the portraits are following them around the room."

The Queen had tightly wound herself up, and her dresser was not making matters any better by saying that, "My Lady, the portrait of Princess Charlotte, which was given by the Queen of the Belgians, has been said to have done just that."

The Queen looked at her, astonished. "Do you mean to tell me that you have fallen for this superstitious humbug? We are not living in some Gothic castle. This is my royal residence, and I shall not have the staff believing in such things. Next thing you know, they will be saying that apparitions are sweeping the hall at night. That would make a stuffed bird laugh. I do not believe in such things as poltergeists, so pass the word along that I forbid such talk under this roof. Matter of fact, bring in more flowers. Flowers brighten the spirits."

The Queen realized her homophone in the word spirits but did not try to explain it away. She was satisfied that her dresser plainly understood what she meant, with no pun intended.

The Queen walked quietly over to the bedside table and eyed the panic button which she had installed. The button gave her confidence. She would not confess out loud, but the talk of paranormal things made her uneasy.

While the maid was in the next room to draw the Queen's morning bath, the Queen contemplated these possible hauntings in her mind. In the adjacent room, her Personal Assistant and Curator of her Wardrobe were busy laying out the first outfit of the day. The day continued in normal fashion; the Queen would change clothes at least four more times during the day, dressing properly for each occasion, whether it be her breakfast (which she took in her own private dining room, where she began her meal after the footman who brought her the hot plate had left the room) or a change of dress when guest visited.

As she ate, the Scottish regiment of bagpipes could be heard off in the distance. She loved the bagpipe and made this a daily morning ritual. As annoying as it sounded to some, her alarm clock was the bagpipe. She was left to enjoy her breakfast while in the sitting room, her Chippendale desk covered with stacks of paperwork for her to consider over the next two hours.

After her breakfast, the Queen moved into her sitting room and went about with her favorite fountain pen, and among the clutter and disarrangement, she went to work. She read through the mound of papers; some she skimmed through. Over the years, the Queen had learned the art of speed reading, and once she was satisfied, she pressed a button within arm's length and said, "Would you like to come up?" Her private secretary would appear. He was carrying a small, well-crafted wicker basket that contained paperwork for the Queen to initial.

"Your Majesty," he said, presenting the basket to her.

"Have you heard of this nonsense that some of the staff are seeing ghosts?" Her question caught him off guard.

"Ma'am, I have."

"Have you experienced anything abnormal or paranormal?" she plainly asked him.

Straight to her face, he answered, "On occasion, Ma'am."

"You too? How ridiculous. I am the Queen. One would think that apparitions would appear to me, not the servants," she said with the arrogance, a podsnappery, that one would expect from Royalty.

"Send for my page," she ordered with stubborn intent.

The page came right away and stood before the Queen, who had remained at her desk.

"Your Majesty, you sent me for?"

Bordering on intemperate, the Queen made an odd request; unblinking, she said, "Yes indeed, I need a priest. Not just any old priest. Order me a priest who specialises in exorcism and such. I need some answers because there are things going on under this roof that are disturbing me."

Without questioning her, the page obediently said, "Right away, Your Majesty."

By the time lunch rolled around, the Queen was sipping her Malvern water and waiting patiently after a light meal for word about her request to bring a man of the cloth to her so she could trouble him concerning superstition in her palace. The Queen could be a perihelion, charting new cosmic territory and surprising even her closest staff.

Without delay, a priest arrived, and the Queen ordered that he be sent to the garden where she would meet him for her mid-day walk. The Queen, accompanied by her personal assistant, rendezvoused with the priest within moments of his arrival.

—

"Your Majesty." The priest bowed. "How can I be of service to you today?" The priest was a middle-aged man, well groomed, his greying hair cut tightly to his head. His countenance was serene, a man of contentment and peace. He was tall, lean, with a stoic face and a pronounced chin. His nose was like a parish pickaxe, but straight with no hump. His eyes were dark, set squarely where they should be, not oddly too far apart or suspiciously too close together. His smile was bright, with perfectly straight white teeth. The Queen thought he would have made an excellent dramatic actor; he had such a characteristically charming look that he would have radiated on the stage.

"I have spooks in the attic. It appears that some of London's cemeteries are missing their dead. There is a mystery brewing within the walls of the palace, and as much as I like an intriguing mystery, I do not enjoy being part of one." The Queen stopped her slow pace and turned to the priest.

"I have a deep abiding affection for my servants, but I can see many of them have been stirred up because of this talk of the palace being haunted. This is causing ludicrous distress, not to mention with this industrial revolution happening before our eyes. I heard that the cause of the Indian Rebellion started out as a rumour, that the cartridges of the Bengal Army's new rifle had been coated in pig and cow fat; you see, the spread of such things, conjecture, speculating causes, these hoaxes have a tendency to snowball and to materialize. I shall not live in a haunted house. Is there anything that can be done to sweep the dead from the palace and return the disincarnate back to their rest?"

"There is, Your Majesty. There are a few potentialities and possibilities I can think of. Firstly, we must know who is haunting the Palace, imperishable or temporary, and if there is more than one entity. Secondly, why are they inhabiting in the first place? There is a perplexity at play. Have you yourself seen orbs, spectres, or the unimaginable?"

"I am the Queen; not even while in a dreamful state have I ever questioned such things. I believe in truth. I see truth, I understand truth, I love the truth. I am not permitted to be scared or frightened. I reverence the divine and have stood face to face with my Creator, and that, to me, is essential, eternal life. My life is the apex, and it troubles me to come down to a level I am unfamiliar with."

"I understand, Your Majesty. I suggest we do not look outside of religion to resolve this matter. Science will only confuse the situation. We can put this into God's hands. He alone, flowing in innumerable forms, has laid the foundations of the earth and built upon it. We can put our faith in Him, and in doing so, we can pray for his consuming fire to cleanse these walls, for that fire is essential to love."

***

Things were organized and set for what the priest deemed to be the purging of restless spirits from the Queen's residence. Everything was done in absolute secrecy, a skilamalink, and the staff had to take a vow of silence concerning these matters. If news got out among the common people that the church was coming to the palace to conduct a séance and a possible exorcism to vanquish demons, ghouls, and ghosts from the premises, it would cause a circus and an outcry across the land. This was not the sort of press that the Queen wanted. The supernormal challenged her authority and could make her look weak in the eyes of her subjects, and the thought of ruin crossed the Queen's mind. She was resigned to filtering out this tumultuous nonsense and to put a nail in its coffin so that her house would return to normal. Her thoughts were, "The important thing is not what they think of me, but what I think of them."

The Queen was at the height of her popularity; her profile portrait featured on the Penny Black postage stamp, even. She saw herself as the patron of her people, giving them the Great Exhibition and steam trains, having led them through the Crimean War and presenting herself as the strength and fortitude of the Home Nation. Simply put, she could not afford a scandal of this magnitude. The very thought that a ghost or many ghosts were in her midst angered her to no end. She did believe, though, that for "the common person, give them plenty of beer, and cheap beer, and you will have no revolution among them."

The pre-prandial hours were past, and night had fallen, and the Queen stood staring out from her bedroom window overlooking Constitution Hill. Her light would be the last to be extinguished, but this night, she wanted to read a bit before she retired. She contemplated the idea of ghosts: where they might have come from, why they were here, and what they could possibly want. It seemed unimaginable. Surely, there were other places to bewitch and disquiet.

The Queen had been reading A Christmas Carol by Charles Dickens. She thought it ironic that she was reading about the very same thing she would be casting out the following day. So many ghost stories being published were giving rise to vivid imaginations. The people were not becoming more contemporary; they seemed to desire a step back to the medieval beliefs. And there was this horrible situation with Jack the Ripper, out on her streets killing innocent women, being the headline of every news story. No wonder such chilling thoughts with their macabre appeal had slipped into the minds of her servants and had draped an elegiac shroud over their lives.

She read as long as her eyes permitted, and without resistance, she fell into a deep sleep with A Christmas Carol lying on her breast. Her lamp still burned by her bedside, which was uncommon, but this night, she was exhausted and was asleep while reading.

Nothing stirred until a lilting sound with a whispery draft passed in a perfect cadence wistfully across the Queen's bed, stimulating her to awake. Unaware of the time but seeing it was still nighttime, she extinguished her lamp and rolled to her side, her back to the smoking lamp. In these nocturnal hours, the crepuscular rest resumed, and vespertine dreams caused her to nightwander into the unknown recesses where a mephitic odour caused her to be uncomfortable. Her somnolence became a restless sleep, and she began to toss and turn, but the smell was growing in her mind. The tranquillity of meditative darkness unfolded like a scroll and became a stark Stygian tenebrous of undefinable terror.

The nightmare was foreign to her. She rarely ever experienced a bad dream. Even more concerning was she could not wake up; she tried to shake herself from the hypersomnia that had imprisoned her in this madness. The stench was a cloak that was moving toward her in a ghostly fashion with the outline of a man, but without specifics or definition. In her vulnerability, she thrashed about in frantic movements as mad as hops, but with a flash of blinding luminescence, like a camera trough filled with Blitzlichpulver (more commonly known as flash powder), in a temporary explosion of sorts, she found herself exposed on a deserted alleyway.

A London fog added to the harrowing imagery, and scintillas of energy sparkled like fairies in the air at the end of the alley. She had never felt more isolated, more alone, more helpless. There was an interval of flashing lights, and that is when she got her first glimpse of a man, and this sighting caused unbearable grief to her soul. The form seemed to be snarling as he approached her; cloaked in darkness like an animated shadow, he gestured something with his hand.

It spoke. "God save the Queen."

Her blood ran cold; she was no longer bricky, fearless, or adroit. She trembled. Under her breath, she said, "Cheese and crackers."

Her heart plunged headlong therein further in a descension she believed there was no returning from. Necromantic chaos ensued as this form materialized into a Liston knife-slinging Jack the Ripper. But he was not coming for the Queen, for there was another person in the alleyway with them that she had not noticed until now. It was a distasteful scene of warped mental anguish as The Ripper attacked the young woman from the back as she casually stood unaware, ignoring the danger, and now the monster was upon her. He choked her with his bare hands, his cold, calloused fingers gripping her throat until she turned blue in the face. Her eyeballs were bulging, and she went limp; her face was twisted and contorted, frozen stiff in that moment of anguish. Using the Liston knife, The Ripper slashed her throat with exact precision, and that was that. There was no coming back from such unmerciful brutality. There was no yelp of pain or alarm; the young woman was dead by the tightened fingers of a serial killer. A police whistle pricked the Queen's ears, and she turned to see, but no constable was there. When she turned back to the dreadful murder scene, standing inches from her face was the face of The Ripper. He was so close she felt his steaming breath upon her own, but his face was blurred, as if her eyesight had failed her in that moment. An indefinite period of time whipped by, and she found herself in her own bed. Her lungs were heaving, she was gasping for air, and she was compelled to scream but suppressed the notion. Still panting, she arose from bed, where she sat on the edge, her toes fiddling for her house shoes.

It was the worst dream she had ever had. It was so outrageous it was incomprehensible, incomparable to anything she had ever known. It was autonomous in definition, but she was not seeking to delineate it or concretize it; she wanted it erased from her memory, dissolved into forgetfulness.

She listened. Something was emitting a sound, a tapping noise from her bedroom door as if fingernails were encroaching upon her sovereignty. In mutual recrimination, her body, soul, and spirit were in agreement to repel the unidentified irritant. An eerie whisper floated through the crack beneath the door and rose to her sensitive ears. It was a woman, moaning in grief; a sorrowful rue set the Queen backwards, and she crawled across her own bed to the opposite side. The Queen was painted in an inglorious fear, but oddly, no prayer could reach her lips for mercy. She thought, "God of mercy," but it was an exclamation, hardly a prayer. Her servants could be called, and they would rush to her side, but she did not want to involve them in something unmentionable. The scratching against the door changed to a racking, grinding sound as if a pitchfork was being slid along its surface, and the raking became clawing, which could only be described as if a monster of some description was attempting to tear through the hardwood to gain access to her bedroom. Imprisoned alone, this profusion of sound surely would wake the staff at some point, preferably before the creature on the other side could break through. Her indecision was uncharacteristic, but this predominating horror cluttered her thoughts.

Then she awoke. She could not believe it. She was having a dream inside of a dream; her sense of reality had been destabilized, and the question she asked herself now was, "Am I still dreaming?"

The room was placid but hardly tranquil, and what seemed like an everlasting darkness began to wane. There was nothing endeavouring to smash through her door.

She felt cold. A chill raced up and down her body, and her legs tingled like harmless pinpricks. She had been perspiring and now lay in a puddle of her own sweat. She could not remain in this position. She wildly kicked off the covers and climbed out of bed. She rang her bell because she wanted the bed sheets changed and to be redressed.

Bringing a candle with her, the maid was surprised to find the Queen in such a bedraggled state. "Oh, my Majesty, are you not well?" the maid asked as soon as she saw the state of the Queen and how shockingly dishevelled the bedding appeared as well.

"I am fine, child. It was a hot flash, night sweats, no more than that," the Queen assured her hurriedly. The bed was changed and immaculately restored for sleeping. There were three hours before she normally woke, so she returned to bed, but she could not lay aside the uneasy feeling that she was being watched, targeted, haunted. As she reminded herself with the comforting words,

"Oh! Was ever woman so blessed as I am." She drifted off to sleep, and when she awoke, it was morning, and the sun caused the windows to glow brightly.

Today was the day the church was coming to pay a visit and hopefully rid the palace of any abnormal activities concerning the spirit world and drive unwanted apparitions back to their dark resting places. First, there would be a séance; the Queen had held a séance after the death of her husband in the Blue Room at Windsor Castle. Among the hanging azure damask, cornices gleaming with gilt, she had longed to hear her husband's voice again, for whom, to this day, she still grieved. Disappointingly, she never heard her beloved departed husband's voice, but did get caught up in spiritualism at the time. This was a secret she held close to her heart, and only her most confidant staff knew about. She was friends with a popular medium, but on this occasion, she was not compelled to call on this woman, who was known to be a meritorious and extraordinary clairvoyant; she convinced herself this was a matter for the church.

If she called in a secular medium, people might assume that she had lost her Christian faith. She could not afford any talk of occult practices. Such behavior, leaked to the public, could ruin the royal family as a whole.

Representatives from the church arrived after dinner along with the tall priest whom she had walked with in the garden. In a room seldom used or ventured into, the Queen was sitting alone at a round table when the priest and his associates entered. The Queen's grandson, Eddy, accompanied them. "I wish to see," he said. The Queen permitted him to attend, and the doors were closed.

Eddy was a grown man, a soldier even, and was visiting at this time. Everyone knew him to be a strange man, yet he was in line to the throne.

Candles were lit all around the room; The Queen, Eddy, the priest, and three church representatives sat around the table, and the priest started the session.

"We ask for wisdom, knowledge and understanding as we enter the realm of the spirit. As Saul sought out the prophet Samuel through the Witch of Endor as recorded in First Samuel and in the Book of Sirach and saw Elohim rising from the netherworld, we reach out this evening in the power of the Almighty God to any undetermined and wandering spirit that may be within these royal halls. Are there stateless souls itinerant and drifting without rest among us? Please give us a sign. We plead the blood of Christ to build a hedge around us that any contact will be safe to do so."

No one spoke; they listened, and the quiet was so silent one could hear a pin drop. From across the room, against the far wall where a portrait of the Queen's husband was displayed, a green mist exuded in rolling fashion, tumbling like tiny clouds one upon another from the wall beneath the portrait. The mist swirled from the floor in a thin, funnelled cloud and began to drift upward in an enigmatic motion, forming the outline of a woman. This inscrutable sight was foreboding, but there was no sense of a threat.

This green lady was a horrifying sight, ominously intimidating, but nothing about her caused any thoughts of peril.

The priest addressed the green lady, whose gown flowed angelically around her feet. "Who are you?"

"I am one of five, the third in a series of tragedies. I am a victim who has sought out the one who has taken my essence away. I was living; now I am in oblivion, unable to cross over until I call out my murderer." Her voice was soft but distant and quivering.

"Are you a victim of Jack the Ripper?"

She answered, "I am."

"Why are you here in the palace of the royal family?" the priest asked.

"Because the killer is among us." The green lady began to move toward the table.

"Your killer is in this room?" The priest sounded strained, as if he did not expect this.

"My murderer suffers from gleet and is going mad day by day; my killer is The Duke of Clarence and Avondale."

The Queen's grandson Eddy was The Duke in question. All eyes turned to him. "Albert!" Eddy's name was Albert Victor, and it was the Queen who shouted.

"Albert, is this true?" There was a shuffling of chairs, and the table was accidentally shoved forward. The shocked few were baffled at this accusation.

"Absolutely ridiculous! I was not even in London during the Ripper's reign of terror. You have summonsed a lying demon from hell, not a victim of the Ripper's deadly hands!"

Eddy stood and shouted at the spirit, "You lie! You lie, you evil wench. Burn forever, you foul thing. Suffer the torments of hell!"

"Restrain yourself, man." The priest took Eddy by the wrist. Eddy cleanly pulled away angrily and started for the door.

"Spirit, are you lying?" the priest asked.

The Queen stood. "Do you know who I am?"

The spirit floated around to the side of the table to the Queen's left and remained there behind one of the church officials.

"What reason would I have for not speaking the truth?"

Eddy stopped before he reached the door. "I have an illustrious future ahead of me; why would I throw it away by murder?"

"Your future will be cut short, and you will die prematurely for your sins. You will be known as 'The Lost King, the King That Never Was.'"

"Leave us, you ghoul!" Eddy shouted.

"Wait!" the priest said. "Will you leave us for good? Will you cease to haunt these rooms and to stop frequently frightening the staff?"

The Green Lady answered, "You have nothing to fear from me. I have only come for a warning to The Duke. There is another more terrifying than I to whom I avoid within these walls."

"You have not then been haunting the Palace?" The priest was perplexed.

"No, it is not I, and after tonight, you will see me no more." The Green Lady began to dissipate.

The Queen begged her to stay, "My husband, my sweet departed husband, please tell me about him?" But her words were in vain, and the Green Lady was gone.

"Do not believe that one; she is a liar," Eddy said as he stormed from the room.

"I need not have to remind you that events here tonight are never to be breathed to a living soul," the Queen warned.

The Queen was terribly troubled over the unbelievable accusations from the Green Lady that her grandson Eddy was Jack the Ripper. The following day, she met with her own Royal Private Investigator and gave him permission to, as she put it, to "snoop around." Still, the tormenting ghost question had not been answered. If the phantom who continued to show itself was not the Green Lady, she had no clue as to who it could be.

Some nights after the incident with the Green Lady, when all of the lights had been put out, the Queen was asleep in her bed when she was startled from her sleep by the rattling of chains. Her first thoughts were, "Oh no, not again," but this time, she got herself out of bed, lit a candle, and paid close attention to the anomalous noise. There it was again. It was the unmistakable sound of a heavy chain being dragged down the hallway, with laboured, heavy-limping steps. This was accompanied with a heavy sigh, which sounded directly in her ear, and a cold breath on the back of her neck, which made her spin around, snapping her head to either side, but no one there.

"Do not play games with me, you accursed spirit. I am the Queen," she proclaimed. She was trying to be assertive, but she was verging on tears. This imperishable, abhorrent, unseen entity needed to show itself, and The Queen had had just about enough of the invisible foreplay. Whispering loudly yet angrily, she demanded, "Show yourself!"

The chains no longer sounded from the adjacent hallway. The rattling was now in her room. The Queen, being startled, found her way back onto the bed, and on her hands and knees, she gave the room a good look over the best she could with only a single candle lit.

A shapeless vision manifested before her eyes. It was one of those things she tried to convince herself that should be taken with a grain of salt. She was alone in the room with some strange disturbance, and she did not know what it was. It was indistinct, to say the least; just a very dark patch in the air that hovered slightly above the floor, defying the laws of gravity. "It was a plausible hallucination... or maybe I am having a dream inside of a dream again?" she asked herself, without a given answer. Although this caused her a great deal of distress, she demanded an explanation, and that these days and night of phantasmal displays must, without question, cease and desist immediately. She marvelled at the vision, holding the apparition in high regard because these were forces of unframed dimensions.

"Are you here to bless me or to curse me?" asked The Queen.

A shaky voice of a very small man answered, "I have not the power to do either. I am trapped, locked to this place, helpless to find the key to my release and freedom."

"Trapped? A key? From where do you come?"

"I have been here before this palace was built. I was a monk; I was made to wear these chains and died in these chains, and as you can see, I wear them now throughout the ages, unable to free myself."

"Free yourself? What binds you here? Are the chains symbolic?" The Queen could not imagine in a hundred years that she would be interrogating a ghost, but in some unnatural way, she sympathised with the poor wretched and his abjuration.

This observable dark patch was slowly becoming transparent, and within the film of transparency, there stood a little man; a monk, to be exact. The shade stood perfectly still; his imprecation had been noted by the Queen, but how could she be for sure? It was possible he was no more to be trusted than the lying Green Lady, but if he was being disingenuous, what would his motives be? This mystical gleam around this image was unusual, she thought; it was the first light she had seen outside of her candle. The ghost had no standout attributes; he certainly seemed a pious monk who had been imprisoned. She needed to know why he was shackled.

"What were your crimes?"

"It was love, love of a woman. I broke my vows to the monastery and had planned to leave it when I was apprehended and chained until I was vividly dead, as you can see." The monk appeared self-loathing and upbraided himself, and she did not have the heart to demure him further.

"I know of love. I was married once, but my poor, sweet husband left this world some time ago," the Queen reflected, sombrely changing her mood.

"I loved a woman, and they took her away from me and, in the end, condemned me to death. I wander these grounds to find the key to my irons, that I might be free to find her across the gulf and to reunite with her." The monk looked down at the floor.

The Queen thought for a moment. She had an idea. "If I can find the key you seek and set you free, will you promise to leave us in peace?"

"I do," the ghostly monk humbly said.

"Please hide yourself away. I may indeed have a solution to conclude this rebuke against you and to release your indeterminate body."

The Queen called for her maid and her dresser, who rushed immediately to her upon being beckoned. She explained to them that she thought she had a remedy for the restless haunts. Once the Queen was dressed, the three of them left the bed chambers and went far into the belly of the palace. The Queen, truth be known, was a bit of a hoarder and did not like to dispose of or throw anything useful away. She had said, "It is better to have it and not need it than to need it and not have it."

Once in what was fondly named "The Room of All Things Forgotten," the three women went on a search for what the Queen had remembered from many years ago. It was a box of old keys; no one at the time knew what they were used for. Matter of fact, they were tried in many doors, but opened not a one. But the Queen ordered that they remain stored away, properly accumulated until needed, and that is exactly what her servants trustingly had done. The three women looked high and low, and the Queen's dresser excitingly announced,

"Here, I have them!"

The box was cigar box-sized and dusty, but it was packed with keys of all shapes and sizes. In haste, they returned upstairs, the Queen thankful for the subservient faithfulness of all involved.

The Queen dismissed her maid and dresser and entered her bedchamber in solitude. The monk appeared again and saw that the Queen was holding what he would define as a treasure chest of possibilities to change his circumscribed position and release him from his curse. She displayed the open box of keys on her washing table to his dazzling eyes.

"Take the one you need," the Queen laughed, and when she did, her shoulders bounced up and down from happiness.

The monk trawled through the keys and tried using a couple, which looked like they might work, but the first ones were to no avail. He excavated further, and when he tried again, he produced the very key that he needed. The shackles did not fall to the floor with a bang or clang; they simply vanished. The Queen celebrated with more laughter.

"I thank you, Your Majesty. I must be on my way now."

The Queen then asked something of the monk before he departed.

"If you see my husband along your way, can you tell him I will not be far behind?"

ONE DAY

M ilton was making his rounds through the old facility, which housed the lunatics and those who were deemed too dangerous or unstable for the community. In this psychiatric hospital, this lunatic asylum, this mental institution or, as others endearingly called it, 'the sanitarium,' Milton was seeing its service recipients one by one. Milton had no office, just his clipboard, a notebook, and a well-sharpened #2 pencil, not to mention a stethoscope.

These irreclaimable, involuntarily committed, ill-behaved patients with their diagnosis of borderline personality disorders, schizophrenia, anxiety disorders, eating disorders, PTSD, and depression (and not limited to substance use disorders) were all housed neatly together, collectively in this infrastructure and organization designed to not only keep the residence of the facility situated in a controlled environment, but also to keep the confined from making their way into society, where disturbances would certainly transpire due to the torrential, irrepressible loss of control which would occur if the patients failed to take their medicine on time. Ungoverned and unmonitored, those who lacked the ability of consistent, rational thinking had proven they were unable to coexist with the public at large. This is the very reason that within "Comfort House," people inside regained a part of humanity that was lost to them on the outside, thus bringing a sense of virtue, ethics, and morality back into their lives. Religion and spiritual beliefs were not encouraged as much as the science of getting well in an environment designed to bridle the behavior and bring a sense of compassion, empathy, and altruism into their lives.

A placard was posted on the wall of the recreational hall, which was a quote from Martin Luther King Jr. It read, "Every person must decide at some point whether they will walk in the light of creative altruism or in the darkness of destructive selfishness."

Milton approached the residence of 'Comfort House' with a soft touch, a kind manner and an ease that was never obtrusive, pushy, or aggressive and with a stethoscope dangling from around his neck. He had studied the patients and understood their habitual quirks and their severe mannerisms, knowing that each personality was different. Some were excessive and severe, and everything to them was exaggerated to the point of madness. This is where the pills came in. One pill to sleep, one pill to wake, one pill to eat, one pill to digest the food and one pill to defecate. Without the lovely treatments, maniacal lunacy would be the prevailing doctrine, and these characters would show the appalling, inhuman side of themselves, and this was never pretty. The pills kept everyone tranquil, steady, controlled. Moderate and managed approaches curved the possible menace of behavioral outbreak because without the treatment, malevolence would be unstoppable.

Milton kindly sat in front of Harold, a patient that, even with the medicines, was unable to harness his utterances and force back guttural sounds. So, he would sit with these tics, earning him the appellation of 'Noise Boy.' No one but Milton called him Harold. He was simply 'Noise Boy' to everyone, including the staff.

"How are you today?" Milton leaned in toward Harold, who refused to make eye contact.

"Better today. Better today," Harold repeated, twisting his arms up to his chest and around his body as if he were shielding it.

"What happened yesterday?" Milton licked the tip of his pencil and prepared to jot down some notes.

"Yesterday, I saw them," Harold was sounding out his words with hard enunciation.

"Was it the shadow people?" Milton asked as he pressed the pencil to paper.

"Yes, they gave me the impression that my time was short." Harold seemed thought stricken, frozen upon saying those words, those four words, "My time is short."

"I agree with your sentiment that 'time is short,' but Harold, time on earth is short for everyone. This life is ephemeral, momentary, fleeting even, so do not believe your view of life is any different than the rest of us. We are in the evanescent life cycle. We are the fugitives fleeing one place to occupy another space elsewhere when this life ends. Do not believe in the finality of life. Think of your life as a transition greater than yourself, and once you gain a comprehensive grasp on your own importance, you will see the shadow people are not there to harm you, but to help you, to guide and direct you." Milton stood and patted Harold on the shoulder as Harold looked up at him with hopeful eyes.

"All better now?" Milton asked.

"Yes, better," Harold answered as he looked away again, as if a dream had caught his attention and he wanted to absorb it, remember it before it scurried away out of thought.

Milton left Harold in his reverie and focused his attention on a little old lady whose gossamer threaded hoary head practically shined under the illumination where she sat content in her wheelchair.

"Margaret! How are we today?" Milton asked as he sat across from her at the table where she had been knitting.

With an avaricious move, she snatched her knitting off the table as if Milton had unscrupulous intent.

"Mine," she sheltered the creation of fabric as if through some vainglorious act, Milton was interested in robbing her.

"Oh, no, Margaret, I am not here because I want to take anything from you. I know the knitting belongs to you. I can make no claim on it," Milton reassured her.

With a simpering smile, Margaret eased the fabric back on the table. The significance of her submission was a real breakthrough, and Milton knew it. Just the day before, she found such comfort and relevancy in her work that she hoarded it against herself and never let it go. This craft was substance to her soul, a significant effort on her part to stay connected with the life she had before being brought to the institution. Margaret had been remanded here many years ago after bludgeoning her husband and young son to death in a fit of uncontrolled, accelerated rage. The judge admitted that Margaret had snapped, but he also deemed her not fit for normal prison life due to her diminished capacity to understand right and wrong.

"Would you like to touch it?" Margaret lightly placed her hand on the fabric and gave it a nudge toward Milton, who saw this munificent gesture as a sign of real progress. He made a note of it but refused to touch the fabric.

"It is okay. It will not bite you. Feel how soft," Margaret encouraged him again, but Milton wanted to stick with his protocol and convictions and did not want to jinx this significant breakthrough. He wrote down some comprehensive notes, thanked her for the offer, and said, "I think it is important that you finish the piece before allowing people to touch it. Keep it pure and consequent. Once it is finished, you can show it off to everyone."

Margaret seemed to reason this advice. "Do you know what it is going to be when it is finished?" she asked.

Milton looked at the piece. In all reality, he had no idea. If it were a hat, it was malformed; if a top, it had no arms. He had no clue because it was unremarkable, immaterial, yet he guessed anyway to appease her. "Is it going to be a dress?"

Disparity dimmed her eyes, and Milton believed he had misspoken and something sorely imminent was coming next.

Margaret imparted a smile and said, without descanting or illustration, "Heaven's man, and you call yourself a doctor."

She then uttered something unintelligible under her breath, which to Milton sounded like the word "amateur," but he could not be sure.

"It is going to be a medicinal robe. You know, for protection against the nightmares. I have been in fear, like being trapped in the catalepsy of a nightmare. It has been the most unpleasant of times for me. I am tired of wrestling with it. I am too old, and it is too difficult, and I am losing sleep to this foul incubus."

"Sorry to hear about this. Is it possible a drug such as benzodiazepine or melatonin could be prescribed to aid you in your sleep?" Milton wrote down the word 'sleep apnea' next to her name.

"I was given Ambien; that only made it worse. Firstly, it made my skin crawl; they called it formication. Secondly, I was sleepwalking. My body burned; it itched, and my legs were numb. I do not do well with sleep aids, and when that incubus comes, I need to be wide awake. He has taken a fancy to me, and I can only imagine what he really wants."

Milton assured her he would procure her something that would help with all of that. He called it a 'medical cocktail,' an 'elixir' just for her.

He left her sitting with her craft, and as he walked away from her, something in the background became turbulent and disordered. A torrent of confusion ensued, followed by robust laughter, followed by the tumultuous slamming of chairs and the breaking of glass. The deluge of sound swept over him like a flood, and people began screaming and running. This is when Milton saw Lewis standing, holding a long shard of glass. Blood was guttering down his forearm and onto the floor.

Lewis was a large, middle-aged man, wild-eyed and trembling, incapable of gaining his right mind.

"Don't you hear them?" He raised his voice.

By this time, two security officers had arrived but stopped in their tracks when Lewis's lip curled up like a wild beast, and he swore loudly, "Come any closer, and I will cut your freaking heads off!" Two nurses entered behind them but seemed just as perplexed, waiting for security to act.

It was at this time, Brownie, an 80-year-old schizophrenic who had been sitting at the piano, began a recital of "She'll Be Coming 'Round the Mountain." This melody seemed to incite others to become more aggressive. Brownie seemed thrilled to the marrow with the attention.

Meanwhile, Lewis was unstrung with capsized memories of his past. Brooding and disagreeable, he stomped his foot as if he had the power to cause the earth to quake. When this did not happen, he tilted his head back as if he might do something permanent to himself. There were shrieks as the room became even more charged with electricity. Every eye, with the exception of Brownie's, was riveted on the scene. She had comported herself through a short-lived musical quest when it was shut down by one of the nurses who thought she was about to incite a full-blown riot.

The facility had just come out of a three-week lockdown after a similar incident. Now, with the accelerated yammerings, inextinguishable mutterings and the ceaseless gibbering, Milton could hardly hear himself think.

Milton recognized immediately that neither of these barely post-teen security guards had the proper training to deal with such an explosive situation. They were obviously out of their league, intimidated and insufficiently capable to tackle such a predicament. 'What a mess,' he thought. 'What a horrific palava.'

Milton took a bold step forward and addressed Lewis. He did not believe that Lewis was an evil man, for he knew he could be reasonable, yet the acts that had put him in this zoo had been dark and evil. He came from a tainted pedigree, whore of a mother and a petty thief for a father. "I hear them too, Lewis. They do exist. In your head and in my head. Are they telling us the same things? It is undiscernible, confusing, indefinable even, but I do not believe they are telling us to hurt anyone or ourselves. Do you?"

Milton had hoped he had conveyed the right words to defuse this time bomb. Something in Lewis yielded, and he became complacent and brushed his long bangs back from off his receding hairline. He appeared as a man inebriated, but Milton knew there was no way he could have gained access to alcohol.

"What are the voices saying to you? Maybe it is different because the creatures are not the same as the ones I hear," Lewis asked.

With some exertion, Milton had to think fast. He was not hearing voices at all, and the intricacies of these negotiations were delicate, to say the least. Any impetuous reply may cause harm to Lewis and others. Milton had really stepped in it now. After contemplating, Milton said, "They have told me they have made a mistake."

"A mistake? I know what they are telling me. I still hear them harping in my ears. It hurts. It is painful. Tell them to stop." Lewis sneered as he was surely becoming more vulnerable.

"What are they saying to you?" Milton saw the scene as becoming more ubiquitous by the moment, because Lewis had begun pacing like an animal in a cage.

"My head! My head!" Lewis screamed at the floor, his body language showing signs of great, unmanageable stress.

"What are they telling you, Lewis?" Milton sounded like he was pleading with him.

Everyone else in the room stood helpless to step in. Most were mortified, and the two security officers were simply observing. Lewis was approaching the primal urge to go to the next level, and Milton could see it.

"They are telling me to take as many people with me as possible," Lewis revealed.

"Take them where?" Milton asked, trying not to sound smart.

Things had redlined very quickly. There was annoying chatter in the background, and people were becoming restless. This volatile situation was ready to erupt.

In his dissemination, as his emotions spread like a plague, Lewis answered, "Out there! I will take them out there. With me. Out there."

"Lewis, listen to me. There is no out there. There is only in here, where you are safe. You are safe in here. Out there is dangerous. You are protected and cared for in here. You do not want to go out there. The voices you hear are not your friends. They are a distraction stopping you from happiness and fulfillment."

Lewis seemed to have gained his composure. He said, "Happiness. Yes, happiness." He placed the shard of glass on the table, and this is when security, along with two nurses and a doctor, broke in and led Lewis out of the recreation hall.

"That was a close one," a little voice of a man was heard standing beside Milton.

"Oh, Gary, you are next on my list to see. Do you have a minute?" Milton asked as everything from this last episode faded into memory, and the day continued on.

"How have you been? I have a report that angels are still visiting you at night?" Milton looked down at a blank sheet of paper. At the top of the page, he penciled "GARY" in big bold letters.

"Not just angels. Listen to this. Something stupendous happened last night. I have been wanting to share it with someone. I was reluctant to say anything, but this is big, real big. It is to be disbelieved, but I have to believe it because I lived it." Gary was a little man, balding terribly and was unhealthily thin. His mouth was such that when he talked, it was fish-like, with protruding lips.

"A man could be banished for what I am about to tell you, even excommunicated. It has to do with the church." Gary's character was becoming more enthralled and animated as he spoke. "You remember I am studiously devoted to my religion." Gary then made the sign of the cross. "Forgive my build-up, but this is big," he announced.

"Gary, you have known me a very long time. You know you can share anything with me you feel you need to say." Milton frowned, for as he said this, the tip of his pencil broke, leaving a jagged tip of graphite.

"Excuse me one moment while I sharpen my pencil," Milton said. He quickly darted across the room, and in a desk drawer where most office supplies were kept (minus razors, scissors, and sharp things), he found a Love Sharpener and quickly restored the tip. He returned to Gary, who looked like an abscess busting to burst.

Once Gary saw Milton was comfortably in front of him, he wasted no time. "Judas." Milton paused to understand what Gary meant, then asked, "What about Judas? I assume we are talking about the disciple from the Bible?" "Yes. Judas had an importunate nature. He was not a deceiver; he was a pleaser." Gary waited for Milton, but Milton listened without a word.

"Judas was only following instructions. Jesus told Judas at the Last Supper, 'What you must do, do it quickly.' Jesus was ordering him to betray him. Judas was commanded to turn Jesus in to the authorities."

Milton asked, "How is it that you came to this revelation?" Gary struck a mingled expression of thoughtfulness and delight. "Judas was a friend of Jesus, not an enemy, and I will tell you why. People believe that the devil, Satan, was an angel that led a rebellion against heaven and then a war was fought between the angels of God and the fallen angels, which followed the devil in his insurrection. That is B.S. Remember Job?" Milton read very little of the Bible, but he was vaguely familiar with the story.

"In the Book of Job, God was having counsel with the sons of God, and who showed up to the meeting?" Before Milton could answer, Gary jumped ahead. "It was Satan. Satan was there with the sons of God for the meeting. If he were really a fallen angel, as some propose, how is it he got an invite to return to heaven, stand before God and actually dialogue? I will tell you. He was never an angel to begin with. He masquerades as an angel, but in fact, angel or not, he is an agent of God. God makes it rain on the just and the unjust. God created good and evil, light and darkness, so darkness is there to show us how brilliant the light is, and in turn, we see God more clearly. Judas, though he betrayed Jesus, was an agent of God doing God's will. Without Judas, there would have been no Jesus, Savior of the world."

Milton had a question. "So you are saying Satan and Judas are mere agents of God to cause trouble, but out of this trouble, good comes?"

"Exactly. I will not bore you with other conclusions I have recently come to, but I have enough to fill a book. I ascertain this to be truth. There is no other conclusion to be drawn." Gary looked like he knew it was hard to believe, but he seemed certain.

"Sounds like quite the rigmarole to resolve. But you are the expert, not I. I must concur with you on this, and I have taken note to look into it further," Milton promised.

"If you do study it, it is a real labyrinth. It will take your breath away like a cuirass," Gary mentioned.

Milton did not know what a 'cuirass' was, but later, he would look the word up to find that it meant 'artificial ventilator that forces air in and out of the lungs.'

"I am reluctant to leave you so soon. I have found your insight enlightening. Maybe we can speak on this more tomorrow. I must finish my rounds," Milton informed him.

Milton located Jim Morrow, who was the polar opposite of Gary. Jim despised God. He was angry, full of animosity. He was an omen in itself, an omen of grave portent, and had a security officer near him at all times. Many thought Lewis, who had the episode earlier with the broken glass, was dangerous, but in contrast, Jim's hallmark was not apathy. He was a man with no impulse control. He was a murderer, but for reason of insanity, he never spent a day in prison. He somehow managed to get himself declared insane for life.

Jim was sitting alone as usual, rocking back and forth in front of the TV. He could not tell you what was on the screen, but he never changed channels or allowed anyone else to change the channels.

Milton sat in a chair beside him. "Jim, how are you today?" Jim grunted annoyingly, his frog-like neck swollen noticeably.

"Anything on your mind today? Anything you would like to share?" Milton watched Jim's eyes as a portent to see if he was stepping over the invisible line that might set Jim off.

Uncharacteristically, Jim said, "The pills. The pills, they do not keep us alive. They are killing us."

Milton saw that something was bearing on Jim's mind and that this oppressive weight had dulled him. It was an elevation of a malady, an acute bodily illness that Jim struggled with. Combined with peculiar sensibilities of temperament, intermingled with being prone to murder, Milton felt a bit uneasy conducting this interview.

"My heart is sickened," Jim stated with overtones of abandonment and unredeemable value.

"That is not good to hear. Just yesterday, I thought we had made some progress," stated Milton.

"Yesterday is yesterday. That is the past. I am talking about now. Right now," he emphasized.

"Ridiculous. What could have changed in 24 hours?" Milton remarkably found the courage to ask.

Jim was never superficial or manipulative. Whatever his demons were, they were consistent. That thing that possessed him never changed, and neither did Jim until this conversation, when his nature seemed to have become more reflective. In Milton's eyes, he saw a man deteriorating in front of him. Jim looked like a prisoner who overnight had become somehow decrepit with a fractured spirit, and something tiny left of his manhood was wriggling to escape, but the gap was closing in. Milton was more than astonished. Jim was shattered like a man that had been mentally penetrated, someone who was the butt of a despicable rumor and scorned. He appeared soft, boneless, an insufferable man skulking behind a brawny frame. The animosity he strongly had shown in the past was not even a trickle. This once necrophiliac seemed unaroused, malformed. Milton could not wrap his mind around how the most notorious guest of the facility was no longer accessible and had been replaced by this shell of a man.

"Night terrors come to me. A black gummed hag with an icy touch," Jim cringed and moaned, "I am not just cursed, I am damned."

"Jim, tell me what has happened." Milton was troubled and genuinely concerned for Jim's mental state. It was not until this point that Jim pulled his hands out from his pockets to reveal the crimson stains of what appeared to be dried blood. Milton leaped up. He knew it was the wrong thing to do, but his flight instincts kicked in, and he retreated for safety.

"What unearthly thing have you done?" Milton asked.

"I am prone to it, they tell me," Jim said, justifying whatever evil he had yet to admit to. Milton was stifled with gloom, wanting to call for help, but had to first catch his breath.

"She insulted me. She said I was indiscriminately affectionate and had involuntary impulses." These were relevant facts, most likely, but Milton had stopped taking notes.

Jim gestured for Milton to take a seat, and Milton did not argue. Still with words knotted in his throat, Milton managed to ask, "Who is she? What have you done?"

Jim rocked back and forth in his seat with nervous agitation. "The Slender Man caused me to do it. I had never seen him before. I always knew there was something watching me. Then last night he stepped out of the shadows. These pills make me feel nothing. I am tormented. This is why I have acted out."

"Who is it? Where is she?" Milton asked, recognizing the agony upon Jim's face.

"It was Nancy, nurse Nancy. She is under my bed," Jim admitted.

Milton was impaled with a sickness right in the pit of his gut as this permeating nightmare began to unfold. He was as disgusted by Jim's loathsomeness as he was about hearing about Nancy's death. He had always liked Nancy. She was a new mother.

"Show me," Milton said. Jim stood without a word and, with slumped shoulders, obediently led the way out of the recreational center down the hallway to his room. His door was closed. Milton held up his hand to indicate for Jim to remain in the hallway. Jim complied. Jim did not quarrel; from what Milton could ascertain, all of Jim's fight had been left inside his room.

Milton entered, and it was as Jim said, except much worse. The blood stains were everywhere. There would be no need for investigators to use luminol; it was obvious this was a crime scene. Milton had only stepped in the room, and not wanting to disturb or contaminate the crime scene, he backed out into the hallway and checked his shoes for blood. Luckily, there were no signs. He stooped down and saw the headless torso of Nancy beneath the bed, lifeless; the ichor had drained from her broken skin.

"Jim, it is not good, my friend. You have crossed the line with this one," Milton calmly said.

"No one is immortal," Jim weirdly remarked.

Even more odd, Milton agreed.

"Where is her head, Jim? What have you done with the head?" Milton thought how ridiculous that sounded. Never in his life would he ever have imagined that he would be asking a serial killer face-to-face where was the head of his last victim.

Jim took a look into the room as if he had no idea what I was talking about.

"Her head? No way, man. That was not me," he professed with irradicable conviction.

This was a monstrous mess, and Milton had no choice but to proceed. He settled Jim at the main nurse's station and explained to the head of the department what Jim had confessed to and what he had uncovered in light of being taken to the scene of the murder. Milton felt his heart going crazy in some sort of arrhythmic discord, as if he were the guilty party. But this was because Milton had not taken his meds on this day.

Because of the seriousness of the crime, acts of lasciviousness and murder, Jim would be leaving their facility, and Milton would have to relinquish the stethoscope he had acquired without approval.

Milton was an omnivorous patient of the facility himself, who made his rounds daily masquerading as a doctor. The patients were used to him playing doctor and treated him with more respect and leaned upon his expertise, advice, and diagnosis more than they did the nurses and counselors who actually operated the facility.

It would be a few weeks before Milton was allowed a stethoscope, a pad of paper, and a pencil because of the severity of Jim's heinous crime. Milton was placed back on his regular medication and was happy to draft a report each day.

Milton could put his mask back on after the investigation had concluded and was allowed to practice his unsanctioned rounds throughout "Comfort House," as long as, at the end of each day he gave his report to the head nurse and turned in his stethoscope. It was understood by the staff that Milton was trusted by the residents, and he often found out more about what may be going on in the minds of the mentally disturbed than the staff could.

Milton had a way of taking the distortions and psychotic dreams that came to him in formless animated tales from the other patients and writing them on paper in such an uncontaminated way that the nurses could gain incredible insight. His writings magnified what was too infinitesimal for the staff to see. They seemed to see things through the wrong end of the telescope. The deranged was not always outwardly crazy, and the crazies were not all introverts. Milton made sure his reports reflected the distinction.

And concerning the missing head of Nancy the nurse... that is an unresolved mystery still.

LOOK AT WHAT THE WIND HAS BROUGHT

One might say they hear the wind, but I argue the wind is silent. So, what is it that one hears? I make the claim it is the sounds of what the wind carries with it in its invisible torrent. One hears the roaring, the whipping, the gushing, the whirring, which is nothing more than the science of friction.

Where does it come from in its swift surprise? What is its genesis? It can fan the flames, drive a fire, stir an ocean, but where does this phenomenon originate from? It is hard to imagine that a simple motion of air can bend the treetops. When we hear the shouting of the wind, heard from the trained ear, is it just the old oaks creaking or the faint murmuring of the grasses?

Have you ever wondered how phantoms travel and traverse? Do not tell me that you do not believe. If you can bear to listen intently enough, you will hear the whirring of their breath and the beating of their wings. They ride the sweeping winds, which raise the seas and pull the sailors beneath the dark waves. They move the air and cause it to spin and twirl like a top, filling itself with destruction and debris. It has the power to take lives, but it does not always act without permission from a higher authority. As indiscriminate as it may seem, the wind is governed.

These terrors leave desolation if they leave anything at all. How do these phantoms spare a child with a silent heart who is gazing from a window at the raging storm, yet when the winds hit, carry away everything else, leaving the child orphaned? This thought leaves me numb in utter sensibilities.

My story may not be unique, yet it is unequaled for one such as I. If I say I have been left perpetually haunted, it would not be a lie. Never had hope been more decimated in my life than when the storm blew in. It is not what the storm brought in, but in retrospect, I say it is what it left me with. Allow me to explain.

In my current state, I had just returned to my computer after taking a long look at the horizon, which was crimson in hue, like blood smeared across the troubling skies. The forecast for the day was clear and sunny skies, yet it appeared the storm of the century was brewing. I would have to keep my eyes peeled concerning this one. There was not anything I could do to protect myself. I had no basement or a storm shelter.

I could hear it picking up momentum, roaring and rumbling like an approaching freight train that was about to leave the tracks. I sat facing my computer, hoping if I ignored all of the signs, the storm would simply go away, yet my keen psychometry was getting numerous vibrations.

I am one who believes that inanimate objects resonate and have moving parts. If you do not believe me, cast a dry piece of wood into a fire. Hear it change, hiss, crackle, and sizzle. Yes, infinitely delicate vibrations seek other receptive objects and this way, they have purpose, reason, a connection. Credulous minds cannot fathom such quasi-science, yet those with vivid imaginations—you know the type, the thinkers, the dreamers, the creative ones—have the advantage. If a man does not dream, he merely sleeps his life away without connecting to anything around him. It is only awakening from a dream with breathless excitement that one knows they are alive.

With everything in the room singing in my ears with warning, I continued to research on my computer. My right hand was positioned on my wireless mouse while my eyes were glued to the screen. To restrain my anxiety, I looked up 'famous quotes of hope.' An odd one appeared, mixed in with the running column of quotes. It was a Bible verse: 'The wind bloweth where it listeth, and thou hearest the sound thereof, but canst not tell whence it cometh, and whither it goeth: so is every one that is born of the Spirit.'

For the time being, I was comforted by this verse. Wasn't it with the breath of God that man became a living soul? No one sees the viewless wind. We can record it, predict it, but dark sylphs ride with the prince of the power of the air, masquerading as angels of light. I was conflicted suddenly because outside, a foreboding darkness seemed to have its way with the light of day. I am reminded that darkness is no match for a single lit candle. But the wind, on the other hand, with its Aeolian modulations, removes all imagination and hope for its manifestation and snuffs out the flame from the wick, dispensing the twirling smoke as if it never was.

Atmospheric changes were happening, but I remained disinclined to move, for where could I go? If I were to be honest, I was solidified under this intolerable suffrage. The house shook, it rattled, it creaked, it swelled as if the walls were about to burst. This is when the most unexpected weirdness manifested itself. From the computer screen, which was still locked on the quotes page, an actual hand appeared, bodiless. With its uncommonly long fingers, missing the first finger, it stretched forth and penetrated the glass of the screen and came into my world. This grey, bony, leathered appendage with yellow nails rested upon my hand, which was still gripping the mouse. The haunting hand moved my hand, clicking on different things on the screen until it reached a quote, clicked on it, and it appeared enlarged before my eyes. 'If a man knows not what harbor he seeks, any wind is the right wind' by Lucius Annaeus Seneka.

I had no idea what this could mean. I was horrified and frightened beyond belief. This was unimaginable madness. I was insane with fear but could not pull loose the grip, which forced me to surf the net with incredible speed. Under an oppressive uneasiness suffering from an attack of nerves, I was helpless. I gazed fixedly at the screen. This appendage imposed its will upon me in so much as to guide my hand to websites of blasphemy, indignant scrutiny of pain and suffering, to sites of foul, carnal, fleshly lust, and into screens where the web content became darker than I could have ever envisioned. It held me captive, fastened tighter than a pair of handcuffs. The storm outside was in plangent fury. The house was under full assault. If it blew away now, I was sure I would go with it. I could hear the ruthless smashing of glass. Something must have crashed through the window. There was the sound of personal items being blown off their shelves, and the doors were slamming shut within the interior. I could only begin to envisage the damage. At the computer, I turned my head from the offensive content, but every time I did the hand, that decrepit hand squeezed mine tighter, as if to show who was in control. It certainly was not me. If I did not want my hand and wrist broken, I had to watch the screen. This accursed extremity knew every time I shut my eyes. Resistance was a waste of all my strength. Why did it want to fill my head with such abominations? This protruding death lock had clamped me for many minutes before releasing me and receding back within the computer. It disappeared as if it had never existed, yet it left a severe bruise around my wrist and the coloring extended into my fingers.

The storm settled straight after the unexplainable episode, and I went to the freezer to collect ice cubes to apply to my contusion.

I was not remotely interested in finding anything further on this macabre bizarreness. I was certainly distressed in my clarity. It was totally and completely intolerable, this confusing, evil episode.

I do not know any other word to describe it. It was almost like a seductress was luring me with the disgusting depravity of the world.

I rested until I heard a braying laughter from outside. I leaped to my feet in fright. I knew not whether to run or to find a weapon. The important thing was that I keep my head on straight and not lose my cool. I went to the front door because the laughter originated from that part of my property. Then again, anything was possible. Before I reached the door, I asked myself the question if I had actually heard the unnerving laughter at all.

I opened the door slowly, and to my surprise, a man stood on my doorstep. I was taken aback, but instantly took notice of his appearance. His face was too full to be handsome. It was a cascading face that was at mutiny with itself. His forehead was deeply rippled with a runaway nose. His eyes squinted, forming thin lines around his eyes like a traffic junction, and the color was undefinable. His cheekbones were as dull as butter knives, but he had a captivating smile that stretched from ear to ear. He was neither handsome nor loathsome, striking, or ugly, yet for some reason, he bore an attraction. I suppose it was because he was charismatic, not in a religious way but rather in a 'I do not give a damn way.' If he had not been shaken loose from infinity, then I was sadly mistaken.

The first thing he said before I was able to address him properly was, "I am here from the winds of unknown spaces." He proceeded to smile malignantly, showing his copious mouth of crowded, jagged teeth as if time was on his side. I said a silent prayer of salvation, for I did not know if this was to be my hour of death or not.

He knew right away what I was mumbling. He remarked, "Save your breath. No one is listening. Anything supreme deserted mankind ages ago."

That was a troubling statement. If he was truthful, which I scarcely doubted, then I would hope for the immortal oblivion of eternal rest.

His chin tilted outward as if he was measuring my soul. I thought how impossible, how irrelevant, as trying to understand the movements of birds in flight. He laughed again, and it was such an obscene squawk it could have only been a guffaw which no one could ever be accused of letting out, unless stoned on the 'green fairy.' I am not sure if it is even translatable. I shrank back atrophied with great concern. This was absolutely unusual in every sense of the word.

I gasped and shut the door straight in his face. There came a rapping again. It was bony knuckles against wood. I did not know what to do, so I ran back to my computer room. It seemed everything started here; maybe I could end it there. I immediately unplugged the machine, yet the screen still glowed with perversion and images that made me nauseous. The knocking continued.

Obviously, it was not going to be as easy as unplugging the lurking entity. I retrieved a kitchen knife of formidable length and, with sure and practiced steps, returned to the front door. Although it was a solid wooden door with no way to peer inside my residence, when I approached the door, the knocking ceased. There went my element of surprise.

I yelled through the door, "What do you want?" I pressed my ear to the wood to hear the answer; however, the ear not pressed to the door heard a troubling whisper. "I beckon thee to come with me."

With feigned surprise, I collapsed to the floor. My hand became too weak to hold onto the knife. It dropped from my hand. I was now in a crouched position with that which was outside, now appearing inside and standing over me glaringly. I was panic-stricken in so much my breathing became rapid and shallow. My head became fuzzy and light, and I prayed death would not be painful. I have always been an intuitive soul; you know, first impression, the gut feeling, sixth sense sort of thing and how I was reading this situation made me shiver. With a wry expression growing on his face, this man of privation reached down with his right hand and lifted me back to my feet. It was ever more evident now that this man was not from this time.

I instantly retracted in a way that was clumsy and embarrassing, more afraid than before. My elemental strength would be no match for his certain wizardry. That is what I thought at the time, that this must be a magical enchanted person from another world. He ignored my initial resistance, and seeing for the moment I was unapproachable, he stood, patiently waiting, it seemed, for me to collect myself. I had to think, to reason this out. I had no concealed methods of dealing death other than the knife I had loosely allowed to fall from my grip.

Strangely significant, I began to realize if this towering figure wanted to bring me to my demise, he could have already accomplished it. Mortified beyond anything I had ever felt, I mustered the voice to speak.

"What do you want?"

"There is something at work in my soul that I cannot describe. I am carried by the phantom winds in search of the hand, that wretched, deplorable thing which terrorizes the living."

"The hand?" I realized he was after the same hand that had possessed my computer. I carefully studied the man but could read nothing of his intentions.

"I am a raconteur from a former time. I exist but do not exist because I am incomplete. Do you understand?"

I understood nothing as the man cast his hard gaze upon me. I did not have a clue, but because he was holding all of the cards, I answered truthfully.

"I do not know what you want?"

"I am Sir John Rowell, a character in a book." "I cannot help you. I do not know what you expect of me?" "The hand has visited you. It is a murderous hand and must be contained." "You are a character in a book, you say? How have you sprung from the pages and now stand in my house? If you are a character in a book, then you are only a figment of someone else's imagination, a creation invented in the mind of this author you mentioned?" I was not a big reader; thus, I had never heard of . My knowledge of the literary world was considerably lacking.

Sir John responded with, "The hand must be gathered, the hand must be returned. I have no peace otherwise. Where is the hand? What have you done with the hand?"

This was some kind of fresh terror now. A dead man who does not really exist is chasing a severed hand in some phantasmagorical land, which just so puts him here at my doorstep, in my home. If this had been any other intruder, I would have demanded that he was to leave immediately, but seeing this had to be a bad dream, I honestly did not know where to direct him to. It was not like I was hoarding information. I believed Sir John knew much more about this insatiable matter than I did.

"The phantoms collected the hand. These mystical creatures sent from Abaddon's lair exist in the 'without world' where demons rule. Seldom are they permitted to cross over. Yet the hand wrote about, and this story I am in, was real. It is the hand of Baal, which I once possessed and had nailed to my wall. I came into possession of it through mutual trades when I was brewing a unique blend of alcohol. Gypsies from the Balkans had traveled through our land, and once they heard I had the very best spirits anyone had ever tasted, they were quick to make me an offer. They traded me the hand, saying it had only been a curse for them, yet swore it was the right hand of Baal."

Sir John implicitly believed what he was conveying to me. I was oblivious to any of the history which he described. I was convinced I was not in immediate harm's way and was able to generally relax without becoming complacent or comfortable.

"I have what is called a computer. It is very technical, and I will not go into great detail concerning how it works, but can say this was the place I was accosted by the hand."

Sir John winced as I pointed to my home computer.

"But it is only a box. Is it magical?" he asked.

"Nothing supernatural or like a sorceress, yet it has a lot of power. It is called the information highway or the Internet." My explanation was very simple, and even with this uncomplicated approach, I could see Sir John had not a clue as to what I was sharing. I was unsure how to relate the mysteries of the computer world to this 19th-century individual. There was a plenitude of information, yet I hardly knew where to begin. Simple perambulation was my approach, and I hoped it worked.

***

I first logged onto the computer with my password, which Sir John immediately found fascinating. He was elated at the screen and how I used the mouse. At first, he believed the mouse was a planchette associated with a Ouija board. I assured him it was not. I did not want him to think I was a spiritualist. He might have me talking to the dead. Then again, it appeared I was already conversing with the dead.

I described the unintelligible dread I had suffered earlier before Sir John arrived when the hand manifested and grabbed me, showing him the bruising on my wrist. Carefully, I surfed through pages, though for what reason I did not know because I could not be sure if this hand was lurking on my computer or not. In some regards, I thought I might go mad, insanely facing this intolerable dread. I just knew at any instant the hand would lunge from the screen and drag me into the cyber world. There was no perfectly logical explanation for this, so I assured myself I had no cause to despair. The abominable notion of living this night added to the unnecessary terror I was dealing with.

Within minutes, the house rumbled as if in the mist of another storm, but there was no wind nor rain nor torrent of any kind outside. It was the house itself coming under attack. The walls shook; more things were rocked out of place and onto the floor. The lights flickered off and on several times, and the moment it stopped, the hand as gruesome as before lunged from the computer screen and ceased upon my sore wrist. I struck it this time with my free hand. I gave it a battering of three or four serious whacks before I saw Sir John slap a handcuff around what was left of the dangling wrist flesh. This was attached by a chain snapped to his trouser belt loops. The struggle was on. I resisted with all of my might, aided by the formidable Sir John, who was tugging against the amputee limb with all of his might.

I am sure if I had been able to step back away from the scene and actually see how absurd this was, I would have found it ridiculously amusing. As we fought against invisible forces to extract this demonic malware from my computer, the gruesome hand was fingering with the mouse and surfing through the perverted websites again, sex, violence, war, murder, and disgust as if it were addicted to everything unclean and could not get enough. From the corner of my eye, I witnessed Sir John reach to his right hip, and from there, he produced a sidearm. It was a shining pistol of some sort. I knew right away nothing good could come from a deadly weapon. Personally, I avoided guns and had done so all my life. In this instance, however, I was hopeful Sir John knew how to use it without accidentally wounding me.

The irredeemable hand jerked wildly, adding incredible tension to the strenuous fight. Once we freed the hand from the screen, the sound of a gun blast practically concussed me, and I went stone deaf with a constant ringing assaulting my ear drums. The instant smell of sulfur from the gunpowder filled my nasal cavity, and I smelled another type of smoke as well. When I surveyed the damage, my computer had been shot to pieces. Whether the ghoulish hand had been dealt with or not, I could not discern. I could clearly see there was no hope for the computer. The bullet went straight through it.

There was no sign of the cursed hand. It was loose somewhere in the house.

"I missed," Sir John admitted.

"Seriously?" I moaned.

I heard scuttling down the hall. The decrepitude appendage was invasive and quick. I was not about to be the first one after it—I had no idea what it was capable of—but not Sir John. He was eager to keep up the fight, and off he ran with his pistol raised in the air over his head. I followed Sir John at a safe distance in case there was another assault. I had no desire to become an unintended victim.

The morbid thing had taken up refuge in my bedroom, still with the chain around the wrist. When I reached the doorway, I saw the infernal, distal limb attached to the corner of the wall in what could only be described as a pouncing position. Sir John said to it, "I have something for you, you miserable... you unmittened manus."

I did not know what that meant, but I took it as an insult of some sort. Sir John then bent over at the waist and coughed a few times extremely hard. He held a hand over his own mouth, and what I witnessed next practically made me lose my lunch. He coughed up something that was long and crooked. It was comparable to a finger. I thought, "Good Lord Almighty!" No wonder the maimed hand only had four fingers. Sir John presumably had bitten that finger off at some time since his association with the double amputee.

"Is this what you were looking for?" In a dastardly tone, Sir John seemed to tease and taunt the atrophied hand, which scuddled noisily, with the chain dangling, along the wall to the parallel wall, then took up a position on the ceiling as if watching Sir John and measuring him up. Holding the finger slightly out in front of himself, baiting the hand, Sir John cocked the hammer on the gun and slowly aimed it at the hand, which had clenched itself into an indignant fist.

"It's all yours if you want it," he slyly gestured. The withered hand, using its fingers as legs, galloped along spider-like across the ceiling toward Sir John. He fired his weapon once again, but unfortunately, the arachnid-like thing sidestepped the bullet with lightning-fast reflexes. Again, the blast caused torturous ear pain, but I was better prepared and less shook by the concussion. When I took a deeper look through the cloud of white powder, I saw Sir John wrestling with the malformed extremity, which had moved on him with tarantula-like speed and had clutched itself with vice strength to his throat. I did not know if the revolting hand had been wounded or not, but I sprung into action and immediately grabbed the chain. Instead of a constant steady pull, because that did not seem to be the trick earlier, I yanked violently on the chain, trying to free Sir John from the deadly choking that was taking place. With every effort I gave, the aberrant hand fought back using superhuman resolve. After a dozen or more vicious pulls, the metacarpus which had fused itself forcefully snapped loose from the strangulation of Sir John's gullet but seemed as though it had turned its focus directly on me. I had no way to defend myself, but I quickly grabbed a table lamp, and when it came toward me, I did not hesitate to use the lamp as I would a baseball bat and swung for the fences. I made solid contact, and the hand went flying across the room. With unintentional and terrible aim, I had swatted the hand back onto Sir John's chest. Sir John scampered on his backside away from it, slapping it, brushing it away with a look of fright in his eyes. Again, it leaped to his throat and began to strangle him again.

"You've got to be kidding me," I grumbled and took hold of the chain once again. I cannot believe there was a ghastlier scene. Sir John, red in the face from lack of blood due to the asphyxiation, and me, straining my guts out, attempting to dislodge the hand from Sir John's throat for a second time. There was little doubt that this morose scene, as eerie as it certainly was, was becoming fatalistically comical. If I was unable to free Sir John from this demented death grip, not only was he going to perish, but I would easily be its next victim. So, the scene was Sir John laying flat on his back, pinned supine by a single severed hand which wore a chain, me tugging with two hands on the chain in an attempt to save Sir John from being killed. On the floor beside us was the dismembered appendage which Sir John had regurgitated moments before. As ignoble as it all was, I managed once again to free Sir John, who bolted for his gun that he had been forced to give up at some point. I never saw him drop it, but obviously he had. The hand dragged me along, racing Sir John for the pistol. Never would one imagine a cadaverous appendage could demonstrate such power. I dug in my heels just enough to slow the hand and, in doing so, allowed Sir John the advantage to collect the pistol. He did not hesitate or necessarily take aim. A third shot, a fourth and a fifth shot exploded in the room, and I felt no more pulling on the chain. The tension ceased, and I stopped there to look at what had occurred. At least one of the bullets had hit the deformed hand, for it lay on the floor without even a twitch. Promptly, Sir John collected the hand, which had turned completely black. He tightly ran bailing string around the bag and knotted it closed. He secured the newly packaged hand into his hunting bag. He looked quite satisfied as he threw the strap over his shoulder and tucked the bag underneath his arm.

"What are you going to do with it now?" I did not really need to know since it was obvious my work was done, but I was cautiously curious. After I asked the question, I honestly did not expect a response, but politely he answered.

"I will return it to where it belongs, nailed to the wall in my house in a story written long ago," Sir John said as he made his way to the door.

"But won't the phantoms come for it again?" I enquired.

"Let them. I will not forget this night. I will be ready for them." Sir John picked up the finger and grotesquely and, with some trouble, swallowed the finger again.

"Why go back to a place like that? Why can't you go any-where you wish now?" "Someone else is writing this narrative. I can only go and do what is written of me," he kindly said as he opened the front door.

"Do you need me to give you a lift or anything? I have a car?" "My departure is at hand," he declined as he stepped through the door. A savage gust of wind howled in out of nowhere, and just like that, Sir John was swept from the step, never to be seen again.

It was late, very late, and I was hit with incredible slumber. I would worry about my computer and the few gunshot holes tomorrow. As for now, I only wanted to sleep. Maybe tomorrow I will pick up The Hand by Guy de Maupassant. Something tells me the book will be much different than the events to which I was inadvertently contributed as an unwilling participant.

SEEK AND YE SHALL FIND

Mortimer Abbott was filthy rich. Matter of fact, in the town where he lived, he had more money than all of the other residents combined. He did not flaunt his wealth. He did not live large. He did not have servants, or gardeners, or even caretakers, yet the mansion and its humble grounds were always manicured and immaculate. Not once could anyone remember seeing Mr. Abbott doing any sort of yard work at all. Matter of fact, no one hardly saw him at all. He had been spotted at the farmer's market a few times and he had attended an auction of a neighboring farm, with this as an exception, to get a glimpse of the old fellow was rare. His home, which was called The Abbott House, had been in his family for decades. It was something to behold. Mr. Abbott lived in comfort under self-imposed isolation and security, which led people to talk that he most likely never used a bank. If he did not have his money in the bank, it was assumed the fortune must be stacks of cash hidden away in the fortified walls of his home. The window blinds were usually pulled down and shutters were shut tight. Once in a while, a window or two may be open, but no one could gain a vantage point to even get the slightest peeps through the tall windows. People supposed, as rumors circle, he slept on his wealth in a four-poster bed with Egyptian sheets and goose down pillows. The home itself was built with stone and slate and boasted a magnificent courtyard which spilled out into a small orchard. The property was prime real estate, sophisticated without being gaudy.

Mr. Abbott was set in his opulent castle, but one day his time simply ran out and he passed away of a heart attack. No one knew just how old he was, but they were sure, without question, he had outlived all of his childhood classmates and may have been the oldest man in the county. It was not known until his will was read, and to everyone's surprise, Mr. Abbott, when he was younger, had been married for a time. His wife had passed away from tuberculosis. After her untimely passing, he had remained unmarried and unaffiliated with any woman for the remainder of his days.

His funeral was a quiet affair. There were thirty or so mourners who came to pay their respects but no relative attended. When his will was read, it was found out, as was assumed, he did have some money in the bank. It was not nearly the sum which most expected him to have accumulated but as per his wishes according to his notarized will, the property was to be maintained by the county until the funds were exhausted, and then the mansion would be gifted to the county as a historical landmark, mainly due to its age. However, no one for any reason would be permitted inside the house during this time period. These were strange requests, yet the county agreed they would look after the mansion until the day came when the county could take full possession of the estate.

Virgil Weed and Angus Gunter were two "good ol' boys" always compelled by greed and opportunity. They had read in the local paper Mortimer Abbott, the eccentric man of wealth and means had died and peculiar his house had been left vacant and in the care of the county for upkeep. They concocted a plan. They always had a plan for better or for worse, and usually it was the latter.

They contrived a scheme to make their way into The Abbott House and to search for the cash they had convinced themselves existed somewhere within. They assumed it would be hidden well, possibly in the walls, under the floorboard, potentially the attic or perchance it could be in the old man's mattress. They were opportunist having never earned an honest wage. Their hands were always dirty, not for labor, but because of the petty criminal lives they had led since dropping out of school several years earlier. Neither Virgil nor Angus could be said to be the follower or the leader. They fundamentally were equals when it came to the ideology of innovative crime. Both of the young men were fresh out of the county jail after doing 60 days for breaking the windows of their local Baptist Church. They were also ordered to pay for the windows with other restitutions imposed. If they could only find the old man's money, they could buy their way out of trouble and move away from this place, which they determined through trial and error was not the best for them to be living in. Too many people knew them as thieves.

No one wanted to hire them because they were thieves. Virgil and Angus were considered the most undesirable fellows in the area. No one liked to see them coming, but everyone loved to see them go. The town folks knew it was a matter of time before the boys would do something so stupendously stupid, they would be serving time with the hardened criminals.

The plan was a simple one because Virgil and Angus were incredibly simple. They would wait until dark and jimmy the lock on the backdoor. Virgil had already given it an inspection earlier and determined unequivocally, that the backdoor was definitely going to be the easiest way into the home without being detected. There were no neighbors on the back side of the house and the lighting was not particularly good.

Clothed completely in black with beanies on their heads and wearing gloves, they made their way on foot through the dark of night to the rear of The Abbott House. Virgil wore a small tool belt which held a claw hammer, a short crowbar and two screwdrivers. The house had an impression of eeriness shrouding it at night.

Curious shadows gave power to the imagination, as if dark figures were lurking behind every tree and the corners of the house. Both young men were unsettled at the unworldly tenebrous hovering spookily over the place.

As to be expected, they had chosen a terrible night for a burglary. The weather had turned later in the evening to pouring rain, rumbling thunder and impressive display of lightning which streaked across the sky and illuminated the house like something from Tales of the Crypt. By the time they had crossed the grounds, through the backyard to the rear of the house, they were drenched through. Neither had thought to bring an umbrella. The lightning flashed, illuminating their silhouettes as Virgil worked on picking the lock. A wind whipped, and rain slapped against them with practically gale force. The sibilant wind seemed to be blowing from every direction. The thunder rolled sounding like a bowling bowl rolling down its perspective lane and a sudden thunder clamp made their bones rattle. It was the sort of boom which made the two bumbling 'want to be thieves' practically jump out of their skin.

"Gazooks!" exclaimed Virgil, who had instinctively hunkered low when the thunder cracked the sky.

Angus looked nervous when he said, "This place gives me the willies." Virgil looked over at him as he was working on the lock to the back door. "Yeah, like the heebee-geebees," he continued to poke and prod until the door popped open with a crack. "Heebee-geebees easy peasy," Virgil sneered. Cautiously moving inside the house, dripping wet and chilled to the bone, Virgil and Angus quietly sneaked through the kitchen. They both carried small torches and tried not to shine them toward the windows. The house was furnished with the best of everything as far as their unprofessional minds could surmise, but they were here for the big prize, the cash! With little light, the house was arguably morose and expressed an aspect of gloominess. The two looked for the staircase because they assumed the old man's bed would be upstairs in the Master Bedroom.

Caught up in their own adrenaline, they lumbered through the house trying not to break anything along the way in case they wanted to come back for other valuables later. On tip toe they proceeded, being quiet and careful, although they could only assume they were alone. They quietly joked, indisputably they did not want to wake up the ghost. The floorboards creaked and squeaked with every other step until Virgil spotted the banister to the staircase. Angus was having trouble focusing his eyes. Between the dark, the dim torches they carried and the consistent lightning flashes outside the continuance of the ever—changing luminosity or the lack thereof made every step he took deliberate.

"Good Lord man, this Old Man Abbott had a lot fancy antiques," Virgil made mention. "You can say that again. What do you call that?

Virgil answered with a horrible French accent, "That is an armoire."

"When did you learn Spanish?," Angus ignorantly asked.

"Do not be stupid! It is not a Spanish word, it's French, you dummy." Virgil barked. Their folderol was interrupted by a banging from upstairs. It reverberated through the walls to the ground floor.

"What in the name of Judas did we just hear?" Angus withered.

"Stop being a scaredy cat. Probably a branch from the old oak tree on the side of the house." The knocking continued out of cadence as the two crept up the stairs, step by step.

"I heard it again Virgil?" Angus paused. Neither said a word and involuntarily were holding their breath to listen. A scratching sound from overhead and the sound of prevailing winds outside had stopped them midway up the staircase. Virgil reassured him, "Just small branches grazing the roof. That is all." Right then, manifestly, the room flashed brightly because of a thunderbolt outside and there was a crack and bang as if it had struck something. The lightning strike was synchronized perfectly with both men facing a portrait painting of a young, beautiful woman displayed on the wall. The woman in the picture looked as though she had leapt from the painting at the precise second of the lightning crash. The illusion caused both men's hearts to leap in their chest and knotted in their throats in such a way, the suppressed scream aching to be belted out was stifled, strangling them from making sound. After they gained their composure and courage, they tried to laugh it off, although the house seemed to seep moroseness.

At the top of the stairs, the decision was made to go right, shining their torches along the hallway, trying to light a path. The first door they came to was a closet. Obviously disappointed they had to try again, they walked on, hearing the rattling sound of something behind the next door. The two young men stood staring first at the door, then at one another.

"You ready?" asked Virgil.

He answered, "As ready as I'll ever be. Let's just get this over with. I am creeped out."

Virgil turned the creaking doorknob, and the hinges squeaked something terrible as he pushed through into what was discovered to be the master bedroom.

"Ah, this has to be it." Angus said excitedly.

"Yes, but what is that in the bed?" Virgil's voice sounded unsure.

They stared at the bed and what they saw went against all reason. For lying in the bed covered in a sheet up to the neck was a person. "What the devil is going on?" Virgil did not go further; his blood was singing in his veins. More so, Angus was terminally petrified where he stood.

"No one is supposed to be living here." Angus groaned.

Virgil shined his light right on the person in the bed. "They are not moving. They must be asleep. Come on, let's take a look. There's two of us and one of him. What is he going to do if he wakes up?"

"Yeah," Angus agreed. "Two of us, one of him."

Together they approached the bed, ignoring everything in the room. They wanted to get to the mattress. Virgil withdrew a large, shiny hunting knife he had thoughtfully brought along to cut open the mattress. He now had it out in front of himself and followed the blade close to the bed.

In the bed lay an old man, face gaunt with deep wrinkles, the skin looked grey or claylike. The lips of the man were bluish, almost black, and his eyes were closed but deep set and his mouth was pierced open like a slit. "I don't hear him breathing." Virgil whispered. "He looks dead." Angus retorted. Over the bed on the wall hung a painting. The man in the painting looked very much like the man in the bed, except the man in the painting looked alive in contrast with the man covered in the bed, who was obviously dead.

Their bodies felt weak, attacked by horror. Their knees shook uncontrollably.

"This looks like old man Abbott." Virgil said, feeling as though he could have a blood stroke at any minute.

There was a light tapping now, which got their attention, coming from the direction of the closet door.

"Check it out." Virgil suggested to Angus.

Taking an obdurate stance, Angus refused. "No way man. We have a corpse in the bed and a tapping at the closet door. That ain't no water pipe sound."

"Could be the air ducts or mice." Virgil reassured himself.

"What are we going to do?" Angus said nervously.

"What we came to do."

Virgil stabbed the knife into the side of the mattress with a large amount of force. The knife went into the mattress like butter. He began to rip and tear and shred the mattress, pulling its content out. He dug his hands in madly trying to locate the hidden cash. Angus watched in terror as the tapping seemed to become more amplified as Virgil destroyed the bed.

Angus began to poke Virgil on the shoulder hard and rapidly.

"What is it?" Virgil stopped his assault of the bed and saw Angus pointing at the dead man.

The man was still laying stiff as a board, but his eyes were opened. The eyes were revoltingly black and stared directly at the ceiling.

"His eyes just popped open." Informed Angus, who had taken a step backward away from the bed.

Virgil's mouth was gapped unnaturally wide, profoundly stunned as he stated the obvious, "This is not cool. This guy is dead and buried. What is he doing here?"

"Yeah, and why are his eyes opened," Asked Angus?

"Okay, we got to get a grip. It is an old dead man. The eyes of the dead open on their own sometimes. Maybe I rocked the bed or something?" Virgil said, having a hard time believing his own words. The sound of air could be heard, being released from the mouth of the old man as if someone was letting the air out of a tire. The room became offensively malodorous. The unpleasant putrescent gasses drove Virgil back as he covered his mouth and nose. Still obdurate, Virgil seemed to have turned his fear into anger. He ripped the sheet off the old man in a rage and had the knife in the air ready to plunge the blade into the frail bony chest when gale force winds roared through, blowing the windows open and causing a vortex in the room. The dust and pollen which had lay undisturbed and accumulated for some time all gathered at once, as if it were being shaped by an invisible hand. This tornadic whirlwind whooshed around the room with enough thrust to push Virgil away from the bed.

"Shut the windows!" Yelled Virgil to Angus, who had not been caught in the spiral. Angus eventually got the windows clasped shut, and the wind was blocked from wrecking any more havoc.

A sickening sweetness hung in the air, which practically gaged the two men.

"This is not right Virgil. I think we need to call this off, count our losses and get out." Advised Angus.

"Count our losses? You have to gain something to lose something, and we have not gained a thing yet. I am not leaving without the cash. I know something is not right here. The old man should be in the ground, not lounging in his bed. But he is dead. Ignore him. We have to get back to business." Instructed Virgil.

The madness had set in on Angus. He began to become irrational. He was babbling on to himself about the dead, ghost and the macabre.

He was going on in a state of delirium when Virgil abruptly slapped him across the face. The sting from the open hand pained Angus, but at the same time caught his full attention.

"Pull your bloody self together, man. What the devil are you going on about?" Virgil did not want an answer. He demanded compliance.

Angus, with crazed eyes and a reckless smile, spewed out, "My God man, can't you see what is going on here? I am not the brightest bulb on the tree but I know for sure, nothing about tonight is of the norm. There is a freaking dead man in the bed! It cannot be explained. Are you so greedy and hell bent on scoring the big haul you cannot see we are in some sort of purgatory, some sort of haunted realm?"

"Bull crap!" Virgil raged, "This body in the bed could be anybody and there is a storm outside. Everything feels like a haunted house tonight. If you were in the holiest of sanctuaries under these unlit conditions you would swear devilish things were afoot." Virgil reasoned.

"Go ahead and try to convince yourself, but there is something demonic going on here." Angus sounded angry.

Virgil pushed Angus to the side and then moved around him toward the closet, where they had heard the tapping previously. He swung open the double doors without a care in the world and began to fling, every stich of clothing hanging there out onto the floor.

"You see Angus? There are no ghosts behind the doors. It is the wretched wind! Why do you have to be so simple-minded? Not everything that goes bump in the night is a phantom waiting to lung out and devour you. I came here tonight to find treasure and I swear I am going to find it!" Virgil was more decided than before. His anger had spilled over into greed and desire, and he was not about to be stopped.

Angus had no choice but to go along with him. Like a whipped pup, he clamored behind Virgil as Virgil smashed walls and ripped out drawers. He swung open doors with evil intent looking, feeling, seeking the treasure his heart so desperately craved.

After a futile attempt, the cash was elusive. He stood in the middle of the upstairs hall with sweat dripping off his face from his efforts. He began to convince himself, poor Angus's existence was superfluous. He did not know why he brought such an incompetent coward to such an important robbery.

"What good are ya?" Virgil asked Angus, who looked dumbfounded by the question.

"I don't know what you mean?" Angus pathetically responded.

"I am doing all the work and all you are doing is following me around waiting for the payday!" Virgil's temper was at a boiling point.

"I have been with you through thick and thin. I have not always agreed, but I have followed." Angus felt like he deserved some credit.

"Yeah, you have followed alright." Virgil gave Angus a look of distaste.

"I am not sure what you are talking about, but you are scaring me, Virgil." Angus said, intimidated.

"Just stay out of my way until we find the cash!" Ordered Virgil, taking a severely harsh tone. Virgil continued to ransack everything in sight, thinking the old man had hid the money in vases, drawers, behind doors, in walls, yet nothing was found.

"I am going back to the upstairs, to the master bedroom. We've missed something there. I am sure of it. With Angus at his heels, Virgil stormed up the stairs, his feet pounding the steps with hard deliberation. Virgil re-entered the master bedroom and the first thing he saw was the old man still laying in the same position, undisturbed, he had left him in.

———————

Virgil walked over to the bed. The old man lay there looking as white as powder. He looked brittle and broken. He was not much more than a shell of a man. Everything had been flushed out of him, and he lay cold, resonating death.

For a split-second, Virgil wondered, what kind of man was this Mr. Abbott with all of his wealth and fancy things? What sort of man would accumulate such riches and live alone like a hermit? Why not live large? He could have had fancy dinner parties, be the talk of the town, inviting the best of the best every weekend to wine and dine. Why die in such obscurity?

As his mind wandered into the fantasy world, he dreamed of what it would be like to be rich, what he would have accomplished with such prosperity and abundance. "Oh, I would have had the cars, the girls, thrown parties for the judges, the doctors the lawyers, I would have had this place on party mode 24/7."

Virgil then smashed another vase, only to find it empty as well. "It's got to be in the walls," Virgil shouted as he pushed by Angus. Virgil was carrying a hammer on his toolbelt. He withdrew it and began to smash the walls of the bedroom. Angus excitedly joined in by tearing at the gaping holes with his hands, ripping the plasterboard away from the studs. The terrific sounds of crashing, shattering and destruction were so bombastic no doubt, it could have awakened the dead. And it did!

Mortimer Abbott had become surfeit; he had allowed this to go on long enough. His treasure was still secure and all affluence untouched.

"Enough!" A commanding voice raised over the melodramatic obliteration. Virgil lost the hold on the hammer, and it dropped to his feet with a clunk. Angus spun around and the hair on his neck bristled. Their blood seemed frozen in this instance and a wash of terrifying dread coupled with unutterable horror seized their minds.

Mr. Abbott was no longer on the bed. He was standing at the foot of the bed, just as ghostly white as before. Nonetheless, he did not appear to be as rickety or enervated, nor as dead as before. "What have you done to my house?" Demanded Mr. Abbott with an articulation of a deliberate frightful tone.

Speechless, the two boys shifted slowly in unison toward the bedroom door. Knowing the hallway was just a few feet away, they were only thinking of escape. The bedroom door slammed shut and the sound of the lock could be heard turning inside the door mechanism.

"Look, look, look." Angus stuttered. "Let's reason this out," Virgil's voice was desperate.

Mr. Abbott paralleled the boys and once again made a statement. "Who do you think you are? Breaking into my home! You are uninvited! You are trespassers, invaders of my home." Mr. Abbotts word were straightforward, deliberate.

"We are sorry. Please don't hurt us. We'll leave. We'll never come back. Please!" Virgil begged, his eyes watery with ceaseless worry.

Mr. Abbott never took a step. He simply glided as if he were wearing roller skates face to face with Virgil, who refused to look him in the eyes. Mr. Abbott glared at Virgil. Angus was petrified, looking straight down at the floor seeing for the first time, Mr. Abbott's feet were hovering a couple of inches off the floor.

"How dare you wake me from my sleep! Get out of my house," Mr. Abbott's voice sounded insistently grizzly, it growled deep with the guttural sound of the abyss. His breath was notable as the putrid rot hissed forth not from a living soul but of the foul sulphur which rises unimpeded from the inferno below. It was a fetid stench of astringent rotting flesh laced with a sickening perfume, an off-putting remoulade. Like an aerosol, it rolled from his mouth like a green transparent fog.

The window shades swished and rolled up and back down on their own, letting in the lightning flashes from the blustery storm outside. The rain fell like bullets from a machine gun on the roof, causing temporary deafness. Mr. Abbott's bed shook violently and the bedroom door, which previously had been supernaturally closed and bolted, now flung open and slammed against the door frame over and over. The room had become helter-skelter with tumultuous clatter. Things had become so abysmally tense that Angus could take no more. He attempted to flee through the banging door, but it slammed shut right before he got to the opening. He smashed headlong into the door, concussing himself. His slipshod attempt at escape would have been comical to Virgil, except the severity of the moment was now upon him. Virgil was retreated back against the wall, his eyes as big as golf balls. Over Mr. Abbott's shoulder, he saw a glowing white figure of a woman in a white dressing gown. She approached him as Mr. Abbott had done, without touching the floor.

With a sinister voice speaking through his teeth, Mr. Abbott asked, "Have you met my wife, Lilly?"

Virgil was too frightened and panicked to answer. His tongue felt swollen in his mouth.

The woman said not a word but came and stood with Mr. Abbott.

Mr. Abbott gave the command. "Take your accomplice and get out of my house. Never come back or you will never leave this house. And you tell others the same fate awaits anyone who breaches my walls ever again!"

Precisely at that moment, the bedroom door opened. The upheaval and ruckus ceased. The sound of the storm was muted, and the silence was almost as painfully dreadful to their nerves as when the raucous cacophony of madness had ensued.

"It is time for you to vacate," Mr. Abbott's voice also became gentle, soothing almost harmonious. Virgil was not sure, he was confused.

Mr. Abbott's eyes turned red and with timbre in his voice as a song of war he asked, "Have I not made my myself clear!"

At that, Virgil took the hint, managed his courage, gathered his senses, and darted for the door, dragging Angus by the back of the shirt collar out of the master bedroom, down the hall; by this time, Angus was alert and his feet were moving. The two skipped stairs as they raced downward, passing by the painting of what must have been Lilly. They tripped and stumbled at the bottom step but regained their balance and exited through the back door which they had entered the house. As they raced across the lawn, Mr. Abbott had the final word. "Get out of my house!"

Virgil and Angus ran through the soggy, sloppy yard as fast as their feet would carry them. The rain started again, and it was colder than before. They left the grounds and vowed to never return. They would tell no one of what they had saw nor of the night they had underwent.

Inside the house, Mr. and Mrs. Abbot walked down the stairs to her painting on the wall. He pulled on the painting and opened it like a door. Behind the painting was a safe. Inside the safe was the wealth. Assuredly one day someone would find it.

But not this night.

THE LIGHTHOUSE, THE DIARY AND THE DEAD

"Death may be the greatest of all human blessings"—Socrates

The Lightkeeper was retiring. He had two wickies assisting, young lads whose job was (but not limited to) the responsibility of tending and trimming wicks for the light. All three men were being relieved from their duties, and they would be off Flannan Islands in the remote Outer Hebrides on the coast of mainland Scotland very soon. This archipelago was remote and uninhabited. The three men were looking forward to leaving this barren rock. For the past twelve months they had been on duty, taking shifts. They were done with solitary life for a while. They wanted to get to the mainland, mix and mingle and have one good night's rest in a comfortable bed. Their bodies were worn, and their eyes were tired from guiding trans-Atlantic ships toward the harbour in Leith, Scotland.

The relief vessel, 'The Hesperus' carried the Lighthouse Tender, who was going to go ashore and take over the duties until a full crew could join him. There had been some terrible weather in recent days, and this delayed the relief ship an entire week. Concern had been raised as the steamer, 'Archtor', had reportedly passed by the Flannan Isles Lighthouse and her light was not operational. This was a cause for concern because a dark lighthouse means real problems.

When 'the Hesperus' came upon the landing platform to the Lighthouse, on the day Ratcliff McLean was to go ashore and relieve the 3 men, he noticed, as well as the rest of the ship's crew, none of the men on the island were waiting for them on the dock, as procedure dictated. The captain sounded his horn, and a flare was released into the sky, but no reply reciprocated from the island. Another peculiarity was the flagstaff was missing the signal flag. The crew of the Hesperus knew this was an ill-omen. Ratcliff demanded the supply boat be lowered into the water; without delay he would immediately go to shore. Ratcliff was not afraid, but apprehensive based on the oddities he had witnessed from the island. Some might say he was a brave man, but he was, in fact, better described as conscientious but not a risk-taker. He was going beyond the strata of his own safety. He carried a locket which contained a picture of his deceased wife, who ironically had drowned two years ago in a freak accident when the boat on which she was a passenger tipped over, and she plunged into the water, never resurfacing. She was a beauty; long, dark, flowing hair and fair skin. Ratcliff took a look at the picture in the locket. He made eye contact with his wife, which for him was a sign of good luck. Closing the locket, he placed it in his vest pocket and prepared to launch for shore.

He went alone, rowing through relatively calm waters, pointed toward the black face precipices and craggy clefts, barren of vegetation. Part of the island was hidden in a sea of vapour, but he steered directly to the dock. Upon arrival, he made note of more irregularities. Both the entrance gate and the gate leading up to the compound were shut. This submerged him into suspension. Ratcliff remembered he was carrying a loaded revolver and if there was trouble, he would not be hesitant to use it. There was an unexplained eeriness causing the hairs on the back of his neck to stand up. With a sky turning grey, with a backdrop of gloom, he ascended the long staircase leading up to the Lighthouse. Every step of the 160 total steps was a foreboding reminder that he was most likely alone, and possibly something tragic or sinister could have happened to the three men. He was breathless once he finished his exhausting climb to the lighthouse itself. His nostrils were filled with the smell of the sea mingled with limewash and tar.

The tower was a beautiful sight, standing 23 meters tall, like a monument erected to the God of Light. The wind was picking up and Ratcliff felt the raw power of the turbulent flow as he got closer to the structure. It consisted of a circular three-stage tower with a one—story keepers house on the northwest corner. The second stage consisted of a corbelled walkway and steel railing and topping the tower was a cast iron deck.

He could not imagine where the others were. They should have greeted him the moment he came ashore. Cautiously, he entered the Lighthouse through the unlocked door to find many other disturbing things. The air was cold, no fire had been lit for some days and a dampness crawled into his clothing. Initially he found no signs of a struggle or foul play. There was no indication from first view, no evidence there had been a mutiny or violence of any kind. The beds were unmade, the mechanical clock had wound down in the kitchen, there was food on the table and a chair had been left knocked over. This was an indication that whatever happened to the three men must have caused great alarm and happened unexpectedly and quickly. There was a set of unused oilskins still hanging on the peg, which meant one man must have gone out without any waterproof clothing during the storm. It had been a bitter cold winter, so why would anyone, under any circumstances, think it was a good idea to go out into a storm without their oil skins on—especially since this was December in the Outer Hebrides? How could three experienced lighthouse keepers have just disappeared from their posts?

Ratcliff concluded; possibly when the storm hit, two men must have gone out to store equipment. When they didn't return, the third man left his post, which was a severe violation for leaving the Lighthouse unattended, and in breaking this rule he must have been swept away, possibly by a rogue wave. This was the only explanation Ratcliff could conclude. It was simply a tragic act of nature. Storm conditions, gale force winds, must have swept the men away. The geos or narrow gullies could create gigantic waves due to how the water was channelled. He was obligated to submit his findings. Ratcliff sent word back to the ship he was staying on to perform an investigation. He suggested the Hesperus return to port and he would give his findings to the Northern Lighthouse Board so they could start an investigation. In the meantime, he would gather as much evidence as he could and wait for the Investigating Superintendent to arrive from Edinburgh.

After further investigating, he concluded that there was no other life to be found on the island. He crawled over rocks, walked the shoreline; he even fired a flare, but received no response. Down by the landing platform he discovered the mooring ropes, landing ropes and derrick landing ropes were strewn about and tangled on the rocks. These ropes were usually held in a brown crate 70 feet above the platform on a supply crane. The iron railing around the landing was warped and twisted out of shape. It also appeared a sizeable piece of rock had come loose and tumbled down the jagged cliff face, smashing at the bottom. He also made note that a life buoy was missing, torn free from the path's handrail. The iron railings around the crane platform from the terminus of the tramway to the concrete steps up from the west landing were twisted as well. Maybe the lighthouse keepers had gone down to save the crate and tragedy hit them? But if this were the case, where were the bodies? He assumed there would be a good possibility of them washing back up on the shore, yet no one was found.

According to the clock, which was frozen in time, whatever had happened a week prior was at the same time the storm had blown through. Ratcliff returned to the Lighthouse and located the logbook and found it to be quite unsettling. Some of the last logs entered were terrifying: 'Severe winds the likes of which I have never seen before; gale north by northwest. Sea lashed into a fury. Waves very high, tearing at lighthouse.' It also appeared from what was written the men at one point were all together, crying. What an odd entry, thought Ratcliff. These men were quite tough. It must have been a storm from the abyss.

Other log entries showed desperation while the storm raged on, and the men resorted to praying for their lives. Questions arose in Ratcliff's mind. Why would these seasoned Lighthouse Keepers be afraid of a storm? Fascinatingly, on the dates they described the storm hitting, there were no storms reported in the area by anyone. The storm which had delayed him from arriving to the island on time had hit 3 days later than their entry indicated.

The weirdest log entry was the final log which read, 'Storm ended, sea calm. God is over all'. What was meant by 'God is over all'?

Puzzled and concentrating hard, nothing made sense to him. Three men, snatched off the rock of Eilean Mor without a trace. This sort of thing just did not happen. Eilean Mor was the largest of 7 rocky outcrops with 45 rocks and islets. The men could have road out the worst of storms and the mystery was, why did they leave the safety of the lighthouse? Ratcliff could not get over the fact that the crew had recorded a storm, but no storm had come until many days later.

Ratcliff made his way up the tower to the watch room and found everything to be in order. The raison d'etere was protected by a dome cap and a weathervane. He ventured out onto the balcony and saw nothing to cause distress or concern. The astragal—which is a metal bar dividing the lantern glass into sections—was undamaged. He noticed a faint paraffin odour in the air; not so unusual since the light used this fuel to operate. He looked about the chariot, which is a wheeled carriage at the bottom of the Fresnel lens assembly, an optic consisting of a convex lens and umpteen prisms of glass, which focus and energize the light through reflection and refraction. All appeared to be operational, capable of allowing the clamshell shaped lens to rotate around a circular iron track atop the lens pedestal. He was positive the height of the focal plane would be accurate. Everything appeared unremarkable with the light itself. For now, Ratcliff knew he would have to be the Interim Light-keeper until relief came in a few days.

He returned to the kitchen in order to make himself some dinner. He had lost track of time and night had fallen. He did not want to move many things around in fear he may impede the investigation when the Investigating Superintendent arrived from Edinburgh in the next few days. He did keep a journal and on day one he began to fill the pages with his own investigation and findings.

His first entry was December 26 and read...

"Arrived at Flannan Isles Lighthouse, all is not well. All three Light Keepers have vanished without a trace. I have searched the island and the lighthouse itself. It is apparent that they were under great distress from a storm, all three men abandoned the lighthouse at some point. The living quarters are dishevelled, signs of panic all around. It is likely that their last meal was interrupted. I will include their Log Journal in this investigation to testify to their mental capacity in their final hours. Much of what I have observed shows possible madness caused by the fear of a storm and possible isolation syndrome.

December 27... I awoke this morning to find the lighthouse in full operation. The lamp was burning bright. 144,000 candle power shooting its beam 20 miles out. This is impossible. There was a white flag flying on the flagstaff. How this got there and raised is beyond my comprehension. I skipped breakfast and investigated the outside surroundings. The weather is bitterly cold, and the water spray is enormous today. My main concern is how did the lamp burn all by itself, and how did that flag get raised?

December 28... I had a miserable night's sleep. I tossed and turned and when I finally slept, I was restless. I was sleeping, yet not sleeping deeply enough to wane off the hints of nightmarish images and visions which taunted me. I may have drunk too much coffee before bed. I will not make that same mistake again. I woke up exhausted, so I decided to do very little and catch up on my sleep and start afresh tomorrow.

Late entry... right before bed as I was about to extinguish my (IOV) Lamp, for a brief moment I swore I heard a man's voice. It was faint and the tempest was whistling outside dreadfully, but if I had to guess one way or the other, I swear it was a voice. I went to the window and looked out, but all that was visible was darkness and the splatter of rain against the window pane.

December 29, Oddly, there was absolute silence when I woke up this morning. I got myself dressed. I heard no wind nor rain. I went up into the lighthouse tower to find that the light was not illuminated. I wasn't about to touch a thing, much less carry fuel up and down this cast-iron serpentine staircase. I would have breakfast, which I did. Afterwards I dressed warm and made my way outside to attempt to recreate what those three men were possibly doing when they were snatched away. I combed the rocks again, looking for clothing, a boot, a hat; something that may have blown out of their pockets on that fateful day. All I could see were rocks, rocks, and more rocks. Rock formed from cooled lava and dolerites intruding Archaean gneiss, a type of metamorphic rock created by extreme pressure. I am not sure what I expected to find. I covered many acres and found not one single hint as to where the three poor souls went. I am now back inside and trying to stay warm.

December 30... Something terribly disturbing for me to wake up to; all three beds were made upon me waking. I swear I did not touch their beds. I am sleeping in a cot I found in the supply closet. All three beds were perfectly made. Someone or something is playing a trick on me. First there was the lamp burning without fuel, then the distance voice of a man and now the beds. I am either in a haunting or I am losing my mind. I interrogated my mind, looking for any objective that would bring me resolution.

I searched the closets, under the beds and checked the locks on the door which I pathologically lock each night. I am a man of routine. I am the only person in the lighthouse. It is perfectly clear; I have been visited.

December 31... I am sleeping with my revolver now. Not that it would have any effect on a spook. I do not believe in such things. People allow their imaginations to run wild, and they invent all sorts of scary monsters and devilish feigns. I have never had interest in such rubbish. I am a man of principle, fact, a man of science. I sat listening most of the morning for sounds or moments or anything amiss. Late afternoon I went to make myself a coffee and the coffee pot had already boiled. I lie not! I did not boil the jug, but when I went to make coffee, the water was steaming hot!

January 1st... the New Year. The temperature is freezing, I still have fire, and food. I expect the relief ship with the Investigator soon. Hope they arrive expeditiously. I feel as though things here are darkening. I will be honest, I am bewildered. There is an imponderable evil enmeshed in the soul of this place, cackling at me, watching me, and drawing the darker things closer.

I am no Pharologist, so I am no expert. Yes, I can maintain and operate a lighthouse, but I know nothing about haunted lighthouses. Today, in the kitchen, I found the chair which had been knocked over during the time the three lightkeepers went missing to be upright and pushed to the table like the other chairs. I purposely have not touched the dining set, not wanting to contaminate any evidence that might remain. I feel a presence, something unseen but acknowledged in unspoken respect of the unknown. I am going outside less. I am not going to the light at all. I think there is something not quite right about this lighthouse.

January 2nd... it has been too many days now. I would have expected my relief with an Investigating Officer to have already arrived. There must be some sort of delay. I can sense the weather is changing outside. It doesn't look good. Bad weather will delay their arrival. This is something I had not counted on, nor can I afford such a long wait. My nerves are getting the best of me. I catch myself humming stupid little songs just so I don't go mad. I have some reading material I thoughtfully brought with me, but reading often puts me to sleep and now I am uncomfortable with closing my eyes. When I do close my eyes, strange and peculiar things happen. This has led me to the wildest conjectures and greatest disappointments. I could no longer depend on my theoretical extrapolations. But all I had was conjecture, no positives or proofs.

January 3rd... I was startled out of my sleep by the voices and wailing of men. My mind was in the early morning fog and my eyes were adjusting to the peculiar spectacle. This was beyond the scope of the ordinary. I had to be dreaming, I thought. I knew no one else was on the island. I was alone. Where were these copious, incessant wails coming from? I had to be careful, not foolhardy. Had someone come ashore while I was asleep? It was doubtful, but not impossible. You would think a strong man with a revolver would never feel fear, uncertainty, or extreme apprehension, but it would not be the case. I stuffed my fingers in my ears as an experiment. If I could still hear them, it would suggest I had gone mad and all of this congruence I was experiencing was merely in my head. It would be an undeniable concern for sure, yet treatable. If I stopped hearing the sounds of mournful men, the solution would be these men were real and somewhere nearby. As soon as my fingers were inserted, the wailing ceased. What is their game? Why the trickery? They are not fooling anyone. I am off to see if I can uncover this horrible trick and expose it for what it is; a con, a farce, nothing but deception. Late entry... I have once again searched everywhere within earshot of my last position and have come up empty.

Jan 4th, I just realized this is the New Year. I find it ever so strange to enter a New Year alone on an island with the paranormal present. I smelled a strong, meaty smell of bacon. I examined to kitchen, and no bacon was found. Maybe it was wafting from the walls where the smell had imbedded itself through the full year of frying bacon for breakfast.

I heard a rattling of chains outside. I put on my oil skins and proceeded outside. It was frigid and damp, but thank God there was no rain. I searched over the right slope of the lighthouse because the sound seemed to resonate from there, but I had no success.

Jan 5th I had a dream of little people. Little people with an unrecognizable dialect. They had surrounded my bed as I slept. These Fey people in the dream did not appear to want to cause me harm, but I had an unpleasant uneasiness with them standing there looking at me while I slept. I am sure it was just a dream.

Jan 6th I am getting tired of eating canned fish daily but with no sight of my relief I must ration. I cannot imagine what the delay could be. I have not seen evidence of a storm. I will light the lamp tonight and send out a distress code for any passing ships. Matter of fact, I have not noticed a single ship while I have been marooned here.

Jan 7th I am afraid now. I am terrified. My pertinacity is caving in; I am weakening. The blackness I sense has sponged my bravery away, leaving me consumed by fright. I had lit the oil furnace, and as the room heated, I heard a rap at the door. My heart leapt with excitement, for I believed it to be my relief. But when I answered the door, no one was there. On my life I swear, on my eternal verities, in my peripheral vision I saw a fleeting dark-haired woman rush out of view. Although I was not dressed for the cold, I went hurriedly in pursuit. I swear I saw her, a woman with long dark hair in a white dress. But my pursuit was in vain. She was not to be found. I am convinced more than ever I am bewitched in some capacity. In the uncharted vastness of my inner habitation, somehow, she had touched me intimately. Was she engaging in some dreadful malignity? My apperception and conception of time were retreating me into a prison of abstraction. I am forever accursed and alone. The island seems to possess dark secrets, hidden intrigue and troubling surreptitious mysteries. She looked much like my beautiful lost wife.

Jan 8th The storm of the century has come to this place. I have lit the light and began sending distress signals out across the water, but no ship would or could sail these waters.

I mopped water from the kitchen before bed. A window was cracked open, which I did not open myself and had not noticed this entire time. The kitchen was very wet.

Jan 9th Daytime is gloom and dark, for the storm still rages and the sky is a torrent of foulness. I suffer through the elemental sounds mixed with chthonic fury and it intensified incrementally from rudimentary beginnings into crude distortions of unimaginable scale. I am urged by the tingling of my weary nerves to brace myself as catastrophic gale force winds and devastating noisy rain batter the place unapologetically. I cannot take more of this blitz.

The storm has crescendo'd and I know I am to die; moreover it relinquishes its magnitude of terror and as far as I can see, the lighthouse still stands.

The light has turned red without me touching it. How this is possible, I do not know. It is no longer illuminating white, it is a red glow as of a fire. I have been locked out of the lantern room, and I cannot find my key. I did not lock the hatch, but it is bolted shut and my key is lost. It is imperative I open the hatch. The tower still glows red. I cannot compass these intriguing happenings. The parameters of my expertise are being stretched. The infinite pathos of my emotions have been strung thin.

Jan 10th I have stopped sleeping. I am eating very little. I wonder if my relief are lost at sea, or worse, maybe the maelstrom has dragged them down into the depths? I am praying.

Jan 11th I awoke still sitting at the kitchen table, where exhaustion must have overtaken me. Here is the thing you will not believe. The woman with the dark hair was in the kitchen with her back to me at the stove. Was she here to inveigle me? My only sense was my sight; all other senses were numb and deadened. I focused, trembling at the sight of this woman. I have no idea how she could have entered. Everything was fastening tight. Her unnatural taciturnity troubled me. She never said a word. She stood unconcerned, not at all acknowledging my presence. This was an insoluble enigma. I cleared my throat to get her attention, to make myself known. When I did, her body flinched, then disarticulated in a sickening display of contortion as if she was having a severe delirium episode. Then the image evaporated, as if she never existed. In desperation and despair, I sat frozen in disbelief, constricted in my throat. I could not make a sound or release even a whimper. But I saw this with my own eyes. I do not exaggerate. The light in the tower still burns a majestic beacon of red, flashing twice every 30 seconds, and my key has still not been located.

Jan 12th The storm has ceased. Something beckons me, drawing me to the window. I hear the screeching sounds of birds outside. I first imagine it is sea birds which have flown in from the neighbouring island, so I go outside to have a look. Up to this point, I have not remembered seeing any birds on the island. To my astonishment, there are a dozen or so enormous birds of prey sitting on the wall which surrounds the tower. They are not guillemot or shag. These birds are much larger. They sculk and twist their heads as if measuring me up as their next meal. The birds have the head shape of a southern cassowary, but a leaner body like a Lammergeier but twice the size. I noticed before heading for cover that their talons are unusually long like grizzly bear's claws. These birds mean one thing, they are meat eaters, killers, practiced in the art of savagery; and no way am I returning outside until I can be sure they are gone.

Jan 13th The birds are still out there. These menacing creatures are not sea birds. How have they come to this island? Today I observed through the window the birds are off the wall and edging closer to the door. I feel they are waiting for me to step out. I cannot leave for fear I will be eaten. This has caused me to become upset, like a foreign umbrage has assailed me. I do not have enough bullets for all of these raptors. I need more paraffin oil, so I will have to make an attempt.

Jan 14th No birds lurking today. I made a successful trip to retrieve more oil. I still have not figured out how the light is working without being maintained. I dare not speculate in my mentally dishevelled state. I am becoming more unstable, emotional, my comprehension must be more in focus. I must pry the hatch open and evaluate this mystery closer.

First time was a feeble attempt but the second time, Success; I pried the hatch and broke the lock and entered the lantern room. The moment I entered, the light shut off its red glow. I closely examined and scrutinized every inch, every nook and cranny. I heard a bird chirp. Not one of the massive prehistoric vultures outside, but a small whimsical chitter. It was a canary. It landed on my shoulder. I was startled at first, but it seemed harmless. I assume one of the men had brought it as a pet. I polished the lens to the light and returned downstairs.

Jan 15th Heavy impenetrable veil of fog has set in. I am debating whether to start the light again. I need more oil. Retrieved the oil, no signs of the giant birds. The little canary is doing well. It is eating, and I located its cage. I am in incipient danger in some intangible way. I am thinking of myself as a denizen of this place, like I belong here. Then it all could be some narcotic-like dream, ethereal and not subjected to the outside world.

———

Jan 16th The fog won't lift. I have started the light again in hopes someone will see it. It is beaming white light. I am still perplexed over the red glow from days ago.

I saw wet footprints through the kitchen area as if someone barefoot walked through from out in the rain. The size of the prints was small, like a woman. I have to imagine it was the dark-haired woman. I ask myself, am I completely mad yet or have I developed lyssophobia and will soon be schizophrenic? Is this how it starts? The delusions are growing in intensity. I saw a figure, not the woman, but something else, like a shadow figure; a black mass djinn peering around the doorframe. When my eyes caught sight of it, it moved back out of sight. I know I sound pusillanimous, but I physically jumped. The contemptible dark thing was seen for only an instant, yet purblind, daunted by this sense of mystery and shock, it has plagued my mind.

Jan 17th I have grown more nervous and anxiety is hard to beat back. The fog won't lift. I ventured outside, needed air, needed more space. I saw the dark-haired woman in white on the steps going down to the sea. I called to her and for a brief moment she stopped as if she heard me, but she never looked around. I called again and began to chase after her. As God is my witness, the woman began to dissipate before my very eyes. She went into a run, bounding down the steps, lifted her arms over her head and turned into a ball of light which shot into the night sky like a rocket. I have never seen anything like it before.

I cannot sleep, I keep thinking about the woman I have seen a few times here. She must be an apparition. A human being, unless they are a ghost, just doesn't turn into a spectre and vanish into a ball of illumination. My question is, where has she come from? Why does she look so much like my wife? I must see her face, but I dare not tempt the dead. Before the lighthouse was built here, I know this chain of islands had a miserable reputation and this was called the "Island of the Dead," or "The Seven Hunters," because of how many ships had come too close and hit the rocks, only to sink to the bottom. I do not exaggerate. This is not a figment of my imagination. Could it be, some who perished on these deadly rocks before the lighthouse was constructed, walk the rocks of Eilean-Mor today? If I never believed before, I believe now in the existence of the living dead; as in necromancy, magic or otherworldly phantoms, maybe stuck in a purgatory? I do not know. I am no expert on the matter of occult practices or mysticism; I can only believe what I see.

—————————

Jan 18th I have been abandoned, exiled away from the living. I heard footsteps in the living area last night. They sounded like a single person walking about. I was too overcome with fright to cry out or to look for myself. I went up to the Parapet to get air and breathed in the fresh air and listened to the crashing of the waves below. I cannot stay here forever. I will soon be out of supplies and will starve. I suppose I could use a bullet, and if the enormous birds return, I can shoot one. I have no idea how the other birds would react. They may attack me? If it comes down to it, I will kill one of the birds to survive.

Jan 19th another rough storm has blown in. It woke me with the sheets of lightning, reiterating the rolling and cracking collapse of thunder like cannon fire. This was a brooding, torrential, malefic fury. The building, as sturdy as she was, shook and shivered. I piled logs on the fire to gain more heat and light for the room. I heard portentous laughing through it all. The sound of more than one man laughing, in cachinnated mockery. I could not make out what they were laughing about. Gesticulation and laughter and deep collective breathing impinging on my sovereignty as a man. I did get up and walk through the living space. I heard faintly, convulsed laughter, lost, echoing in the cisterns of thought.

I prayed for faith. I hoped the voices would leave me. I asked God for spiritual vitality. I wept for no reason. I was losing myself in the murky purlieus of impossible thought with vain imaginations, when somehow, I began to feel coeval with the lighthouse as if it saw my heart. I gathered my emotions and set out to see what I could discover, since the voices had gone silent.

My curiosity took me to the light. There I witnessed moving shadows in the shape of people hovering before my eyes, not fixed on the wall as they should be, but as if they were beckoning me. My eyes were impeded by the glare of an oil lamp, but I saw long, ink-black tentacles reaching out as if they were attempting to escape. The serried army of phantoms all in rank moved and swelled, becoming stealth-like at times, sweeping, deepening, in blackness which held me in impalpable terror during this slow fest of writhing, faceless torture. Unexpectedly, the shadows were absorbed into the darkness as if a great force bode them swiftly away. I fell down exhausted. My strength was ebbing, and I was cold and stiff. I caught myself trembling. How long had this side effect been going on? I needed rest.

Jan 20th It is with disquiet and dread I continue my journal. I have noticed after checking on the light and winding the clock, the wick needed replacing. I have done regular maintenance and changed out the wick. After saturation, I lit the wick and capillary action is normal. Pumps working normally, still anticipating a relief vessel anytime. I have always frowned upon the thoughts of clairaudience; never have I been interested in the psychical nor am I theosophical minded, yet there had been a deleterious influence upon my rationale; I could not consider any of my convictions absolute. Obstinately I deny the existence of ghosts, apparitions as the figment of fanciful imaginations inflated rampantly, by fraudulent, mendacious, unprincipled and uncouth inventions of the duplicitous.

Jan 21st I am going mad. I awoke early morning to find I had sleepwalked out of the lighthouse. I found myself swathed in mist at the edge of a cliff, looking down at the water as black as Nori. The ambient exhalation from the sea must have awakened me. The shock of my position, inches from falling into the black abyss of tumbling waves, drew from me a smothered scream in frantic admonitions as my hands pressed hard against my mouth. I had been caught in languor and reverie, a dream state. I stood astonied at the panoramic view of the great Atlantic Ocean. As harrowing as this was and as volatile as I had become, I returned drenched from head to foot, to the lighthouse where I stoked a fire and prayed.

Jan 22nd I am ablaze with fever. I am a sweltering, perspiring mess. My skin is seeping from every pore.

While I washed my face in the early morning, at the basin I had filled with hot water from the stove, I heard a repeated tapping. Tap, Tap, Tap. I thought it was coming from the window. I looked out and saw those enormous rooks, or whatever they were, flocked around my door. They were pecking at the door as if they were attempting to break in. I retrieved my revolver and covered the door. The hideous squawks and squeaks of those rapacious fowl needled into my brain. I warned them with loud shouts, but the pecking continued. I thought at this rate they would be inside and upon me in no time. I banged on the door with my fist. This seemed to make them stop, but then they started again, more viciously, with devilish intent. I could not allow them inside. I would have no place to retreat to except the lantern room. I had purposely not repaired the lock I had broken so I would have a way of escape. I aimed my gun at the door at a level that if I fired, it would hit at least one of them in the chest. I had every right to be ornithophobic.

I fired my revolver. With a bang, the bullet tore through the wood and a hideous cacophony of wings beating and thrashing and a clamour of excitement ignited at the door. I ran quickly to the window to evaluate the damage. Two of the freakish birds were down on the ground. They were not moving or fluttering at all. The sky became black. This was the moment I saw the murmuration of thousands of birds twisting and turning, rolling in coordinated patterns high above. The dozen or so living birds took flight, swooshing away with incredible power to join the others. I watched until, while on the edge, they became one and no one bird was distinct. I have never seen such a phenomenon in all of my life. They rose out of sight and were gone. Once I had gathered myself, I retrieved the birds and brought them inside, where I carved them like a Christmas turkey. I was not about to let this go to waste. Despite what I had witnessed, I was desperate and delirious. I was struggling with apoplectic thoughts from the fever, which still clung to me like a steaming hot cloth.

Jan 23rd My fever broke last night, but not until I'd had some disturbing dreams and a restless sleep.

After making sure the coast was clear, I took the leftover pieces of these two birds. I would gladly dine heartily for the next few days. When I returned to the lighthouse, I was spooked to see there were three lit candles flickering on the kitchen table. Impossible! I was not only flummoxed by this unexpected magic trick, but I was truly petrified. I am not alone. I am not in control. I am aghast by what I am witnessing here. I could not be more alarmed than I am right now.

This is what I thought until I left the candles burning and walked to the bedroom where I found three men sleeping in their beds! This cannot be. My mind was endangered, and it exploded like the force of cannon fire. I was thinking more unthinkable thoughts; I had left my revolver on the table. I backed away, returning to the kitchen. I fetched my gun and slowly made my way as quietly and furtively as I could to the bedroom to find the beds empty.

It has been a late night. I am writing with my back to the wall, giving the place a good looking-over. Nothing else out of the ordinary has manifested. Getting tired. Memory is fading. I am forgetting who I am. Who I was?

Jan 24th While sleeping there was a flash, both fire and ice, and my heart was filled in my sleep state with inevitable conviction and unpleasantries so maniacal I couldn't be certain I still existed in the land of the living. The little people which had surrounded my bed in the first few days of my quarantine here returned to my dreams. They call themselves Lusbirdan. They were diminutive pygmies and did not mean me any harm, but they were not happy I shot their birds. They took one of the carcasses and left me with the other. They spoke in monosyllables, reluctant utterances of febrile madness, but I understood all of their gibberish. When I awoke, I found one bird had been taken. This plumbed the depths of my heart, drawing out like water from a well, inconsistencies revealing no rhyme nor reason. I spent the day polishing the lamp, filling the fountain and checking all the binds on the windows.

Jan 25th I have been praying Bible verses I memorized as a child. I sought after a Bible, hoping the Good Book could give me strength and courage, but reciting the Lord's Prayer and the 23rd Psalm eased my worry somewhat. I heard voices again, rattling chains, and there was moaning. I prayed louder. I have my revolver with me now always. Rain is falling again.

I am drowning myself in notes of black caffeine. At least the coffee is in abundance.

Jan 26th I did not sleep. I ate some of the bird I had killed and became deathly ill. I am poisoned, it seems. I am sweating with a fever, yet I am shivering cold. I tried drinking water, but it all came back up. I must rest.

Jan 27th Still alive

Jan 28th Vivid dreams of dying. Peaceful, floating, drifting. My mind has hyperaged, the levy has broken and is pouring evermore infamously like a fractured cataract. Over-swollen, flooding over its banks, running, draining... I pray that I see the dark-haired woman again before my time is done. What if it is my wife? I still have never seen her face.

Jan 29th It is snowing outside. I managed to make it to the window. I ate some stale crackers. I am still praying. God is over all.

On Jan 30th, with a light flurry of snow in the air, the relief vessel arrived with the Investigating Superintendent Benjimin Fairbanks from Edinburgh. He was accompanied by four other men who were keen on gathering the facts and evidence of the disappearance of the 3 Light Keepers. The flag was flying on the flag staff which was a good sign. They walked the lengthy steps up to the lighthouse, where they found the door unlocked. The first concern was a bullet hole in the door leading into the living quarters. It was certainly not characteristic of a lighthouse. Who would need to discharge a weapon if they were alone? Benjimin let himself in cautiously. The other men followed. He called out Ratcliff's name but received no answer. They searched the lighthouse, which was in order. They took note of the broken latch to the lantern room, but everything else was in its proper place. The table was clean, there was wood in the stove, but it was not lit, the clocks were wound, the beds were made. Everything was as it should be, with the exception of the missing Ratcliff McLean. There were no bloodstains, nothing broken, nothing surmisable. There was no evidence he had ever been there except one of the men spotted a revolver; only his revolver on the small woodpile beside the stove. After a quick examination, they determined one round had been fired. The question arose, why would he have need to fire a round? They looked for other bullet holes but found none. A thorough sweep of the lighthouse proved fruitless. They took their investigation outside. They combed the craggy, foreboding archipelago. Benjimin ordered the men to keep up their search as he retreated to the lighthouse. He was in desperation to find the logbook. He wanted to see with his own eyes how the three missing men had recorded their final days. Locating the log book in a bottom drawer of a desk, he sat and opened it up. There he found the journal of Ratcliff McLean. The dates of Ratcliff's entries puzzled Benjimin. It was such an unaccountable thing. The journal was dated from December 27th and Ratcliff's last entry was January 29th. This could not be. Absolutely, it could not be. Benjimin scratched his head. He reasoned how impossible and absurd this was. Ratcliff had a journal for more than 30 days. Benjimin knew for a fact that today's date was December 31, and tomorrow was the New Year. Why would Ratcliff have written things which happened on days that had not happened yet? What gave him cold chills was Ratcliff's last entry, "God is over all." It was the same phrase verbatim that the missing lighthouse keepers had recorded after they wrote the storm had gone.

Ratcliff's locket with the picture of his wife was recovered on a cliff overlooking the water. Nothing of Ratcliff's body was found.

DEAD IS DEAD

Winning an all-expenses paid trip without any catches is quite rare from my experience. There is something unfamiliar with awards, triumphs, and real success for most adults. Take winning the lottery, for instance; how much money does a person sink into that abyss of no return just to win a free couple of lines in the next draw? When you add it up, gambling and gambling addicts are just trying to break even. In my experience, and I am no expert, I have found it nearly impossible. But as fate would have it, profiting or balancing the account when it came to sweepstakes, contests, or raffles hardly produced a stroke of fortune.

Another example might be the old "office pool," where everyone puts some money in during something like the NCAA Sweet Sixteen basketball tournament and then by chance, only one person in the office wins or loses according to who, in the end, is crowned the champs of the college basketball season. "Sweet Sixteen," now there is a phrase as un-PC in our current climate and things you can say and do. But you get my point, right?

Well, now, there is always the exception, and the exclusion, of course, is that somebody always wins. What is the slogan? "If you do not play, you cannot win," or "Got to be in it to win it."

Mark Sweeney was literally 'over the moon.' Life had been a crapshoot for him. He had never won a single thing in his entire life. The main cause of never winning is he never gambled. He would not even bet on a sure thing, yet this one time, he filled out a sweepstakes form online to win an all-exclusive paid trip to a marvelous holiday resort, and he had won. Most certainly the 'luck of the draw,' as they say.

He could not be more thrilled, plus he had plenty of accumulated annual leave time built up from work that he could take. The company he worked for had already sent out a notice to all employees to take their annual leave before Christmas, if at all possible. They did not want the leave to build from weeks to months.

Mark put in for his holidays at work, which were immediately approved, and he told no one what his plans were. He simply said, "I am going away for a couple of weeks. I will see you when I see you."

The trip to this holiday destination began with a flight on a 757 jet directly into the Vail/Eagle Airport, where a car rental was waiting for him in his name. Mark thought, "This is too good to be true." He had not won the Megabucks Lottery, but he had won, and this was going to be, more than likely, a once-in-a-lifetime vacation. He paid a little extra and upgraded the vehicle to a sportier model. He was informed that it should not take more than 30 minutes to make the drive from the airport to Beaver Creek. All he needed to do was head east on I-70. All loaded up and situated in his rental, off he drove. He rolled down the window to breathe that fresh mountain air of Colorado. It was clean, refreshing, and he sucked it in like therapy.

His flight had gotten in late, and the sun was sinking like a ship. Not bothered by the lack of sunlight, Mark decided to jump off the interstate, and he ended up on Highway 6, which was a bit closer to Eagle River. He was glad this trip was happening before snow season. He was not experienced with winter driving. The sports car

Mark had rented was quite zippy, and he was having a great time flinging himself around curves and sharp corners. Of course, he should have known better, but he was not considering the risk of throwing the dice, and his driving was becoming foolhardy at best. He loved the feel of this car, the way it stayed glued to the road. He was now driving as if the traffic laws did not apply to him and never considered once that there might be a State Police or Sheriff's Deputy just waiting for some reckless nitwit, barrelling through injudiciously with acute hubristic instincts.

Mark was really laying into this unfamiliar, sinuous stretch of road. The tires were howling as he flew into the sharpest bend yet. Mark realized the instant he was in the tightest twist of the road that the traction beneath him was not holding. Matter of fact, it gave way at an unreasonable speed. The car, with Mark strapped tightly in it, did a tumble, a rollover, flipping more than three times. The squawking tires sang no more, but Mark was filling the car with his own screams. There was severe momentum where metal and plastic were folded and bent, and Mark was captured helplessly in the twilight of the moment. Like a ragdoll being tossed down a flight of stairs, Mark's arms flailed in a twisted and perverted show of animation. As he was contorted in unnatural ways, completely at the mercy of Newton's Laws of Motion (Force = Newtons = lbs = tons), he told himself, "This is going to hurt."

The car ceased its violent tumble and miraculously landed right side up. The car was munted, absolutely demolished. Mark heard a hissing sound coming from steam pouring from the radiator, and the horn seemed to be stuck in muffled klaxon mode, as if something was covering it.

Mark unfastened his seat belt and crawled from the window of the demolished metal. He did a once over, palpating his body, searching for anything broken, but as fate would have it, he was in one piece and surprisingly not hurt at all. He picked up one of the door mirrors that had broken in the crash and examined his face. There was not a scratch or even an abrasion to be found.

He immediately thanked God for coming through this unscathed. "Hallelujah!" he shouted out loud. "What a stroke of luck," he thought as he searched for his cell phone.

This was just great; not lucky enough. He could not see his phone anywhere. Smashing the rental car was going to raise his automobile insurance rates, and now his cell phone was missing. After a disappointing search, he decided since he was losing daylight, he would grab a bag of essentials and head back up onto the road, hoping to hitch a ride from a passerby, and he could return in the morning daylight to locate his phone.

His bag was fairly heavy, and he found himself struggling along the road without a single car in sight. He watched carefully for a sign of a pair of headlights heading his way. He did not care from which direction they came, he just wanted off the road. He had walked a good way and was about to take a seat on his luggage when, up ahead in the distance, he saw a light.

"Saved!" he vocalized, just realizing how scratchy his throat was. He was now desperate for something to drink. This tickling sensation in the back of his throat caused him a slight cough, but he proceeded on being drawn to the light.

———

The house appeared to have a single window lit up, which was evidence of a possible resident being home. As he drew nearer to the house, he took note of how shabby, dilapidated and run-down the place presented itself. A cold chill raced over him as if winter had breathed upon him. He knew before night plunged completely into darkness that he needed shelter, and regardless of the miserable state of the house, he had to take a chance, one more time to tempt fate. He hoped the turn of events, meaning the car accident and him surviving it without a scratch, was not his last miracle of the night.

Mark stepped up onto the wooden porch. The flooring felt soft, rotted, spongy. He rapped a few solid bangs on the door with his knuckles and waited in anticipation of being greeted. He heard the stirring of someone inside responding. The door soon cracked open with a squeak. A young boy answered the door. He was in his pajamas. Mark guessed his age at about 11 or 12 years old. Mark had expected an adult, but the boy would do. "Good evening, young fella, my name is Mark Sweeny, and I have been in an automobile accident. Would you happen to have a telephone I might use to call for a taxi?" Mark asked.

The homely boy with the red, tousled hair stood dumbly, eyes fixed queerly upon Mark's face.

"Ain't got no phone, mister."

The boy obviously had learning disabilities, Mark assumed, and he asked further, "Is your mother or father home that I might speak to one of them in possibly giving me a ride to Beaver Creek?"

The boy looked stiff, sadly lethargic. His nailbeds were grimy and black, as if he had just recently clawed his way out from a grave. He answered with, "Ain't got no mother or father, but I had a maw and a paw, and they are both dead."

This troubled Mark deeply. For whatever reason, his stomach churned like a maelstrom and cramped as if he had suddenly been punched in the gut. Being submerged in this uncomfortable position, with Mark knowing that the boy could not possibly live here alone, asked, "Is there anyone else here that might help me? Do you happen to know of any adult who has a car and can drive?" Mark glanced around at the driveway, not realizing until now there was no car in the drive.

He swore under his breath, trying to mentally fight off the stomach cramps.

"My sister. I live here with my sister, but she is not here right now," the boy said drearily.

Mark introduced himself a second time. "I am Mark. What is your name?" "I am called Buck." Again, this apathetic child was either missing a few marbles in the social category or he was on some really good opioids.

"Hey Buck, how about you let me go to the toilet? If you would be so kind, I really am not comfortable with going out there in the woods," Mark said.

"Sure thing. You might not want to be outside tonight anyhow. Inclement weather is moving in, the weatherman said." Buck opened the door back further, and the unoiled, rusty hinges sang with a note of rapid oscillation similar to that of a minuet. Inside the house with the door closed behind him, Mark found himself in some kind of throwback to early civilization. The room was amazingly spacious, which amplified the clumping of Mark's boots, resounding with reverberations echoing from floor to ceiling.

"Nice acoustics." Mark took note of the taxidermy, which he had a degree of aversion to. Mark was an animal lover, and this did not sit right with him, though he was grateful for the hospitality. The other peculiar thing was there was no electricity that he could discern. The room was lit with a few candles, which were burning bright and guttering down, plus one lamp, which Buck had retrieved from a ceiling hook and now was using as the guide down a hallway where the toilet was found. Mark was over the moon to be out of the harsh elements. Buck handed him the lantern without a word and left Mark to conduct his business.

As he stood over the toilet attempting to relieve himself, he realized he no longer needed to go. He noticed a fair bit of dust and cobwebs, as if this toilet area was seldom, if ever, used or cleaned once in a while. He was glad he had minimal light. If the house was in such ruin in the dark, he could only imagine what illumination would reveal. He gave up on the attempt to empty his bladder; as a matter of fact, his stomach came around as well, and he proceeded back into the main room where Buck was dutifully standing.

"You would not happen to have a phone, would you?" Mark queried again.

"Got no use for a phone. Ain't nobody to call."

Mark thought it inexplicable that a house would have no way of communicating but to each his own.

"So, Buck, is there a power shortage, or have you guys had your electricity turned off?" Mark inquired.

"Ain't had no 'electric' in a good month of Sundays. One day, we had it; next day, nothing. We get by, though. One day, you're living, and the next day, you die. Mah and Paw both died," Buck somberly said.

"I do not mean to pry, but how did they die?" Mark's curiosity of this backwoods scenario had risen to the surface. Before Buck answered, there was a meowing of a cat, and Mark looked down in the dim light to the shadowy floor and felt the brush of a cat against his ankle.

"Oh, you have a cat," Mark stated the obvious, surprised.

"It's Edith's cat," Buck informed him.

"Does it have a name?" Mark reached down and stroked its soft fur as it purred, still circling his ankle.

"Yes sir, that is Familiars," Buck answered.

What an odd name, Mark thought. But then, on the other hand, the day had morphed into a peculiarity that caused him an uneasiness. There was something not right, a languor in the air he could not describe.

"I don't know when Edith, my sister, is going to return. You ought to stay here tonight. You won't want to be out there at night. It ain't safe," Buck suggested.

"Are you saying that only you and your sister live here?" Mark could not understand this unless Buck's sister was quite a bit older than him. His car wreck was now pushed far into the back of his mind. He wanted to know more about how these siblings were living.

"Well, we dwell here; it is home for us." Buck's eyes were still as vacant as when he first opened the door. Mark could not get a read on this kid.

Mark thought about asking the boy for something to eat or to drink, but strangely, his thirst and hunger were not anything he believed he needed to satisfy right away.

"My bedroom is down the hallway across from Edith's room. I would let you sleep in Maw and Paw's room, but Edith said we needed not to disturb it and to keep it as it is. I can offer you our couch," Buck proffered.

"Sure, thank you. The couch is fine. I will be gone early in the morning. I will find a ride then. Maybe Edith will be home by then, and she can give me a lift?" Mark communicated.

"Oh, Edith don't drive," Buck said as he haggard awkwardly down the hallway to his bedroom, where he entered and closed the door without another word.

Mark was truly perplexed. "What a weird little fella," he thought. Mark did not bother to get undressed; he had carried with him a sheet for a bed. The thoughts of laying on sheets hundreds of people had slept on gave him the Heebie-jeebies. He stretched out the clean white sheet across the couch and laid down, hoping sleep and morning would come quickly. His eyelids were tired because of the hours spent wide awake, but the slumber left him as he wrestled with so many uncertainties in his mind, unable to resolve the perturbations that distracted his rest. His mind was very much active, and he spent a good while in rumination with intractable thoughts. The ascendancy of how the rich had it all and the poor had nothing caused him to remain awake for some time. He thought he was just about to doze off when he heard something that startled him into a posture of fright. He listened intently to identify what it was he had heard.

There it was again, like something scooting or sliding, shuffling toward the back of the house. He thought better than to wake Buck, who he assumed was surely asleep by now. He decided to investigate this anomaly. After all, Buck was a child in this house, and some lunatic might be trying to break in and take advantage.

Mark grabbed the lantern and made haste getting to the kitchen, where he found the back door open. Was it possible someone had already entered the house? He cautiously went to the door and stretched the light out in front of him to see more clearly into the dark. There were impressions in the grass from the door, as if something heavy had been dragged away. The grass obviously and recently had been mashed down by something of impressive weight. Mark saw nothing within the light's limitations and made the determination it would be foolish to venture out on such a chilly night. Buck was not wrong. Inclement weather had moved in. It felt like snow, but there was enough moisture in the air that possibly rain might be on its way.

Mark returned to the sofa, where his mind's overactive thoughts refused him sleep. It then dawned on him he should check on Buck, for what if someone had entered the house? He hurried down the hallway to Buck's bedroom and found the door closed. He staved off any trepidation by reminding himself that Buck was just a boy and was too vulnerable not to peek in to see how he was doing.

There was a light beneath the door he could see. The radiance was a red-tinted glow, which troubled Mark slightly. "Red?" He thought about desisting but knew the right thing to do was to open the door just a crack; it was not his intention to maliciously spy or disturb his sleep, or even invade his privacy. It was important to make sure Buck was in no danger. Mark clutched the doorknob in his hand and, with some effort, twisted it and gently pushed on the door, laying his shoulder against it.

Deathly cold air forced its way out, accosting Mark's face. His eyes instantly teared as the frigid temperature of Buck's room escaped. What Mark saw was an unexplainable mockery of all that was holy. The unhallowed scene was far worse to Mark's senses than the rush of cold air was. In the ensuing few seconds, Mark's idea of good and evil took on new definitions. Atrociously dripping from the ceiling were pools of blood that clung upside down and rained over the bed where Buck was lying. He was partially sitting up with his head tilted slightly toward the nasty serum massacre over him.

Mark shuddered, unable to mentally process this debauchery of mad bloodlust and sheer sadism. Mark could see arms reaching down from these unnatural ponds of crimson. Buck sat up, his eyes gleaming as the blood drizzled, covering him. He squinted to see, and as blandishment, he spoke directly to Mark. "Now that you see, do you believe?"

Mark stood halfway between the door and the frame with one foot still in the hallway. Fearful of his life, he refused to answer this demon child and backed out of the abysmal room. He closed the door, but furtive whispers had followed. From inside the room, Buck laughed a demonic guffawing and deliberate cackle of horrid vocal accents with such intentional intensity the disdain of his denunciation caused Mark to put his feet in motion. His only concern was to escape this hellish charnel house and its eldritch wickedness.

Quickly gathering his belongings while keeping an eye on the hallway, he was convinced he was not being followed. Instead of using the front door, he was drawn to the back door for a reason he could not explain. In this conscious decision, he felt detached from his own body, although he remained self-aware. Mark raced to the back door, which led into a wooded area. He could not convince himself to head back to the road. He had an urging inside to conceal himself and to hide out of sight. He hoped this gamble would pay off.

As he stepped through the door into the outside, he heard Buck's voice scream out maniacally, "The dead have gone before us! The dead have gone before us!"

Although Mark noticed the same imprint of drag marks in the nearly frozen grass, he recognized the need to distance himself from this living nightmare. Into the woods he disappeared, with a lantern in his hand full of oil to guide the way. The darkness was indescribable. The light barely pierced through the dark, inky eeriness. As he eked through the wooded area, the trees became sparser as he walked until he emerged upon a road.

He did not recognize his surroundings whatsoever. Being lost was the least of his worries after the gruesome sight he had beheld in the house. There was no explanation. He was thankful to have made it out of there alive. He decided to walk east on the edge of the road and prayed to God someone would come by and collect him from this hostile, windy environment.

As it began to lightly sleet, Mark, keeping to the road in full forward motion, observed a light in the distance. It was a house, but it was far too dark to make out what sort of structure it actually was. As he moved closer, he recognized the place. It was Buck's house.

This was hilariously ironic, he thought. Had he gone in a full circle? How in the name of all things righteous and holy could this be? Maybe it was just another ramshackle house that had a similar appearance; after all, he did not take mental notes of the exterior of Buck's house. He had no other choice but to risk it. The sleet was pelting him like needles, and he was frozen to the core. He stepped upon the familiar steps, and with hesitation, accompanied by misgivings, he knocked on the door.

A female voice from inside called out. "Who is there? Can I help you?" Mark convinced himself this could not be the same house. For if it were, it would have been Buck who would have answered.

"Sweet Jesus, yes, I am lost and frozen and have been in a terrible accident. I am not injured, but I need to escape this weather," Mark pitifully answered.

The door sang as it opened with its strained corroded hinges, creaking a conversant melody of syncopation that pierced Mark's ear almost painfully. The demure face of a beautiful young woman greeted him with a wavering smile of welcome, dressed in a long white sleeping gown. Her crystal blue eyes were unblinking, and she was immune to the cold from the churlish, unforgiving outdoor elements.

"Please, won't you come in? You must be frozen."

Mark did not delay; he needed warmth immediately. He did not find it inside the house, however, for it was identical to Buck's house. Lit with candles and lanterns, and as cold as the grave, he realized he had stepped back inside the sinister chamber of horrors.

"I am Edith," she politely said with a mischievously distinguished smile.

Mark wondered, 'Should I say anything about Buck? Does she know that I was in the house earlier and bore witness to her demonic brother in some sort of Satanic ritual?'

He opted not to share his name and hold out to daylight before attempting an escape. He would die in this unfavorable weather. Edith seemed genial and pleasant enough, so without invitation, Mark sat on the very sofa he had attempted sleep earlier.

"Can I get you something to eat or drink?" She said pliantly.

"No, thank you, just shelter. I only need to warm myself," Mark answered, being somewhat confounded at his own loss of appetite.

He sensed another presence, and his heart thumped three quick succession poundings. His acute fear was somewhat relieved when he felt the rubbing of the cat against his ankle.

Reassured somewhat, he rubbed the soft fur, and it began to purr.

"This is Familiars. She is a good cat," Edith shared.

Mark almost said, "I know," but remembered he needed to play it cool as if he had never been here before.

"Would you have the time?" Mark had no clue what time of night it was.

"Time?" Edith suddenly appeared incoherent, which raised Mark's alarm bells.

She did not answer. Mark decided to stick his neck out and asked, "Do you live here alone?" Her face twisted, somewhat uncertain and, in Mark's view, somewhat conjectural.

As if fragments of memories were being fed into her head by an invisible force, she answered, "I live here with my brother." Her tone was deadened as a gloom overtook the room. At that point, Mark understood they were not alone. Something unseen had seized the room and influenced Edith, removing the graduations of her mind and causing her to stand statuesque, expressionless, dulled, and fragile. Mark did not see Buck, but as his imagination ran wild, feeding on the scraps of limited knowledge and the obvious, with great circumspect, he kept his eyes peeled as not to be taken off guard.

Edith spoke much differently now. Gone was her innocent and vulnerable bashfulness. What she said next haunted Mark's soul.

"Death is summoned easily."

"Why would you say such a thing?" Mark asked, still clutching his small luggage piece in his hand.

"I was referring to if you had remained outside in the storm," she answered.

She added, "You can stay here for the night if you wish. I would strongly advise it." "May I use your toilet?" Mark needed to make sure Buck was no longer in the house. For some unknown reason, he did not feel Edith was a threat, but that boy, Buck, might be the devil incarnate.

Holding a candle, Edith led Mark down the hallway past the door where he had encountered Buck, lost in macabre extravagance, and another door further on the opposite side of the hallway was a toilet.

"We have no electricity, as you can see. The storm is responsible. But the toilet flushes," she said, looking steadily into his eyes as if to read his mind. Her voice was colorless, with no defining character. Mark broke the gaze and said, "Okay, then. I will be right out."

Edith's intentions were not known, but her methods were efficacious in that she was successful in causing a disconnect in Mark's thoughts to the point he wondered if any of this was real. He still had his power of observation, though he had lost faith in himself. He had little confidence because the idea of this house and its occupants were incomprehensible. Mark had no need to use the toilet; he merely needed to separate himself from Edith. He tried to bolster up his courage, for he felt deep down a crisis was imminent, and soon he would be immersed in terror-stricken fright of unsurmountable proportions and volume. As of this moment, the majority of his ambivalence were the invisible assailants he had invented himself. He found himself deeply steeped in inexplicable, self-generated, stifling fear.

"Is everything okay in there?" Edith enquired with concern attached to her question.

If only there were a window, he would challenge himself against the frozen night. He fought back his emotions and blurted out, though from an undulation of a wounded cry, "Yes, one minute, one minute, please."

Mark collected himself, got his nerves together the best he could, and stepped out into the hallway.

"Did you flush?" she unexpectedly asked with sententious overtones as if he had been accused of an indictable offense. Mark hurried back into the bathroom and flushed the toilet obediently. When he entered the hallway, Edith's countenance had become an infernal shade of infinite sorrow.

Just when Mark thought he had recovered himself and was able to be more recumbent with this seemingly endless dire situation, Edith just had to go and appear as some malfeasant emanation of unearthly dread.

Mark could not bear much more. Puerile and absurd, she flippantly asked, "Do you believe in ghosts?"

Offended, Mark responded, "What sort of question is that?"

"I do," she said with a vulgar, frivolous gesture of the hand.

"I believe what I see," Mark answered.

"Do you believe that nightmares are real?" she asked mawkishly.

"Please, I do not know what you mean!" Mark was confused, with the fog permeating in his already clouded mind.

"Mark, can you hear me?" Mark heard Buck's voice, but it was somehow in his own head.

Edith asked, "Are you afraid of monsters?"

Banality and despair drifted through the ether of his soul. There was a sudden amalgamation, a uniting of something inside of him with something that had seemed distant that was now looming over him. Mark could not concentrate. He saw Edith before him in an imbecilic exhibition, twirling and smiling and spinning and laughing.

"Help me with this," Buck's voice necessitated in Mark's head. Mark heard the trill of many voices gibbering but only saw Edith in some pathetic display of ridiculous improv dance.

Mark found himself dragging something. He was unaware of how this heavy bag came into his tightened grip. He pulled with all of his might. Why was he pulling this bag? His thoughts were scrambled, and he was astounded with terror. He was on the grass, dragging a weighted sack toward the wooded area out back.

"Pull harder, pull harder," Buck said as he backed into the thickets. It was a titanic mission, but he had managed the mysterious bag, and now he stood over it. What was it? What could it be? What was in the bag?

He glanced around, and this was when he saw an open grave to his right. He was nearly on the edge of the damnable thing.

Buck's voice spoke again, "Put the bag in the hole." Mark refused. This was outrageous, phenomenally unthinkable. He did not know what was in the bag. He frantically began to tear at the ties which bound it closed. Under the copse of trees, in frigid relentless weather, standing next to a grave, Mark ripped the ties off and prowled into the bag as if he had found treasure. But what he discovered was no treasure. He found Maw and Paw, charred, burnt to a crisp. It was his own Maw and Paw.

Edith was heard laughing and scolding him. "Look what you did, you freak! You have killed them! How are we going to live?"

Mark felt the essence of who he was drifting away. Thoughts raced into his mind, pushing Mark Sweeney out, making him extinct. Every memory of Mark faded, and Buck's mind commenced to take hold in great and wonderous detail.

Mark fought back with what little he had remaining. He sprinted from the grave site into the woods and ran like the devil until he was standing once again on the porch of the same haunted house. He did not knock this time. He barged in maddingly and went straight down the hallway. He burst through Buck's door. The room was empty. He went to the next room, which was Edith's bedroom, and in a violent rage, he crashed through, leaving the door off its hinges and splintered.

He was fed up; this deception had gone on long enough. Uncharacteristically, Mark screamed out an injunction. "Show yourselves! Where are you?"

There was no answer. Mark stormed from the room straight to the last bedroom, which had been said to be the parents' bedroom. He froze at the door, knowing this was it. He had no more options and nothing to lose. Taking in a deep, stale breath, he exhaled slowly, and without resistance, he swung open the door.

His eyes could not believe this perverse abomination before him. Buck was standing naked on the bed over his bound parents and was pouring what smelled like gasoline over their bound bodies. The odor of benzene engulfed the room. The parents were still; Mark assumed he had already murdered them. Edith stood to the side of the bed with a large lit candle in her hands. She had a fierce fire in her eyes and ignored Mark altogether.

She cited something aloud: "If only darkness had taken that night away! May it not appear among the days of the year; may it never be entered in any of the months. Behold, may that night be barren; may no joyful voice come into it. May it be cursed by those who curse the day—those prepared to rouse Leviathan. May its morning stars grow dark; may it wait in vain for daylight; may it not see the breaking of dawn. For that night did not shut the doors of the womb to hide the sorrow from my eyes."

Buck turned his blood-soaked body toward Mark and said, "You're not the one." Yowling as if he were in great pain, the demented boy leaped from the bed and charged Mark, shoving him with terrific force from the room and slamming the door with a loud lock of the key. Mark had been pushed to the floor and was now viewing the room under the slight crack at the bottom of the door. Flames lit with a whoosh sound, and Mark could see the bed had been set ablaze. Leaping to his feet, he touched the doorknob with his hand. The heat had already made the knob impossible to grip. Mark ran again. This time, not through the kitchen out the back, but straight out the front door.

He had witnessed the most unfathomable, experienced the deplorable, the unbelievable. As he fled the ghastly house and its devilish illusions, the sun was coming up over the horizon. When the sun lit his face, he never felt more alive.

He continued to run until he heard the sound of a vehicle approaching behind him. He stopped and waved his arms, hoping the driver would stop and give him a lift. The heavy oppression he had been afflicted with had lifted, and he was as light as a feather. The van slowed and then pulled over to the side of the road. It was an older couple, from what he could see. It stopped right before reaching him, and he approached with jubilation. He went to the passenger side, where a couple in their 50s sat smiling at him.

"You need a ride fella?" The man seemed friendly enough.

"Yes, please. I have been through a horrendous ordeal and have not slept all night," Mark said thankfully.

"We just live up the road. You can use our phone up there to get yourself help and be on your way." The man again seemed gracious enough.

"Slide the side door open and get in. The door sticks a little, so yank it hard," the woman advised.

Mark took the handle by his hand and gave the door an aggressive pull. The door was difficult, but sprung open. Because of the van's tinted windows, the occupants sitting in the back seat had not been noticed by Mark. Before his bedazzled eyes sat Buck and Edith, grinning with wide-stretched, unnaturally shaped mouths that were more like slits across their face.

"You kids scoot over and give this man some room," the mom said, staring straight ahead.

"Do you believe in ghosts now, Mark?" Edith asked.

Buck moved over for Mark and said, "Once you are a ghost, you cannot go back. Can ya, paw?" The driver never turned around. He simply replied, "That's right, son. Dead is dead." Mark climbed into the van and slid the door shut. Familiars leaped onto his lap and purred quietly.

THE VISITANT

Wendall Crabtree crossed himself devoutly and took a moment to catch his breath. He had never been overly religious, was not a regular church attendee, seldom gave in the offering plate or donated to any charitable causes, but he also was not a sinner as such. Some would say Wendall was a good man, a family man, with a small but close-knit circle of friends.

Wendell was of average height; he was not too tall, nor was he a short man. He was of medium build, had an unassuming appearance, a forgettable face, and in his defense, he avoided drama and lies whenever he could. I guess you could say that he was a good ol' boy. Morally upright, faithful to his wife of thirteen years; in the early years of their marriage they both wanted children, but not anymore. He and Edith were content, just the two of them, sharing their modest house with Homer, their hairless cat.

It was five o'clock on a Friday, and Wendell was making his way home from work when the most unexplainable thing in the world happened to him on his drive. A careless driver had recklessly pulled right out in front of him.

Wendell was not a speeder because Edith was not impressed with fast cars. She always said, "Slow and easy wins the race."

Wendell was no slowpoke, but he was no boy racer either. In this instance, when the car thoughtlessly pulled out into traffic,

Wendell was already on top of the other driver, and Wendell instinctively yanked the wheel. How he missed crashing into the other guy was utterly unknown, but his car turned to the side, and the tires squalled like the winds of a Northeaster. He fought the wheel with all of his might, wrestling back control of the spinning car. His foot was heavy on the brake, and his mind went into preservation mode.

In this violent battle of survival, he felt the car lift slightly as if practically airborne and then crushingly came back down. Miraculously, Wendell had manhandled the wheel brilliantly, it seemed, sliding and coming to rest at a stop, as if he had meant to park where he had ended up.

The other driver, oblivious of what they had caused and unaware that Wendell's heart was beating out of his chest, drove away without a care in the world. Wendell was less than impressed and took a moment to gather his senses and slow his breathing. He could not imagine how, in all of this evening work traffic, it was possible that he did not hit another vehicle, nor could he fathom how no one else hit him. An even greater mystery to him was how such an idiot as the other driver was able to acquire a license to operate a motor vehicle and then take it out onto the highway.

Wendell quietly reflected on this near-death experience and crossed himself in thankfulness for whatever guardian angel had sprung in action to rescue him from this certain fate. He was alive, and he could ask for no more than that. Although his nerves were rattled, he carried on home without incident.

Because of the near catastrophe, Wendell pulled into his driveway a few minutes later than normal. Edith had dinner waiting for him.

"That sounds horrific. It could have been so much worse," Edith responded after Wendell dryly told her about the ordeal he had gone through. He was not a loud or boisterous man, and for the most part, he had a calm demeanor with hardly any animated or gesticulated movements when he spoke.

"It could have been infinitely more terrible than it already was," he said as he cut into his pork chop with a serrated knife.

"You eat a big meal and just rest up. A harrowing event like that can take a lot out of a person," she responded, reaching for the salt.

"I do feel tired. I guess when a person faces a near miss, it can be exhausting," Wendell popped a good-sized piece of meat into his mouth and began to work it over with his teeth. It was not as tender as he would have liked, but it was tasty nevertheless.

"I have done the same thing before, stupidly pulled right out in front of oncoming traffic as if I had all the time in the world. I guess I should be grateful since I have been guilty of idiot driving as well," he added, then finished off his iced tea.

"If you think about it too much, it will play out over and over again with the same results. It is best you just put it out of your mind. There is no need to dwell on speculations of what ifs."

Wendell helped Edith with the dishes, still unable to totally free himself from the life-threatening events of the afternoon. He decided a shower would do him good. He left Edith to finish up what little was left to do. She needed to feed Homer, anyway.

That night, Wendell slept miserably. He found it nearly impossible to get comfortable, incapable of completely wiping the car incident from his mind.

In the early morning hours, a couple of hours before he was to get out of bed for work, Wendell had sat up thinking it might be easier to fall asleep sitting up and leaning against the pillow rather than lying down, which had proven insufferable. When he eventually found a comfortable position, still unable to shake that intolerable unpleasantness, his eye caught the image of something that looked out of place in the bedroom.

Next to the bathroom door, there seemed to be something black in the distorted shape of what could be seen as a person.

Instantly, his full attention was upon this unnamed form that occupied the space without so much as even a twitch. On prior occasions, the moon shining through the gap in the curtain would cause strange shadows and mystifying sights to him if he applied his imagination. But this was something far greater in intensity, almost like a phantom entity that just stood there watching. This unidentified form was causing Wendell's wakefulness. He stared at the disconcerting intangible thing and said nothing, realizing there was now in the air a rotten staleness, acutely and presently permeating every fiber of his being. He attempted to read it with his eyes, and he did not like what it was saying. Its presence was an intrusion and hinted at malignant and foul intent.

Wendell did not want to react spontaneously, for that could be his undoing, and he had Edith to think about as well. He opted to remain as calm as possible. With the patience of Job, Wendell, whose fatigue was long forgotten, viewed the worrying visitant until it faded away and was no more.

This was bleak and extremely frustrating in every way. He could not convince himself that it was an illusion, a trick of the light and tall shadows, but then again, he had nothing concrete, not anything substantial other than his own eyewitness account that whatever it was had appeared out of thin air and retreated in like manner. Wendell gave himself a moment to allow the fatigue and vexation to pass away, and then he made his way to the toilet, passing by the exact spot now unoccupied where the phantom had stood.

He was entirely dyspeptic, and this irritability caused him to not return to bed. This phantom had prevailed upon him, crept up on him, something like a man but not entirely, a thing of flesh and blood and somehow filled his mind with apprehension to such a degree it was impossible to shake loose the notion of impending doom.

He told himself that he was just being silly, and the entire car incident had been the root of last night's improbable encounter.

It had made him miserable in his own skin, and he did not like not having control of his emotions. It was something he was unaccustomed to, as if an atmosphere of crisis was looming and he was powerless to defend against it. Regardless of what had happened, if the same thing occurred tonight, he had made up his mind to confront it.

The following day was the last day of the work week. Invisible was how Wendell wanted to make himself today. He had a lot on his mind and simply wanted a stressless environment where he could manage his workload and have a nice drive home without hostility or being murdered by another motorist.

The company he was employed by passionately loved to call unscheduled meetings. Management seemed to believe that random meetings grew productivity; however, Wendell begged to differ. In fact, if he were honest (and he was almost always honest), he believed that meetings slowed down productivity and threw him out of his work rhythm. Once he lost momentum, he might as well pack up and leave because he figured his day was shot.

Ever since getting the memo about the impromptu meeting, Wendell had not felt well. These things made him nervous, and he always felt as if his head was swelling because of the pressure they put him under. He described it as having his head in a vice. Walking into the staff room, he had a peculiar sense of raw unease with a trepidation accompanied by simple jitters. As staff gathered into the room, some sitting, most standing, Wendall became oddly fixated on an area of the room which, to him, in his mind, did not seem right. Under acute stress, he drifted hypnotically away from the reality of everyone else, who were shoulder-to-shoulder in the room. Astonished by his own prolonged scrutiny of this area, a sudden flash of heat, like a blowtorch, unexpectantly came over him, to his distress. Now filling that vacant spot of the overcrowded room, cleverly disguised as an ordinary shadow, was the evasive intruder from last night. He thought, "How absurd!" His austerity was being challenged, for to believe in such a thing as this would be to forsake much of what he had been taught to believe as a child. He could have forgotten and erased last night as a simple misunderstanding, but now here, in broad daylight under the unnatural overhead lights within the staff room, how brazen his phantom was to appear. Yet no one else seemed to be the least bothered by the dark gap in the corner. He could not imagine that he was the only one with eyes to see this lucent shadow, vivid yet anciently dark. It stood without features, minus expression, in a cruciform pose, as if mocking all that was holy and everything that was pure. Wendell saw it as a profane, disrespectful entity with malignant intentions and a propensity for horror.

Still, not one person sardined in this overly congregated, festering room of human mildew acknowledged the abnormal shadow. He thought about calling it out, then he thought better of it. How mad would his colleagues believe him to be if he went shooting his mouth off about something invisible to them? How insane would he be to interrupt the president of the company and cry out, "There is a demon lurking in the corner!" He might be committed, institutionalized... but maybe this is what the black demon wanted? How would Wendell know what otherworldly creatures thought at any given time?

He could feel the malice and knew the devilish thing had inappropriate thoughts about him. He wanted to attack it, to take it on, stab it with his ink pen until it lay perished and dead on the floor. But he would have to wait to have this opportunity for fear of not being taken seriously. His skin crawled with nervousness, and his eyes were fastened hard upon the deepness of evil that stared back. Wendell was becoming more dismally paranoid by the second, having not heard a single word spoken by the presenter, and the spine-tingling needles of frenzy were scratching at his nerves in such a manner as to cause him to become fidgety.

He fumbled about with his hands awkwardly and almost ran in place at one point. A few around him noticed his strange, impulsive behavior but said nothing, nor reacted to his queer mannerisms. Remarkably, Wendell struggled to hold it together and did so, using up every ounce of his lactic acid and breaking out in perspiration, which a few around him did take notice of.

Wendell left the meeting and went straight to the bathroom, where he planned to splash some cold water on his face. Once in the toilet area, he doused his bloodless, drawn face over and over again. The water seemed to have the desired effect, and whatever influence had mightily gripped him had let loose.

A co-worker, Bob Hampton, whom Wendell had worked with for the past six years, entered the bathroom.

"Are you feeling okay? You looked as white as a ghost in there." Wendell raised his sopping head from the sink. Using the mirror to address his friend Bob, he made the excuse, "My stomach had turned on me in there. I am pretty sure it was a bad egg this morning." "Do you need anything? Maybe you ought to go home for the day," Bob suggested, genuinely concerned.

"Yeah, maybe so. You do not have the number of a good exorcist, do you?" Wendell was serious, but Bob took it as a joke and laughed it off.

Wendell asked to leave early from work and was granted half a day, but his boss reminded him, "Any more time than that, you will have to bring in a doctor's note."

Wendell was more than ready to leave the stuffy office and breathe the air outside.

Undoubtedly, he knew what he had seen, now on more than one occasion. He believed he was seriously haunted, but did not understand why this evil spirit had attached itself to him. He was at a loss for an answer. Wendell put the windows down, turned the radio on, and began his trip home. Thankfully, it was Friday, so he had time to rest up and hopefully get this demonic pest out of his life.

Stopping at a traffic light, he hummed along with the radio until he checked his rearview mirror. He saw a dark area reflecting in his back seat. His chest felt like it had been squeezed by bony fingers, and he gasped in shock and awe. He was chilled to the bone with a lasting horror, and he embarrassed himself with a frightened whimper.

Wendell gazed at the indistinguishable dark blot sitting there, proud as a peach over his right shoulder.

"What do you want?" He could not believe he had mustered the courage to address the otherworldly menace.

Threatened by the unknown, Wendell was affixed where he sat, parked at the red light in the middle of traffic, frozen to the wheel, unable to make a move. His physical body had become rigid, turned whitely cold and became undeniably weaker than he had ever known, penetrating his inner marrows. He was not a coward, but undiminished fear had clamped down on him like a vice. He felt like a bird trapped in a net. As much as he wished he could fly, he was grounded, feet locked in a miry substance, invisible to the eye but richly sticky and real in his subconscious.

"What are you, you nameless thing?" Wendell was angry and asked with much vehemence, but no name was given, not even a sound to acknowledge that it was truly there. Yet Wendell could see it. He could see it and nothing else. He listened for its voice. Would it be gruff and foul like swallowing razor blades, or would it resonate a sadness, a softness, a solemn warning?

He heard nothing coming from the backseat, nor the multiple horns blaring and honking for him to move on because he was blocking the lane of traffic.

"I will identify you yet. All I have to do is look up the word infestation, and your featureless face will be there." Wendell then heard the sounds of angry motorists as they peeled out around him, yelling and cursing at him. Wendell did not care. He paid them no mind, for he knew he was far more accursed than whatever they were laying against him.

"Get out!" Wendell shouted. "Get out!" he screamed. As he started to demand the immediate exit of his unwanted hitcher again, the phantom vanished as if it had never occupied the back-seat at all.

Wendell was glad that it returned back into the recesses of nothingness for the time being. He was ready to exit the car and leave it behind, and would have done so if the treacherous shadow had not departed. But he was glad it did in many ways... the main reason being a very long walk home.

Without incident or further delay, he pulled into his driveway, some fifteen minutes overdue. Being abandoned by the phantom gave him little relief because he expected the revenant to return again. He struggled if he should inform his wife of recent events or leave it for now.

As Wendell entered his house, everything seemed different. He was different; the smells of the house were not recognizable, and he immediately became distressed and deeply troubled.

Standing in his living room as dark as pitch was that accursed eidolon. It was dimly discernable and cast a resonance of wicked-ness and corruption that made Wendell feel unclean.

He attempted to ignore the worrisome presence, but the concern for his wife became ripe in his mind. In desperation, he began to call out his wife's name. "Edith, Edith, where are you?"

To his relief, she popped her head from around the corner and breathed hurriedly, as if she was right in the middle of something exhausting, "I am right here, dear. Why are you home so early?"

"I was not feeling well," he answered, plopping down in his favorite chair and trying not to give credence to the ominous figment pushed back into the corner from him.

"Can I get you something to drink?" Indifferent, he answered, "Yes, please. I made some iced tea last night. That sounds good to me." He gave a huge sigh. He figured any stronger drink might really throw him into a deeper, unearthly funk.

Edith returned with his iced tea, and he asked her to have a seat.

"Edith honey, there is something I need to tell you, and it is not good. Now, before you go and get all upset, it has nothing to do with our marriage. We are fine, okay?" He waited for her to acknowledge, and she did so by lightly nodding her head.

With the details still fresh in his memory, he proceeded to tell her everything.

"Something has happened. I think it has to do with that wreck I was in the other day. I know I did not crash the car, and thank God that I or no one else got injured, but something happened. Right after that incident, I started seeing something dark and creeping, and the closer and nearer it got, the more of an effect it had on my state of mind. I know I have always said I do not believe in ghosts. Maybe this is not a ghost; it seems more evil, more sinister than a ghost. I do not believe that this dark entity haunting me has ever been human, not a disembodied soul lost and wandering; it has tentacles and can reach wherever I am, work, home and even the car. It will not leave me. I am either going out of my mind, or a devil has come to our home to roost."

A brief silence fell upon them, and Edith breathlessly asked, "What does it look like?"

Wendell had no trouble in describing it. He had seen it enough now... and plus, it was standing to the left of Edith. Just... standing there.

"It has a body but no real features. It has arms, legs, and a head, but no face, eyes, nose, or ears. I do not see fingers, just elongated arms. It neither speaks nor gestures; it just stands there, wraithlike, but not in a mist or a smoke. It is like a suspended oil slick that absorbs the light around it."

Edith looked confused, and she asked the hardest question of all. "What does it want?"

Wendell hesitated; his eyes were bleary with tears. He choked, cleared his throat, and then affirmed, "I think it has come for me. Maybe I was supposed to have died that day from the car incident, but for some reason, this reaper, or whatever it is, missed his opportunity. Maybe it failed, but it returned to finish me off."

"Well, he cannot have you," she stated defiantly.

Homer meowed, as if to confirm her statement.

"I do not know what to do," Wendell admitted with a sensation next to panic.

"Where is this hobgoblin now?" Edith was furious.

"It is there, to your left," Wendell exclaimed, staring helplessly at the eyeless abyss.

Edith stood, facing the direction that Wendell had said, and she let loose a real tongue-lashing upon the intruder.

"You have no right to be here. You leave my husband alone. I will not have you harassing him, threatening him, nor tormenting him. Go back to where you came from. You do not belong here, and you are not welcome in our home. Begone, you, you... parasite. God sees you. You might think you can hide from me, but you cannot hide from the Lord. Now away with you. Get out and stay out!" Her voice had raised, and the veins in her neck had bulged. Wendell had never seen her so bold before.

The two waited. Edith could not see anything, so she asked Wendell, "Did it leave?"

It was at this tragic moment that Edith's body went flying through the air like a rag doll and slammed into a cabinet, rendering her unconscious. Wendell raced to her side and saw she was not good. She violently spasmed, her entire body shaking uncontrollably. Her eyes were rolled back, showing red-veined orbs of white. With dread gnawing at the back of his head, he immediately called an ambulance, and within twenty minutes, he was sitting in the back of the ambulance, riding it with her to the hospital. He held her hand most of the way, but she did not come around.

Her diagnosis was a concussion with some rib bruising, and Wendell ended up having to answer some questions from the doctor, who was quite suspicious of her injuries, and then the police got involved.

Such a violent occurrence could not be explained away so easily. Wendell was cornered by the law and suspected of spousal abuse. He refused to answer any questions concerning the accident because he had no time to think of a plausible reason why his wife took such a jolt; he could not say "The devil did it." No one would believe such an outrageous thing as a demon, having come in on a scalding zephyr from the isothermal underworld, attacking his wife viciously.

Pathetically, he said nothing and, unfortunately, had to hire an attorney just to keep him out of jail. He was on restricted visits to the hospital until Edith came to. She regained consciousness after forty-eight hours, and she, in fact, did tell the tall tale of being batted like a fly across the room by an evil entity.

The authorities were highly suspicious of her account of the evening, but had no other recourse but to drop any pending charges against Wendell.

Sitting by her bedside, Wendell was ashamed that he had no power against the malevolent force in their lives. As a matter of fact, he could see it on the other side of the hospital room, resigned to linger there like some lurking carrion bird, waiting for the rotting meat.

Wendell wanted to yell at it, scream at it, but was terribly afraid that the umbrage that had come upon them would not only snuff out their light but, in a flight of rage and fantasy, drag them helplessly into the bowels of what awaited the unrepentant dead. Their lives had been enveloped with unaccountable dread. The dreams they wanted to live out together had become a nightmare they could not escape. Their minds were dominated and tortured, and, in this bleakest of days, they began to pray to escape the phantasm.

"God, please, no more hallucinations and illusions. Stall our minds so they cannot create delusions and falsehoods. Remove this evil from our lives, destroy the plague that has crippled us and made us fearful. Breathe in us your spirit, and may the evil one recognize your purity in our lives. Let us not be castaways to be mauled by the dogs of hell. Take away our oppression and the oppressor and free us from the constraints of the profound storm that has raged."

Edith prayed this prayer as they arrived home from the hospital. Her sister had come to help take care of her and to get her back on her feet again. Her equilibrium had been affected, and she could not stand for any length of time without feeling dizzy.

Wendell welcomed the help. Mentally, he had shrunk and withered under the cruel sufferings of recent days. Everywhere he went, the dark figure was there, watching in silent intimidation. Wendell went to the mailbox, and as a neighbor stopped him to ask about Edith, there stood the wrong side of darkness, ever-present, pressing ever harder on his nerves. Wendell attempted a conversation but could not remember what the neighbor had asked him. He did hear the neighbor say, "You do not look well, Wendell. Maybe you need to get some rest," but other than that, Wendell did not hear a word.

Wendell left one afternoon and said he was going to the store. He kissed Edith goodbye, and since the store was just around the corner, he decided to walk. This was the first time he heard the voice from the depths of outer darkness speak.

"Escape fate, you cannot. Good intentions will not save you. Be merciful to your wife, and do not put her in harm's way again. You have been absent from this world since the day of your automobile wreck. That was your last real day on earth. Everything afterward is borrowed time, and for every day you remain among the living, your wife loses a day, Wendell."

Wendell was suddenly leaden with guilt.

The voice was in his head, but not imagined. It had tone and content, and it was from regions where no man has ever returned.

"In the obscurity is where you belong. I should not have to entice you to make this decision to do what is right for Edith and for everyone," he said with rapacious glee.

As impossible as this proposal was, and regardless of the con-strictions placed upon Wendell, it left the sharpest impression on him.

Wendell stopped on the corner, engrossed in the moment, and took a deep breath. He was hoping to get two full lungs of clean air, but the air was polluted by the traffic crossing the intersection. It was impossible for Wendell at this moment, being dictated to by the voice in his head within this unfolding nightmare, to cope with the mounting oppression.

Across the road, he saw a man. The man was dressed in all black. He was tall, lean and wore gloves even on this warm day. The man had a long face, and his eyes were as red as fire. Wendell thought he saw actual flames within. The strangest thing was, this stranger was holding a black umbrella, though there was not a cloud in the sky.

Although he looked lifelike, the face of the man was sallow, pallid with thin, fine lips, and he wore no expression. Wendell strained to see the man clearly; the traffic separated them, and the sun was glaring from every direction.

Wendell looked at his watch. It was almost noon. He did not know why the time mattered. The man in black waved a friendly wave and smiled cordially at Wendell. The traffic light changed, and Wendell saw he had the green, indicating that he could walk across the street now. The man in black cast a peering look in Wendell's direction.

It was a look he could not ignore. He believed there had been arrangements made, but he did not know what for. His thoughts fragmented as he stepped out to cross the street. Wendell hoped that his human nature would be counted, and that God's goodness would shine upon him and consider him a mere vapor in an endless sea. He was compelled through necessity to finish his walk, ignor-ing the blaring and sounding of many horns. He never hurried nor looked left or right. He reached out his hand, but the only thing he touched was the measureless void. Wendell heard the voice again, coming from a blankness somewhere out there in oblivion. It voiced, with perfect articulation, "Skin for skin."

Once he locked eyes with the tall man in black, his eyes were fixed, and his mind was convinced. He walked toward the man as if in a vision. In some way, he was able to look down upon himself from way up high, as if he were a drone spying on the last moments of his life.

WEREWOLF THERE WOLF

Mark was an avid jogger. There was nothing he enjoyed more than going through his ritualistic stretching exercises and in his running suit, which clung to his athletic body like a glove. With the potency of a sportsman, he would take his run. It was ineffably exhilarating for him, invigorating to put his feet on the trail and go for it.

He primarily ran the same trail every day; this would assure him a great run, eschewing any of the pitfalls of the lesser trails, which he purposely avoided. He had heard rumors about some of the other pathways that they simply were far too dangerous to run due to steep precipices, sharp cliff faces with unsteady rock, uneven terrain with unmanaged potholes... even dangerous animals on the track such as bears, wolves and moose were common.

The place where he chose to run did not have any of these dangers, and he never felt as though he was running on the cusp of indeterminant declivity or teetering on the edge of bottomless ravines. He had no interest in exploring the chasms of the unknown nor putting himself in perilous situations unnecessarily. He had known a couple of runners who met with tragedy due to the elements. He was not about to fall victim to some sort of testosterone-fueled challenge. He ran for enjoyment, not necessarily for his health. He knew the benefits of raising the heart rate during exercise, but Mark honestly did not correlate what he did with being physically fit. He regarded it as a meditative event that kept his mind purposed, a type of therapy with the intent on wellness of thought and mental sustainability. Regardless of the weather, Mark was never complacent and, with due diligence, committed to his run.

Well-hydrated and geared up, Mark set out on his one-hour run. He enjoyed running in the evenings as the day was cooling, and by the time he had made his traverse, he was facing the sunset, which he truly loved to see. This day began unremarkably, and nothing even now appeared out of the ordinary. He had already covered two-thirds of the track and was coming out of the verdant canopy of trees when something outlandish and extraordinary presented itself.

Mark was stopped cold in his tracks, his resplendent evening getting a rude awakening. He simply could not continue, and he looked for a quiet, unostentatious way of avoiding what he saw before him blocking the trail. As he stared at the alpha male wolf, who was clearly unwell, he shuddered with a sense of dread that one experiences only a couple of times in life. This comparison of healthy and sickly was made in Mark's mind by recalling nature programs he had seen in the past on wolves and their behavior. Wolves ran in packs, but this was a lone wolf. Wolves are supposed to fear man, but this one's posture was that of dominance. This was an imposing situation that Mark had never found himself in... well, ever.

The wolf was a magnificent beast. It was a dark color with keen eyes that stared directly into Mark's fearful gaze. It was reputed that wolves feared humans, but this forbidding beast showed no signs of drawing back. It had never occurred to Mark that any dangerous animals would ever be on this favorite trail of his, so he had made no preparations for such an occurrence, nor was he very good at improvising. He had no weapon, no bear spray, not even a pocket knife. Before Mark could gather his thoughts and collect his courage from the nethermost area of his mind, the wild beast charged Mark in such an unimaginable way, and with such ferocity and quickness, Mark had no time to think, to turn to run or have a chance to defend himself. The fight was all wolf, at least, until the point at which Mark swore that it unnaturally raised upon its hind legs like a man. In this unusual lycanthrope stance, the jaws of the mighty savage chomped down into Mark's arm, and its canine teeth, like daggers, pierced his skin to the bone. The weight of the wolf and its momentum had driven Mark to the ground, and there ensued a brief wrestling match, with Mark attempting to protect his face and guard against further injury. The wolf did not continue the attack and fled, leaving Mark wounded and bleeding. With a beating heart that seemed to want to either leap from his throat or tear free from his pounding chest, Mark staggered along, trying to reconcile what had just happened to him. He knew he was in shock and desperately wanted to make it home before the shock wore off because he feared the real pain had not come upon him yet. In his presence of mind, he removed his shirt, wrapped it around his bloody arm and, without delay, worked his way home.

By the time he had made it to his door, he was dizzy and somewhat lightheaded. He went straight to the kitchen sink and ran water over the penetrating bite marks. Although it stung with considerable sharpness, he was most thankful that the thing had not ripped his arm off. Why he did not go straight to the hospital, even he didn't know, but he opted to treat the wound himself with peroxide and antiseptic cream.

He made the conscious decision to stay home from work to allow his arm to heal. On the third day of self-treatment for the bite, he felt a tingling, like a prickling sensation around the bite area, and it itched something terrible. He had become restless and felt like climbing out of his own body. He knew he had the flu; he just knew it. But then again, as he relived the attack in his mind, his thoughts stirred with a real worry.

This wolf stood upright to attack him. This was a strange, unordinary way for any wolf to go after prey. And then the unimagined crossed his mind. Maybe this was no ordinary wolf at all.

As inconceivable as it sounded when he repeated it, he, in fact, did repeat the word 'Werewolf' from his lips several times. He considered the indescribable event, and he could not imagine what else it could possibly be. It was unfathomable, he reminded himself, yet he believed he could sense a change in his body. He had a headache that was persistent but not throbbing; a fever, but he was not burning up; nauseous, but he had not thrown up; and seemingly, he was more agitated than usual. He no longer had a vague suspicion; he convinced himself that this was no flu. He had been attacked by a werewolf, and now he was changing into such a beast.

Mark was running over the brim with anxiety and worry. He did not know how being a werewolf would affect his life, his work, or even hanging out with the few friends that he did have. How would they feel if they knew the truth of the matter? He had to keep this a secret from the whole world, to be inflexible and obdurate and trust no one. He knew there was no reversal of such a chemical alteration and transformation to his DNA, so he secured his reluctance and was inclined to accept what was happening to him. He was in uncharted waters now, in sepulchral depths over his head. The unknown was before him, and he wanted to face it unperturbed, if at all possible.

After a few days, he wrestled with insomnia and refused to sleep because he wanted to be aware of the change when it came. He checked his teeth daily to see if there were any noticeable signs that his canine teeth were becoming longer. He did not see anything out of the ordinary, but again, this was new to him, an indiscernible mystery. He stuck out his tongue in order to see if it had grown in length. It had not. He examined his body, supposing that he would begin to grow hair in unusual places in the anagen phase, but did not see any signs of new follicles. Possibly, it was a progressive disease. He was now calling it a disease. He thought transmutation would only take hours, but now he was going into days, and the metamorphosis seemed to be a much slower growth than what he had anticipated.

Mark finally left his house to pick up some things from the store. He did not like the thought of canine sustenance, but he figured if he were going to be a werewolf, he possibly needed dog food for sustainability. He did not want to kill humans. He struggled with the thought. But what if he was not a proper werewolf and was more like a mutt, a mongrel or a curr dog? He had not been bitten by a relative, so he had no real pedigree. He feared he might not be a complete werewolf, and he might become a hound, a mixed breed without purebred ancestry. Would this mean he would not be accepted by other werewolves? Essentially, if this were the case, he might be doomed, having to hide and shelter among others damned by the same malady. He also fantasized that it could be considered that he was the lone wolf without a pack who would search for a mate, and together, they would be the key to the genetic survival of the species. A lone wolf is the strongest wolf because it hunts for itself and is hardened by the time in solitude.

Once home, he had the sensation that he needed to chew on something. He was positive that if he accelerated the process along, hurry it, so to speak, he would change much quicker. If he acted like an animal while the fluids in his body transitioned into the DNA of a wolf, in all certainty, he was confident it would progress things along at a more expedited rate. Thankfully, when he purchased the bag of dry dog food, he bought a rubber bone, just in case this sort of thing happened.

Mark gnawed on this dog toy while salivating profusely. He practiced growling, and it was during this lunacy that he had an idea. Maybe the conversion into a full-blown werewolf needed to happen under the light of a full moon. Ignoring sensibilities and all practicalities, he resorted to checking his calendar in the kitchen and easily noted that the next full moon would be tomorrow night.

He was thrilled that it could be that soon. At the moment, he had not slept at all and was feeling decrepit. His muscles ached, but he assumed that as his human form was changing, he would find it a painful, maybe an agonizing, miserable process.

Mark prepared a bowl of dog food to eat and sat at the kitchen table. He convinced himself he needed to start living like a werewolf because the more he practiced the mannerisms, the more practical the character of the wolf inside would reveal itself. In order for the indecipherable change to occur, he understood that his central nervous system would be readily affected and that he might even begin to think as a wolf thinks. These were his thoughts as he popped individual bits of dog food into his mouth and forced hard swallows. He did not know if it was the dryness of the food itself, the thought of actually eating dog food, or if his throat was swollen, but he was having difficulty swallowing. Against his better judgment, he retrieved a bottle of whiskey from the cabinet, along with a glass of water. Mark drank the glass of water and then, in an attempt to knock himself out so he could rest for tomorrow's big manifestation when he would become a full-fledged werewolf, he nursed the bottle for the next couple of hours, knocking it back until he was inexorably as drunk as a skunk.

If the symptoms of changing into a nocturnal creature of the night were not already challenging, Mark was not a good person while intoxicated, nor was he an exemplary human being. For reasons unknown, even to Mark, instead of trying to sleep, he decided he needed to go hunting. He walked outside into the evening air, and his inebriated self sniffed the air, hoping his canine sense of smell had developed, but he was unable to pick up those smells that he knew a dog must have. They were indistinct. Staggering along, lost in fascination, uncertain of his destiny, he walked the stony path insatiably smitten with the idea of biting someone. As outrageous as it sounded, he persuaded himself that practice made perfect. His unassailable conclusion was that he believed he was turning into a werewolf, but that he would retain his human qualities. These were ontologically distinct from one another, meaning he might be in conflict with himself according to which aspect was more dominant.

He spotted a woman walking alone. He said to himself, "Easy target." He used no prestidigitation, no sleight of hand or tricks, nor did he use camouflage or concealment. Committing a purely rookie mistake, he mindlessly charged the woman, mouth opened, growling pathetically, and lunged at her. She was carrying an umbrella, which he had failed to determine before the unwitting assault. She whacked him several times across the top of the head, using both hands masterfully to repel the would-be debutant werewolf and fending off the assault, pummeling Mark without hesitation, causing him to scamper away with his tail between his legs, so to speak.

His own charnel actions and behavior repulsed him. Sitting in a furtive area of the woods, he knew he had done the most foolish thing he could have done. The woman would have seen his face, would be able to describe him in every detail. He needed to make his way back home. He decided to pass through the forest for cover, running along the backs of the houses that faced the main highway. The vegetation was dense, but he was well hidden from sight. Distinctly, he heard the sound of chickens. Insatiably, he felt a vestigial flicker, and his appetite wettened again. The urge to feed was upon him, smothering his intellect, which aroused the instinctual qualities of the beast he saw within. He followed the clucking until he spotted the hen house. Stealthily, he moved with the twilight of the evening closer and closer until he reached the fenced-in area. He probed his teeth with his finger, but he had not grown longer canine teeth yet. Disappointed, he lamented impotently, but he was not dissuaded. He opened the unlocked gate to the chickens and sneaked inside. His plan was to snatch a hen, wring her neck, or smother the fowl, then chow down. When he entered the coop, the chickens were nesting idly. Completely out of character, and positively unethically, he grabbed hold of the first hen with both hands.

There was an infusion of mayhem and incomprehensible chaos ensued, which seemed like an interminable duration of time but, in all reality, was only a few short seconds. Every chicken in the coop, sensing a predator and that danger was in their midst, took to flight, flapping their wings, cackling loudly and pecking away at Mark, who let loose the hen he had momentarily seized. The only thing now for him to do was to retreat and free himself from the confined space, which he did expediently. With chicken feathers matted to his hair, he had no choice but to take to the woods again. He had to be clandestine because, by now, surely the woman had reported the attack, and the chicken farmer may have seen him sprinting for cover. Without detouring, he made it home in one piece. He was traumatized by the fowl attack because he never knew chickens would and could fight back. He dismissed this as an amateur move on his part and told himself that he would learn to be a fantastic werewolf over time. Besides, tomorrow was the full moon, and it would be then he would reveal his ultimate potential.

Still, with fever and a sickening headache, he somehow managed to sleep, and in his dreams, he was seen reveling in unholy celebration with others likened to himself. In grand extravagance, he was the Master of Ceremonies at this appointed time, and he found effectual comfort in knowing he had been readily accepted as one of them.

When he finally awoke, he was, as they say, "sicker than a dog." He was now burning hot to the touch with fever, and his muscles were seizing up. The uninterrupted dream had given him hope, but he was disturbed by the enhanced symptoms. Weakly, he forced down a handful of dog food, which he ate from a bowl, on all fours while on the kitchen floor. He lapped water from a second bowl but had an impossible time swallowing. He was convinced that these severe flu-like symptoms were all part of his changeover into a wild, untamed beast. He told himself it was imperative to make it to the trail this evening, and there he could relinquish his identification as human, as a mere man, and embrace this moment of imputation he now longed for. His soul would experience the consummation with the animal mutating within, and without portent, he would humbly allow himself to become that which all men fear. He repeated these things in his head and hoped for an acceleration of the process. His human side was dying for sure, and he needed the wolf to be fully, maturely, born. He wanted desperately to see through the eyes of the wolf, to hear the sounds amplified and defined. He wanted to unmute the sense of smell and to inhale and breathe through powerful lungs, to discern the scents and identify recognized odors of the world in a supernatural way.

He wondered if he would remember himself as a human after the complete transition had occurred. He was compelled by a feeling of sorrow that he may not remember the past; however, it would be a new life, a new way of adventure that he had never known before. As the sun was setting and the day was expiring, Mark tenuously proceeded to the running track, which would take him far into the forest. By this time, he was gaunt, feeble, emaciated, and his face shriveled and ghostly pallid with a frozen sallow expression. He smelled of putrescent dissolve, like something which had crawled from an immemorial burial site and needed immediate fumigation and cleansing... but that had to wait.

He wondered if the final change would hurt. He imagined that it would. He self-proclaimed himself as a visionary and saw himself grotesquely contorted, broken, bones protruding while shapeshifting, thrashing about and uncontrolled convulsions, raising the wolf from dormancy while his bones exploded into stronger, more durable ones. His joints surely would unimaginably ache as they swelled to fit the new and improved body. His skin, the largest organ of the body, would rip and tear then peel away, and he would emerge a terror for all to see. This new life would be the validity he foresaw in his dreams. He no longer would have to scrutinize his existence, for he would know exactly what he was. He was willing to be dissolved or absorbed so that he would gain the sight that the wolf had, that fiery dilation of eyes that he saw days ago. He longed for the instinctual fortitude and the erudition of the beast undisturbed.

When he made it to the spot where he had been bitten, which was on a very high plateau, he saw the moon was full and nearly at its lunar zenith. His thoughts were scrambled, and he ponderously swore, while in a haze of confusion, that he saw the same wolf that had bitten him. But in peevish discontent, his eyes were blurred, and he staggered and swayed carelessly, invoking the unnamed spirit of the wolf.

"Come forth from me, appear!"

Mark reached out his hands toward the moon.

"I am the species, the 'Canis' of a new morning."

He felt the abruptness of the wind and believed it was answering him. Mark howled vigorously, and it unfolded poorly, like a desperate plea to be put down. He howled again, pathetically, then gasped for breath. He went down on his knees and held his head in his hands. He prayed that his cranium would swell, expand to receive the wolf inside. Dyspeptically, he fell to one side, moaning and groaning in agonizing pain. Guttural calls to his kin rumbled from what life was left in him. He gave a derisory whimper and began to whine like a nervous dog whose owner left and had never returned. Now, he prayed for the silver bullet to the heart to ease his suffering and make it all go away.

Lycanthropy never occurred. Mark did not become a beta wolf, for he never had been bitten by a werewolf. He was bitten... bitten by a rabid wolf with full-blown rabies.

MORE CHILLS FROM VELOX BOOKS

MORE CHILLS FROM VELOX BOOKS

MORE CHILLS FROM VELOX BOOKS

www.ingramcontent.com/pod-product-compliance
Lightning Source LLC
Chambersburg PA
CBHW031033310726
48969CB00007B/1971